The Secret POND

WITHDRAWN

GERRI HILL

BELLA
BOOKS
2017

Copyright © 2017 by Gerri Hill

Bella Books, Inc.
P.O. Box 10543
Tallahassee, FL 32302

All rights reserved. No part of this book may be reproduced or transmitted in any form or by any means, electronic or mechanical, including photocopying, without permission in writing from the publisher.

This is a work of fiction. Names, characters, businesses, places, events and incidents are either the products of the author's imagination or used in a fictitious manner. Any resemblance to actual persons, living or dead, or actual events is purely coincidental. The publisher does not have any control over and does not assume any responsibility for author or third-party websites or their content.

Printed in the United States of America on acid-free paper.

First Bella Books Edition 2017

Editor: Medora MacDougall
Cover Designer: Judith Fellows

ISBN: 978-1-59493-563-3

PUBLISHER'S NOTE

The scanning, uploading, and distribution of this book via the Internet or via any other means without the permission of the publisher is illegal and punishable by law. Please purchase only authorized electronic editions, and do not participate in or encourage electronic piracy of copyrighted materials. Your support of the author's rights is appreciated.

Other Bella Books by Gerri Hill

Angel Fire
Artist's Dream
At Seventeen
Behind the Pine Curtain
Chasing a Brighter Blue
The Cottage
Coyote Sky
Dawn of Change
Devil's Rock
Gulf Breeze
Hell's Highway
Hunter's Way
In the Name of the Father
Keepers of the Cave
The Killing Room
Love Waits
The Midnight Moon
No Strings
One Summer Night
Paradox Valley
Partners
Pelican's Landing
The Rainbow Cedar
The Roundabout
Sawmill Springs
The Scorpion
Sierra City
Snow Falls
Storms
The Target
Weeping Walls

About the Author

Gerri Hill has thirty-two published works, including the 2017 GCLS winner *Paradox Valley*, 2014 GCLS winner *The Midnight Moon*, 2011, 2012 and 2013 winners *Devil's Rock*, *Hell's Highway* and *Snow Falls*, and the 2009 GCLS winner *Partners*, the last book in the popular Hunter Series, as well as the 2013 Lambda finalist *At Seventeen*.

Gerri lives in south-central Texas, only a few hours from the Gulf Coast, a place that has inspired many of her books. With her partner, Diane, they share their life with two Australian shepherds—Casey and Cooper—and a couple of furry felines.

For more, visit her website at gerrihill.com.

CHAPTER ONE

Lindsey McDermott walked along the rocky trail, a four-month-old black Lab running along beside her. She wondered how long her heart would be heavy—hollow—as she traveled these familiar paths. Lively conversation and laughter used to fill the air...now, nothing but emptiness surrounded her.

She glanced down at the puppy that had bumped her leg. Oh, not totally empty, she acknowledged. If she let it, the dog could bring a smile to her face with his antics. If she allowed sounds inside, she could hear the call of scrub jays and crows as they scolded her from the trees. She could hear the frequent sounds of the titmouse and chickadee as they flitted between the cedars and oaks and the clear, whistling melody of a cardinal as he sang to his mate. Occasionally, the shrill, sharp call of a red-tailed hawk circling overhead would have her searching the sky, hoping to catch a glimpse.

But it was the absence of sounds that saddened her the most. Children's laughter, lost in the trees; playful banter between her brother and sister and their spouses; her father's booming voice;

her grandmother's gentle laugh; her mother chasing after the giggling grandkids; her grandfather singing as they walked... sounds that haunted her now.

Empty sounds that had been haunting her for months. Sounds she would never hear again...yet sounds that would forever echo in her mind.

She took a deep breath, cursing the direction of her thoughts. Nearly every day she walked the trails that littered her grandparents' property...trails that she'd help build over the years. It was an ideal piece of property in the Hill Country, bordered by the cool, clear waters of the Frio River on one side and little rock-filled Buffalo Creek on the opposite. In between were acres and acres of rocky hills dotted with oaks and ashe junipers—always referred to by the locals as cedars—prickly pear cactus, the thorny mesquite trees, the lovely mountain laurels and bigtooth maples and the many ancient cypress trees that lined both the river and the creek. Paradise, her grandmother had called it. Now it was her paradise. And she'd found that paradise was a very, very lonely place.

Once again, she thought that maybe it had been a mistake to move here. But what else could she do? She wasn't able to function out there. She wasn't able to do her job. Hell, she barely had the will to live most days. No, her life had been torn to pieces. Shredded. She wanted to hide in a dark place and retreat from the world. Many a night she wished for it to end, hoping she wouldn't live to see another miserable day. The sun rose again, of course.

She walked on, pushing out her thoughts as she usually tried to do. Max picked up a stick and carried it along as they walked. She needed to spend more time with him. He loved to fetch and she'd found an old tennis ball in the garden shed. When she could muster up the energy—and the want-to—she'd toss it to him in the evenings. He was a smart dog with boundless energy, and she should be using this time to train him. So far he'd mastered "sit," which he'd do for all of three seconds, and he'd learned to "shake," his new favorite thing. Of course, "ball" was the word that got his attention the most and even when she didn't ask him, he'd often find the faded yellow ball and bring it to her. She ruffled his head now, then attempted to pull the stick from his mouth. He clamped his teeth down tightly on it, emitting a playful growl as he tugged it away from her.

Then she heard it. Laughter. A child's laugh. At first, she thought it was a cruel joke. It sounded like Eli, her nephew. Her heart ached and she looked around, halfway expecting to see him running behind her, his grin contagious as he flew into her arms. No...the trail was empty. However, the laughter rang out again. Max turned, his floppy ears at attention, his stare going into the woods.

The trail they'd taken that day was on the eastern side of the property, adjacent to Buffalo Creek. As was normally the case, she'd taken her grandfather's Kawasaki Mule to one of the cross trails and was walking from there, making a loop around that could take anywhere from one to two hours, depending on which route she took.

She decided to investigate the sound. It was coming from the creek, most likely. The creek separated her grandparents' place from the Larsons' on the other side. The McDermotts and the Larsons did not get along. She'd learned at an early age not to play in the creek if Old Lady Larson was out and about. She was a mean old biddy, and frankly, Lindsey had been afraid of her. She wondered if she was still alive.

When they got close to the creek, she silenced Max, holding him to her side as her gaze went down to the water. She was shocked to see a boy, eight or ten years old, tossing rocks into the water. A yellow dog, probably a puppy like Max, was attempting to catch them, causing the boy to laugh. She stood there, tears filling her eyes as she watched him. Eli would have been seven. Jett, nine. She could see them tossing rocks into the Frio River, not the creek. She could see them splashing in the pond or swinging off the rope into the river, laughing as they plunged into the cold water. The sight of this boy with his shaggy blond hair shining in the sun, the dog bouncing beside him, made her so incredibly sad, she felt her heart breaking all over again.

She retreated, away from the creek, her tears flowing down her cheeks. Max whimpered beside her, as he normally did when she cried. She went back to the trail, thoughts trying to crash in despite her best effort to push them back out again. The phone call, the tears, the funerals, the emptiness…and the loneliness.

As often happened, she simply couldn't take it. She slumped down against a tree, sobs nearly choking her as she cried. The black dog lay beside her, his teeth nibbling at her hand. She didn't know how long she sat there. It could have been hours. Long enough for her tears to dry. Long enough for the emptiness to surround her heart again.

CHAPTER TWO

Hannah Larson had learned a long time ago to tune her mother-in-law out. It was an art, really, to pretend to listen while letting her voice—and words—fade away as if they'd never been spoken. James had taught her how, saying he'd learned to do it with his grandmother when she would go on and on about something. Margie, his mother, had apparently learned the art of nagging from her. She had it down pat.

"Well? Does it not concern you?"

Hannah blinked her eyes. God, was she *still* talking about Jack and the creek? "He's nearly ten."

"And? He's not familiar with the area, Hannah. I can't believe you'd let him go out like that!"

She sighed. "I walked down there with him. I put markers out along a trail so he wouldn't get lost. I put markers along both ends of the creek, telling him he could go no farther than that. He'll be fine."

"Not to belabor the point, but he grew up in the city. This is—"

"I know, Margie. I know. It's just a little creek, though. It's not like it's a river or anything."

"They say you can drown in an inch of water. They say—"

"Margie, please," she said, holding her hand up. "We moved here because you wanted us to be close. You wanted him to experience living out here where his dad grew up. James told me on numerous occasions how he would roam the hills out here unsupervised."

"That's completely different. James was born and raised here. Jack, as I said earlier, wouldn't have a clue what to do if he came upon a rattlesnake, for instance."

"Yes, he would. He would run like hell."

Margie's face scrunched into a frown. "You know I don't like you using that word, Hannah. I hope you don't use it in front of Jack. I'll say it again…he needs some structure in his life. He needs…"

Oh, God. Was she going to start in again on them going to church with her? She could almost picture James's face as he stood behind his mother, making faces and rolling his eyes, she trying her best not to laugh. Once again, Margie's voice faded away as she let her mind drift to James, his handsome face etched in pain, his slick head the result of chemo, his once-bright blue eyes dull and filled with agony. Her only consolation was that he didn't suffer long, but suffer he did. The last month, the tumor in his brain caused him so much pain that he lived on morphine. The last two weeks, he'd been in and out of consciousness, she and Jack watching as he slowly, painfully slipped away from them.

She should have listened to her mother. She should have stayed in San Antonio. She had friends there. Jack had friends there. Her family was there, her support system. But nagging wasn't Margie Larson's only talent. No, placing blame and laying guilt as thick as molasses ranked right up there. James was Margie's only son. Jack was her only grandchild. James's grandmother, Lilly—Jack's great-grandmother—had recently been put into a nursing home. The house was vacant…a house that James practically grew up in. How could she say no to Margie's insistence that she and Jack move there? Still, she agonized over the decision. Their house was filled with James's ghost, and she often found Jack sitting in it in a daze, tears running down his cheeks. It had been two months, and he seemed no closer to getting over James's death than he had at the beginning.

That was the reason she decided to sell the house, decided to move. Jack needed a change, and she thought living out here, where he would have land to explore and where he could play where his own daddy had grown up might help him heal. He would make new friends, different friends. Utopia was a tiny community in the Hill Country, only a couple of hours from San Antonio. With a population of three hundred, she hesitated to even call it a town. She had told Jack they would give it a year. If either one of them wasn't happy after a year, then they would move back to San Antonio, no questions asked. He agreed and they'd begun packing the very next day.

After a week of being here, though, she was already having second thoughts about her decision. Margie had been over every single day, something she'd feared would happen. The Larson place was over six hundred acres yet the prime spot was along Buffalo Creek. James's grandparents' house, which she and Jack had moved into, was less than a mile from James's parents' house. A very short mile.

"And I think that would be the best place for him to make friends."

Hannah stared at her blankly. "I'm sorry. What? A camp?"

"The church camp. It's only for a week. I've already reserved him a spot."

Hannah shook her head. "No, Margie. We haven't even gotten settled yet. I'm not sending him off, alone, to a church camp where he doesn't know a soul. No."

Margie smiled, a patronizing smile that she had grown to detest over the years. "That's how you make friends, Hannah. It's only for a week. He'll be fine."

"No. He's not going. I'm sorry." She made a show of looking at her watch. "I suppose I should get started on dinner. Thanks for dropping by, Margie."

Margie's smile faded a little. "I get the impression you're throwing me out."

"Of course not," she lied. "I have things to do, that's all."

"You know, you and Jack are welcome to have dinner with us. In fact, when I envisioned you living here, I thought you'd come over quite often. So far, you've only managed to join us one time."

"Well, we've only been here a week, Margie. Not even settled in yet. Besides, if I want to make this a home for Jack, then I need to get back to our routine, and that involves me cooking dinner."

"I imagine it's hard to cook now with James gone." Margie's face dropped and sadness prevailed. Hannah wondered how much of it was forced, just for show. "I do miss him. Jack looks so much like him."

I must have been insane to move out here, she thought as the guilt started to pile up. Before Margie was through, Hannah found herself agreeing to dinner, and yes, she'd be there early so that Margie could talk to Jack about the church camp.

Oh, how did her life turn into all of this? How did she end up here, living near her in-laws, so far from the normalcy of her own family? It was easy to blame James, of course. If he hadn't gotten sick...

She shook her head. No. She wasn't going to go there. She wasn't going to feel sorry for herself. She would save that for the nighttime, when she was alone. Jack wasn't there to see her tears then.

She closed the door after Margie left and leaned against it. Eventually, to save her own sanity, she would have to talk to Margie. There was no reason for her to come over every single day. If there was one thing she and Jack needed right now, it was some space. Time to get used to living without James in their lives. She'd come to terms with it. Even before he died, she'd accepted what was going to happen. She and James had talked—and cried—at length and she'd made peace with it. That didn't mean she was over it. That didn't mean she didn't miss him. There was an emptiness now that hovered around them, a dark cloud of sadness. She could see it in Jack's eyes even though he bravely tried to hide it. And no doubt Jack could see it in her eyes too. She hoped this summer would help them heal. There was no school, no job, no doctor's visits, no hospital to rush off to. There was only her and Jack…as they tried to learn how to be a family of two.

She smiled. Well, three, if she counted Barney. And Jack *did* count Barney. The dog slept with him, ate with him, and played with him. That was one thing she had been adamant about to Margie. Even though Great-grandma Larson—Lilly—did not *ever* allow dogs in her house, Barney was to be the exception. Because right now, Barney was Jack's only friend.

CHAPTER THREE

Lindsey sat on the back porch of her grandparents' house, the ceiling fan buzzing lazily overhead. The covered porch was part of the original house. The expansive deck had been added later. She remembered when they'd built it. She was just a kid, barely six, but she had memories of helping to carry boards. Most likely she was getting in the way, but she'd been a part of the remodel, like her older brother and sister had been. Everything had been a family affair. For as long as she could remember, that's how it had been. Every birthday, every anniversary, every *event* required a family gathering. To say they were close-knit would be an understatement.

She picked up her glass of amber liquid. Death required bourbon. That's what her grandmother said when they'd buried her only sibling. Lindsey had been twenty-three at the time and after the funeral for Aunt Lena, they'd all sat around the table here, passing around an expensive bottle.

Death required bourbon.

She wasn't sure if that was true or not…but it sure as hell didn't hurt. She took a sip now, savoring the taste a few seconds before she swallowed. Max was stretched out beside her, his legs twitching as he dreamed of chasing a rabbit or something equally elusive.

She really needed to slow down on her nightly visits with the bottle. It could become a habit. Wine. She enjoyed wine more than bourbon. Her grandparents had quite an extensive wine collection. She'd eyed it a few times. She'd even opened a bottle once. But she'd been saddled with guilt...so much so that she couldn't finish the bottle. Then she got angry. Angry that she'd felt guilty.

But guilt was what she carried with her. Survivor's guilt. Her uncle, her only remaining relative, had tried to tell her to let it go. Easy to say, she'd told him. He was removed from it. Her father's younger brother, he'd left the nest at eighteen, never to return. He'd made a life in New York City...far, far away from tiny Concan. Growing up, she'd rarely seen him. The occasional Christmas visit was about it. He had come down, though, after she'd called him. He'd stayed two weeks, helping to make the arrangements. They didn't talk much. She'd been too distraught. Too traumatized by the events to make idle conversation.

It was Uncle Louis who had talked her into moving here. He had no hard feelings over the will. The bulk of her grandparents' estate went to her father. Uncle Louis said that's how it should be. That, of course, meant that it was now hers. At the time, she couldn't even consider it. She could barely make it through a day without being medicated. Come here? Alone? Where the memories would flood her?

No way.

He'd left her in Dallas and headed back to New York. But he called every day, whether she wanted him to or not. His words finally struck a chord with her.

For your own good, you've got to go out there. That's where they were happy. That's where they loved and laughed. That's where you loved and laughed. That's where you were happy. Those memories are still there, Lindsey. You just have to find them...find them and let them in.

So she'd quit a job she could no longer function at. She gave up her apartment. She sold most of her furniture. She got a dog.

She reached down, running her fingers through Max's soft fur. She got a dog and they packed up and came out here. The first month was brutal. She couldn't even remember how she got through it. She didn't remember eating. She didn't remember sleeping. She remembered crying. A lot.

And she remembered the dark thoughts she'd had. Awful thoughts. If not for Max, she wondered if…well, she wondered if she'd still be here. Some days…some nights…she wondered still.

She had a plan, though. A plan she'd been mulling over for weeks. She hadn't been able to get going, however. Tomorrow. Always tomorrow.

Well, tomorrow was a good day to start. She would take the Mule over to her parents' cabin. It had to be done and she'd put it off long enough. She didn't know why it was so hard for her. Their house in San Antonio, she'd cleaned out and put up for sale without much thought. Of course, her uncle had helped get it started. She'd been too numb to even sort through their things. He'd boxed up pictures and other keepsakes for her. The rest they'd either sold or given away. She hadn't felt much attachment to the house. It wasn't where she grew up. They'd sold that one not long after she'd left home. No, here was where the memories were. Here, at their little weekend cabin. When the family gathered, she always stayed with them. Her brother and sister, both with kids, would stay here at the big house with her grandparents.

So she'd go to the cabin tomorrow. She'd taken the trails along the river, but she'd always bypassed the cabin. It would be neat and tidy, as her mother usually left it. No doubt there would be food in the fridge that was months past good. That would definitely need to be cleaned out. She would open the windows and let in some fresh air. She wasn't certain what she'd do with it yet. She really didn't have to do anything, she supposed. The cabin sat at the edge of the Frio River. During the hot months of summer, she thought maybe she'd stay there instead of here. The cold water would be a refreshing change.

She pushed her glass away. No. She couldn't. All the tubes would be there. The floats that the kids used. That section of river was wide but calm, just downstream of the rapids they used to float through. Many a lazy summer day was spent in that river, the kids laughing as they tried to flip her out of her tube. She closed her eyes, picturing her family, all fourteen of them floating idly in the water, her brother handing out beer from the cooler he towed behind him. Laughter…splashing…her grandfather singing…always singing.

"Christ…I can't do it," she murmured.

She sighed. Maybe tomorrow wasn't the best day. Maybe it could wait another day or two.

CHAPTER FOUR

She didn't know why she'd taken the creek trail again instead of the river or even up north through the hills. The views up there were great and now was a good time to go, before the summer heat would keep her near the water. Without much conscious thought, she'd stopped the Mule at the crossroads, taking the lower trail toward the creek as she'd done yesterday. Max was already bounding ahead of her. There were spots along the trail where she could see the shallow water of the creek, then trees would hide it once again.

When she was little, before she'd learned to swim, they would come down to the creek instead of the river and she'd splash in the clear water. Inevitably, Old Lady Larson would hear her laughter and she'd come down to inspect. Her grandmother used to say that she wanted to make sure we weren't crossing the creek onto their property. Her grandfather, however, said she came down because she couldn't stand the sound of laughter and she wanted to put an end to it. Regardless of the reason, whenever the old lady showed up, they'd take their leave. There were lots of spots along the creek where she could have played, yet her grandparents always brought her here. Perhaps they liked provoking Mrs. Larson. They sure did laugh about it later. She smiled as she pictured her grandfather singing some old country classic at the top of his lungs as they climbed back toward the trail, Old Lady Larson glaring at them from below.

She stopped at the same place, the one where she'd first heard the little boy's laugh. She tilted her head, listening. All was quiet except for a scrub jay that had been following them. She was about to walk on, then decided to head toward the creek anyway. She was oddly disappointed to find it empty, no sign of the boy and his dog. She was about to turn around when Max looked up alertly. Before he could take off, she grabbed his collar, holding him beside her. Sure enough, the yellow dog came running down the hill on the opposite side, the little boy hurrying after him. Today he was carrying a fishing pole. The creek was wide, twenty- to twenty-five feet across in places, but it was too shallow, too rocky for fishing.

The boy placed his fishing pole on the ground, then proceeded to pick up some pebbles and rocks and began methodically tossing them into the water. As before, the yellow dog pounced after them, splashing the boy in the process. It was too much for Max to resist. He jerked out of her hold and ran down toward the creek, giving a high-pitched puppy bark in the process.

The boy ran back, startled. The yellow dog met Max in the creek, both their tails wagging wildly as they sniffed each other. As is often the case with puppies, the sniffing quickly turned to play and they were soon chasing in the water, running back and forth from side to side.

Instead of calling Max back—which she had no doubt he would ignore—she walked down to the creek to get him. The little boy looked at her suspiciously, and she gave him a smile, hoping to ease his fears.

"Hi," she said. "I see our dogs have met." The two dogs ran by the kid, nearly knocking him down. "What's your name?"

He tilted his head, watching her from across the water. "My mom said I shouldn't talk to strangers."

She nodded. "I guess that's a good rule." She motioned with her head behind her. "I live back there though. So I'm not really a stranger. Where do you live?"

He turned and pointed up the hill. "Up there. My great-grandmother's house." He chewed his lower lip as if deciding whether to talk to her or not. "My name is Jack."

She smiled again. "I'm Lindsey." She pointed at the black dog. "That's Max."

He pointed to the yellow dog. "That's Barney."

She walked to the edge of the water. "How old are you, Jack?"

"Nine."

"Nine?" She looked around. "Kinda young to be out here by yourself. Easy to get lost."

"I'm almost ten," he said, as if that changed everything. "I have a trail marked. Mom cut up some old dress she found in one of the closets." He grinned. "She said if Grandma caught her doing it, she'd be pissed as hell." Then his eyes widened. "I'm not supposed to say those words. Or damn or…shit," he said, his voice lowering to almost a whisper. "She says just because she says them that doesn't mean I can."

Lindsey couldn't hide her smile so she gave up trying. "So who's your grandma?"

"Grandma Margie."

Lindsey nodded. "Margie Larson." She married Old Lady Larson's son. From what her grandmother had told her, Margie was as sour and bitter as the old lady herself.

"Yeah, that's my grandma."

The dogs were up on the bank on her side, playing tug-of-war with a stick. She looked back over at him, her gaze going to his fishing pole.

"You like to fish?"

He nodded. "It's too shallow here. I haven't caught anything." He looked downstream. "I can't go any further, though. Mom marked it." He pointed to a tree and she saw a piece of blue fabric tied to a branch. "Down at the other end, she put another one. I can't go past that."

That was smart of the mother, but she was surprised that a nine-year-old kid had obeyed. "That's good," she said. "Even though you're almost ten, if you get lost out here, you'd be hard to find."

"That's what she said but I want to go exploring. I hope later this summer she'll let me go farther." He kicked at a rock. "My grandma said I wasn't to cross the creek, though. She said mean people used to live over there. She doesn't know who's there now."

Lindsey laughed. No, the McDermotts and Larsons never did get along. Her smile faded though. "Those...those mean people, as she called them...they...they died," she said with difficulty.

"Oh." He kicked at another rock. "My daddy died. That's why we're here."

They stared at each other across the creek and it was only then that she saw—and recognized—the sadness in his eyes. Was that why he made this solitary trek to the creek? To think about his dad? Did he do it much like she made her solitary walks in the woods...to reflect on her family? She cleared her throat. She wasn't in the mood to talk anymore.

"I should get going. Come on, Max." She beckoned, but the dog ignored her. He and Barney were wrestling in the water. She looked over at the kid—Jack—and smiled. "I guess I might see you again. Looks like the dogs have made friends."

He nodded. "I come down here every day. I can't stay too long or my mom worries." He tapped the large watch strapped to his thin wrist. "One hour at a time, then I have to go back and let her know that I'm okay."

"That's good. Well...maybe I'll see you tomorrow then."

She pried Max away from Barney, holding him while Jack called Barney back to his side of the creek. Barney apparently was better trained than Max. He went obediently over to Jack while Max struggled against her.

"We need to work on that, Maxwell," she murmured as she pulled him up the trail. At the top, she glanced through the trees, back to the creek. Jack sat cross-legged on the ground, his dog squatting down beside him, licking his face. She didn't know why the sight of that brought tears to her eyes, but it did. She wiped them away, then headed on down the trail to finish their walk.

CHAPTER FIVE

Hannah twirled the spaghetti on her fork, her eyes not on the pasta but on her son as he snuck a meatball down to Barney. He looked up, smiling when he saw that'd she'd seen him.

"Barney likes your meatballs too."

"Barney will eat anything," she said. "Except his own dog food," she added.

"Well, he's not stupid."

She smiled, pleasantly surprised at Jack's good mood this evening. Dinner was usually a quiet affair...for both of them. She watched him now as he held a long spaghetti noodle up high and sucked it into his mouth with a slurping sound.

"So you had a good day?" she asked.

He nodded. "I guess. Did you?"

"I spent most of the day boxing up ancient kitchenware so that we can put our own stuff out. And as an added bonus, Grandma Margie did not come over."

"This house is old."

"Yes, it is. It's also free."

He looked at her, his face serious. "With Daddy gone, will we have enough money to live?"

"Oh, honey, we'll be fine. I didn't mean it to sound like that."

"Are you going to have to get a job?"

"Have to and want to are two different things," she said. "Once school starts and you're not here, I may go crazy being out here by myself." She grinned. "Or your Grandma Margie will drive me crazy."

He laughed. "She drives me crazy too. Please don't make me go to that stupid church camp."

"I'm not going to make you, Jack. It's your decision."

"She said she'd already paid for it."

"That's her problem, not yours."

"She also said that we were going to go to church with them on Sunday. Are we?"

Hannah nearly choked on her meatball. She took a large swallow of water, pausing before speaking. Jack was an intelligent boy and very intuitive. She tried to keep her expression neutral.

"Do you *want* to go to church with them?"

He studied her. "Do you?"

"Your dad and I...well..." How do you tell a nine-year-old boy what agnostic means? "Your dad and I didn't feel that it was necessary to spend our Sunday mornings in church. Or Sunday mornings, Sunday evenings, *and* Wednesday evenings, like your grandma does," she added. "We also decided that when you were old enough, you could decide for yourself if you wanted to go to church or not." She looked at him pointedly. "So the question is, do *you* want to go to church with them?"

He shrugged. "No. I'd have to get dressed up then."

She smiled at his logic but said nothing else. She was, however, a bit peeved at Margie for indicating to him that they would go. She knew James had spoken to his mother on numerous occasions about their feelings on the matter and she also knew that Margie blamed her. She'd even gone so far as to insinuate that James's cancer was a result of them "shunning God" and that that was their punishment.

Yeah...she should have listened to her mother and stayed in San Antonio.

* * *

Hannah kissed Jack's cheek, then pulled the covers to his waist. "Don't stay up too late, sweetie," she said.

"I won't," he mumbled, but his eyes never left the iPad he was playing on—the same game he'd downloaded to her own device, a game she had yet to master.

At least he was content with that. For now. He hadn't mentioned the "Playstation" word in quite a while now. James had told him when he turned twelve, they'd get him one. He'd rolled his eyes and said he'd be *way* too old by then. She watched him for a moment longer, pausing to pet Barney's head as he lay snuggled against Jack's legs. At the door, she stopped.

"Good night, Jack. I love you."

At that, he looked up. "Good night, Mom. I love you too."

She went back to the kitchen and took the bottle of chardonnay from the fridge and poured herself a glass. She turned the lights out as she walked through the house, taking her wine with her into her bedroom. As Jack had said, the house was old and the bedrooms were small. Her king bed and one end table barely fit against the wall. She took a sip of wine, her eyes going to the picture on the dresser. It was taken only a month before James got sick. James was smiling. Jack was smiling. She was smiling. A month later, there were no more smiles. It was a long fifteen-month battle, one that had taken its toll on all of them. Jack had been too young to really understand at first. Daddy had a headache, that was all he knew. But Daddy didn't get better and Daddy couldn't play catch with him and Daddy couldn't take him to the park and Daddy missed his soccer games. When she'd finally told him the truth, that Daddy would never get better, that Daddy would be leaving them very soon, he'd stared at her with his big, blue eyes, trying to be brave. They'd had a good cry that night…she and Jack. She'd held him in her arms, much like she'd done when he was a baby, rocking him back and forth until they'd cried themselves out.

How long ago was that? A few months before James died? Her glance slid to the bed. She still wasn't used to sleeping alone. They'd gotten married their third year of college. Jack was born three years later. They'd settled into their new life, their new family with ease. After only two years of teaching, she'd quit her job so she could stay home with Jack. James's salary afforded them that. Her plan was to go back to teaching once Jack was older and got settled in school. In fact, she'd just started applying for positions when James got sick.

Now? Well, now she'd wait. She had a feeling that after their year here, they might very well be heading back to San Antonio. There simply wasn't enough out here. Tiny Utopia had only the basic necessities. She could drive to Concan or Leaky, which weren't far, but they only offered slightly better options than Utopia. She could drive all the way to Uvalde, a nice-sized town that had everything she needed, but it wasn't a trip she could make on a whim. She sighed as she looked at herself in the mirror. She could admit it, at least to herself, that it had probably been a mistake to move out here. She could have simply sold their house and moved closer to her parents. That didn't really seem like starting over, though. She thought she needed to give Jack this time. Jack didn't see enough of his grandparents as it was. With James gone, she could see a time where they never saw Margie and Dennis. So she needed to give Jack this time and she needed to give Margie a chance.

She looked again in the mirror, rolling her eyes at herself. James had always been the buffer between them. With him gone, she imagined she and Margie would clash like never before.

And that was going to make for a very long year.

CHAPTER SIX

Lindsey pushed through the branches of a cedar tree, smiling at the sight below. She was surprised at how much she was looking forward to seeing Jack again. She had been afraid he wouldn't be there...afraid she'd be disappointed. She didn't even try to restrain Max. He took off down the hill, his large feet flopping out as he ran. Barney met him in the creek and they immediately began wrestling, tails wagging wildly.

Jack stood up, shielding his eyes to the sun as she made her way much more slowly down the hill. She could see the smile on his face.

"You came back!"

She nodded. "Told you I would." She'd also come prepared. Instead of the hiking boots she normally wore, she'd put on her sports sandals. She paused at the edge of the creek for just a moment, then walked into the water. For early June, it was still a little cold but not nearly as cold as the Frio would be. With the sun beating down, she wished she'd worn her water shorts too.

"Have you been in the water yet?" she asked as she moved closer to him.

"No. It's too shallow. And Mom…well, I don't think she'd want me getting in."

She sat down on one of the larger rocks. "You could take your shoes off and hang your feet in. Like this," she said, dipping her feet under the water.

"Okay." He had on dirty, scuffed Adidas shoes and he tossed them and his socks aside, wiggling his toes before sticking his foot in. He jerked it back out. "It's cold."

"Not too bad," she said. "Now the river…that's cold."

"What river?"

"The Frio. It's over on the other side of our…of my property," she said. "Frio is a Spanish word." She smiled at him. "What do you think it means?"

His brows drew together in thought, then he smiled. "Cold?"

"Yep."

"Do you go swimming there?"

"Sure do." Her smile faltered a little. "Haven't this year yet." She looked over at him. "You swim?"

He nodded. "I took lessons when I was six. My grandparents have a pool." He shrugged. "We moved, though…so…"

"Where from?"

"San Antonio."

She nodded. "That's where…where my parents used to live." She cleared her throat. "I recently moved here too. A few months ago."

"We've only been here a week," he said.

"Because your daddy died?"

He nodded. "He had a brain tumor. My Grandma Margie said that Jesus called him home."

"Oh, yeah?"

"Yeah, that's what she said." He looked at her seriously. "What do you think?"

Man…how did they get off on this subject? She shook her head. "I don't know. What do *you* think?"

He chewed on his lower lip for a few seconds, then looked up at her. "I don't know either."

They sat there quietly, side by side, their feet dangling in the water as the dogs splashed around them. Then Jack looked over at her.

"Can you teach me how to skip rocks?"

"Sure. You need some small, flat ones."

* * *

Jack and Barney came bursting into the house, dirtier than normal.

"Take your shoes off," she called from her spot on the kitchen floor. He kicked them off and she noticed the wet spots that his socks made across the tile. Why were his socks wet? She shook her head slowly. Because he had gotten into the creek, that's why. It was bound to happen sooner or later. She got up, shoving the box aside that she'd been unpacking. She found him in the bathroom, washing his hands.

She gave him what she hoped was a stern motherly look. "Your socks are wet."

"Oh." He looked down at the dirty socks on his feet. "Yeah."

She crossed her arms. "Yeah? That's all you have to say?"

"I didn't get in the creek, Mom. I just…put my feet in. It was hot. Besides, it's like this deep," he said, holding his hands a foot apart.

"I know it's shallow, Jack, but you could slip on a rock and knock yourself out."

He rolled his eyes at her. "You've been listening to Grandma too much."

She sighed. "So I have. But I don't like you being out there by yourself. I know you think you're all grown up, but—"

"I'm not by myself."

She frowned. "You're not?"

"No. I have a friend."

She stared at him. "A friend?" Who could this friend be? They were miles from another family and according to Margie, most of the nearby residents were older with grown children.

"She's nice. Barney has a friend too."

She? Oh, no. She had been afraid this would happen. Her mother had warned her that this might not be the best move for Jack. He would be out here alone. Of course he would make up someone. Kids had imaginary friends all the time. Yeah. *Young* kids. Not a nine-year-old. Not her son.

With those thoughts running through her mind, she wondered what she should do. Should she call him on it? Should she just let it go and hope it goes away? Was this his way of coping with James's death? Before she could settle on anything, he walked past her and back into the kitchen, with her following. He opened the fridge and stared inside.

"Can we have hamburgers for dinner? And some of those big fat potato wedges that you fry?"

She smiled and nodded. "Only if you help me."

She pushed his imaginary friend to the back of her mind while she got him started on peeling potatoes. There was nothing better than hamburgers and fries to get things back to normal.

CHAPTER SEVEN

Breakfast had always been a major production out here at the big house. Well, dinner most nights too. Lindsey's father and her grandfather both loved to fire up the grill for steaks or chicken or sausage that they'd gotten at the German smokehouse in Fredericksburg or Kerrville. Her grandfather especially loved to barbecue on the wood smoker, tending to a brisket for ten hours or more while her father contributed ribs that were so tender, they'd fall off the bone. The deck would be full of conversation and laughter and cold beer. Fun times, for sure. But it was the breakfasts that she was most fond of.

The breakfasts were her grandmother's specialty. They were never simple and they always involved eggs. Waffles and pancakes, breakfast sausage and ham, homemade hash browns, fresh blueberry muffins, eggs that were sometimes fried, sometimes scrambled, and always a bowl of fruit to "settle it all," as her grandmother used to say. There were the mornings when her grandmother would make biscuits like her own mother had taught her and they'd smother them with a creamy sausage gravy. Some mornings she'd make elaborate breakfast casseroles that were oozing with cheese. Or omelets that were light and fluffy, made to perfection. Or her quiche that would have so much bacon in it, the kids weren't able to pick out the broccoli and mushrooms.

Breakfast was a time they'd gather here at the big house, she and her parents making the trek from their little cabin at the river. They'd have coffee and visit and make plans for the day, then linger over breakfast and all complain about how full they were. Lunch would usually be skipped as they'd spend the afternoon in the water…playing, relaxing, and visiting some more…and planning dinner.

Lindsey admitted that when alone, at her own apartment, she rarely, if ever, took the time for breakfast. She would dash off to the office, in a hurry to meet a client or finish a project.

She'd been living out here since late March. Not once had she considered making breakfast. That's not to say that she didn't think about the many mouthwatering meals her grandmother had provided. She did. She couldn't go into the kitchen for coffee without glancing to the breakfast bar, remembering the countless dishes that had been placed there over the years. She simply couldn't bring herself to cook. It was almost sacrilege to be in her grandmother's kitchen, using her pots and pans, to try to whip up something that resembled the delectable dishes she remembered.

That's why now, this morning, she was shocked to find herself rummaging in the fridge, trying to find enough stuff to make an omelet. On her last trip to the grocery store, she'd actually bought bacon and eggs. The eggs had sat unused. The bacon she'd used on a hamburger and then, once, wrapped around shrimp when she'd attempted to grill one of her father's classic meals. The shrimp had turned out good. Nearly perfect. But sitting alone at the table had brought such grief to her she wasn't able to stomach the meal.

She had onions. No peppers. She had some mushrooms that were just this side of good. They maybe had one more day left before she'd have to toss them. So she pulled out one of her grandmother's pans, one she'd seen her use for omelets before and went about the business of "whipping one up" to use her grandmother's line.

It wasn't perfect, no. It broke apart when she attempted to fold it over. It still looked good enough to her, though. She poured a glass of orange juice, foregoing a third cup of coffee, and took her plate outside to the table. It was still early and cool, the ceiling fan helping to stir the air. Max sat drooling beside her, his eyes on her meal. She peeled off the crust of the bread she'd toasted and handed it to him. He nearly took her finger off as he chopped down.

"We've got to work on that, Max," she said. She pointed to the floor of the deck. "Down. Lay down." He looked at her and tilted his head. "Why is it when Jack tells Barney to lay down, he does?" Another tilt of the head, but his eyes were on her plate. "Okay, we'll work on it."

She actually moaned at the first bite of her omelet. The only cheese she'd had was cheddar and she'd used a sprinkle of that. Her grandmother had always mixed Swiss and cheddar for her omelets. She made a mental note to add Swiss to her next grocery list.

In fact, she could probably take the time to drive into town this morning and do some shopping. She needed the makings for sandwiches. She thought it'd be fun to pack a little picnic basket to take to the creek. And for some reason, she'd been in the mood for a good steak, something that hadn't crossed her mind in months. Maybe she'd even pull out one of her grandfather's bottles of wine. A baked potato. Some easy veggie to go with it.

She glanced down at Max. "What do you think? Feel like a steak tonight?" She took a bite of her toast, then handed him the rest, smiling as he ate it in one bite. "You didn't even taste it." She reached out and rubbed his head, scratched behind his ear like he liked, then went back to her omelet. She took a bite, then stared off into space, wondering if she dared to try to make her grandmother's biscuits. She'd taught them all and she knew where her grandmother kept her recipes. It might be fun to try. She'd add biscuit ingredients to her grocery list too.

* * *

Lindsey was running late and instead of parking the Mule at the crossroads where the trails met and walking, she took it all the way to the creek. She had too much to carry, anyway. Besides the smaller cooler, at the last minute, she'd grabbed a fishing pole and a can of corn. As a kid she'd caught plenty of perch with corn.

There was no official trail going down to the creek here. When they were kids, they only came this way to irritate Old Lady Larson. Other times, they'd go farther upstream to splash around. Truth was, they mostly stayed on the river side. The Frio wasn't really very wide in most places and parts of it were rather shallow. But deep holes, good for both swimming and fishing, were found in many places. The last few days, she'd had an itch to explore the river again. Maybe it was the summer heat that was settling over them—settling down like it planned to stay awhile, as her grandmother would say—that was making her long for a dip in the cool waters. Or maybe it was being at the creek, splashing in the water with Jack and the dogs that made her want to actually get *in* the water.

She was surprised at how quickly she and Max had established a trail. He ran ahead of her, knowing exactly where they were going. A bark from down below told her that Jack and Barney were already there. Jack waved at her when he saw her, and she waved back, a silly grin on her face as she reached the water.

"You're late," he accused.

"I brought stuff," she said, holding up her fishing pole and the cooler.

"Are we going to fish?" he asked excitedly. "I thought it was too shallow."

She walked across the creek, her sandals gripping the rocks easily—the rocks they'd piled up to make a little bridge across the water. She didn't put her stuff down, though. She looked upstream, past the fabric marker that his mom had put out.

"I know your mom said not to go past there," she said, pointing, "but there's a deeper spot upstream. We can fish there." She paused. "Or do you think your mom would get mad?"

His face turned serious as he contemplated her question. "I guess if I'm with you, she wouldn't get mad."

She pointed to his watch. "How much time before you have to get back?"

He held up his wrist showing her the digital watch. "At 1:15 it'll beep at me."

She looked at her watch. It was almost twelve thirty. "Okay, we've got a little bit of time." She started walking and he came up beside her, his own fishing pole in his hands. The dogs ran ahead of them, excited to be exploring a new part of the creek. "You eat already?"

He nodded. "Mom had egg salad. I don't like it very much, but I don't tell her that."

"I've got sandwiches. Turkey and cheese."

He smiled and nodded. "That sounds good. I gave Barney most of mine at lunch when Mom wasn't looking."

"Now listen, you don't come out here by yourself. You stay back there where your mom told you."

"I will."

"You promise?"

"Promise."

"Okay. And don't tell her I took you out here, either," she added. "Don't want us getting into trouble."

She'd scoped out this part of the creek yesterday, after Jack had gone home. She'd walked both upstream and down, trying to find a place where they could fish. This spot had a couple of deeper holes and she'd seen a few bluegill sunfish and some yellow perch. She thought Jack would have fun catching them.

"What are we gonna use for bait?"

"Corn."

"Corn? No worms?"

"No. I think I know where we could get some, but today we'll use corn." They used to get their worms from her grandmother's garden in the old compost pile. She hadn't yet been out to the garden. That was something else she'd felt guilty about. Her grandmother prized her vegetable garden. Lindsey hadn't had the will to even walk in it. Maybe she'd go out there and clean it up. It was too late in the year to plant anything, but maybe by fall she could do something. Her grandmother practically had a garden year-round. Surely she could find something to grow.

She pointed out the deeper holes to him, then walked into the water, him riding piggyback so she could show him the fish.

"I see them!"

"Okay...so let's see if we can catch them."

She put a bobber on his line and threaded a few kernels of corn on his hook, then stood back, trying to keep the dogs away as Jack tossed the hook into the pool. It didn't take long for the bobber to start popping up and down.

"You got a nibble," she said.

"Should I pull it up?"

"Not yet. Let them take it."

The bobber slipped under the water and he jerked his line up, but the hook was empty. "They got the corn!"

"Sneaky little devils, aren't they."

He had better luck the second time and pulled up a small sunfish, barely four inches long. He laughed and clapped and jumped up and down as if he'd caught a monster. She couldn't help herself. She whipped out her phone, snapping a picture of him holding his catch.

He soon became quite adept at it, finding larger perch from time to time. She sat back with the dogs, smiling at him, his laughter like music in the trees. All too soon, however, it was time to go back.

"We didn't get to eat your sandwiches," he complained as they headed back downstream.

"I guess I'll have to eat yours then." She was disappointed their time had come to an end so quickly.

"No. You wait here," he said. "I just have to run up and let my mom know that I'm okay. She'll let me come back down for a little while. Then we can eat."

"Okay. I'll wait for you."

Barney stayed with them while Jack ran up the hill and disappeared from sight. She walked into the shade and sat down on a rock, sticking her feet into the water. She was ready to go swimming, she decided. Maybe this afternoon. Would she go to the river…or did she dare go to the pond?

The thought of the pond made her heart ache. She hadn't been brave enough or strong enough to even think about going to the pond. The pond was almost sacred ground. A wonderful, magical, secret place. It was where they'd all learned to swim. It was where her nieces and nephews had learned to swim too. It was where you snuck off to if you wanted peace and quiet. It was where impromptu campouts were had…wieners roasted over the fire pit, marshmallows stabbed on sticks. The only shelter out at the pond was an old lean-to her grandfather had erected. A metal footlocker held a couple of sleeping bags and some camping gear for cooking. Another held the floats and rafts they used in the water. Other than an old table, she didn't think there was much else out there. Well, except for the four-wheeler. She smiled as she thought of it. What fun they'd had on that thing. There was no electricity. No phone, no TV, no lights. Just a lantern, a fire pit…and fun. She wondered if Jack would like it out there.

Barney barked and took off running, Max right behind him. She turned, seeing Jack racing back down the hill, a grin on his face.

"She said I could stay out another hour!"

He sat down beside her and took off his shoes and socks, mimicking her position with his feet in the water. She took out a sandwich and a Coke for him…she had a beer hidden under the ice for her. The dogs played around them, stopping long enough to beg for a handout. They soon tired and moved to the shade of an oak, lying side by side, their puppy tongues hanging out, eyes getting sleepy.

It was a blissful afternoon. Lindsey couldn't remember the last time she'd felt this at peace. Well, sure she could. It was the last time she'd been out here…before they were all gone.

Christmas. That was the last time they'd all gotten together out here. It was nice whenever they got together, but summer was different. Summer meant lazy days in the water and eating on the deck under the stars…long summer days filled with love and laughter. Those days were surely over now. She sighed and looked over at Jack. Well, today had been pretty nice. Jack had provided some laughter and dared she say it? She was becoming quite fond of the kid.

He turned, finding her watching him. He smiled at her. "Can we do this again tomorrow? Sneak past the marker?"

She nodded. "Sure. We'll try it again."

CHAPTER EIGHT

"So what is it that you do down there?" Hannah asked.

Jack handed her the potato he'd just peeled. "We…we hang out," he said.

"Hang out? You and this…this friend of yours?"

"Lindsey."

She didn't know why, but she thought she'd feel better about him making up a friend if it had been a boy. But a girl? Lindsey? She thought back to his school friends. Was there a Lindsey? Had he had a crush on her?

"I like it when we have mashed potatoes," he said.

"I know you do. You also like fried chicken."

"It's one of my favorites." He stepped off the stool he'd been standing on at the sink and wiped his hands on the towel. "I'm going to go play my game," he said, running out of the room without waiting for her response.

She continued cutting up the potatoes, wondering what in the world she should do. Well, for one, she needed to spend more time with him. Of course, she knew that she did. But…

she paused, looking around the kitchen. It was still more Lilly—Great-grandma Larson—than her. To appease Margie, she'd been taking baby steps with putting the old things away and bringing out hers. Margie never failed to notice. A comment like, "Oh, that meant so much to her…it's a pity you don't like it" would follow nearly every move she made.

That was really her excuse for letting Jack go off on his own. She couldn't live here, in someone else's house, and pretend that it was hers. She just couldn't. All of their boxes were shoved into a spare room and she'd been—little by little—taking her things out and shoving Lilly's back inside. The den was starting to look like home, complete with the large TV they'd brought with them. So were their bedrooms. That was the first thing she'd tackled. The great room? No, not so much. That's one reason she rarely went in there. It was a large house, old but large and roomy. A huge kitchen with enough room for their small table. The formal dining room was still furnished as it had been, including the nice hutch. They had yet to use it and she had no plans to. She'd redone both of their bathrooms. The last place to do was the kitchen. She thought she'd be finished by now, but she'd gotten sidetracked by trying to peel off the godawful wallpaper that was tacked to two walls. Margie had been appalled that she would even take it down, but she'd told her, once again, that if they were going to live there, it would be *her* home, not Great-grandma Larson's.

When she was through, though, she'd make some plans for her and Jack. There was a state park not too far from them—Garner. Right on the Frio River, it would be a good place to go swimming this summer. Margie had warned that it was extremely busy and crowded, but she'd take the chance. And one weekend soon, she wanted to make a trip back to San Antonio to see her family. She knew Jack would enjoy spending a couple of days at her parents' pool. Maybe then he would forget about this so-called friend of his…this Lindsey person that he'd made up.

"Grandma's here," Jack called seconds before Barney barked.

"Great," she murmured, eyeing the glass of wine she'd hardly touched.

Lilly's well-seasoned cast-iron skillet was already on the stove, ready for the chicken she was about to fry. The potatoes were just beginning to boil and she turned them down. She was embarrassed—ashamed—that there was no vegetable in sight. Margie would no doubt have a comment to make about that.

"Well, I see that dog is still in the house," Margie said as she came into the kitchen. "Lilly would have a fit if she knew."

Holding back the retort that was on the tip of her tongue, Hannah reached for her wineglass instead. It had been two days since she'd seen Margie. She thought perhaps she was mad because Jack had declined her invitation to church camp. Or maybe she was actually considering that she'd been over too much and was getting into their space.

"I brought some vegetables from the garden," Margie said, placing a basket on the counter. "I've got way more than Dennis and I can eat." Her words cut off abruptly. "Wine? Should you really be drinking in front of your son? And at this early hour?" she asked, her voice lowering to a near whisper.

Hannah looked beyond Margie, seeing Jack standing in the doorway, trying not to laugh. At that moment, she pictured James standing behind his mother, playfully making faces as she was forced to maintain a stoic expression. She nearly burst out laughing herself as Jack made silly faces at her.

"I know you're still grieving," Margie continued. "Alcohol is not the answer. I worry about you so, Hannah. You could find the answer, if you wanted, by coming to church with us."

She looked at Jack who was making a choking motion at his neck, his tongue sticking out. She had to turn away to keep from laughing.

"You can blame James if you want," she told Margie. "But don't blame it on his death. He thought it was uncivilized to have dinner without wine." She smiled quickly. "I happen to think it's uncivilized to *cook* dinner without wine." She turned the stove on, heating the oil in the skillet. "Do you want to stay for dinner? You can ask Dennis to come over," she offered, knowing that Margie would decline.

"Thank you, but tonight is pork chop night. Dennis expects it." She took a step back. "I really came over to let you know that Nathan and Liz are coming this weekend. It's probably been years since Jack has spent any time with his cousins."

Nathan was James's cousin and his kids were Jack's second cousins. And if she recalled, Jack had met them exactly once, when he was about four. She didn't count the short time they'd seen them at James's funeral. This was why they'd moved out here, she told herself. To allow Jack to connect—or reconnect—with his dad's family. So she nodded enthusiastically.

"Sure. Will there be a party or something?"

"Al is going to barbecue Saturday afternoon over at their place. You're welcome to ride over with us."

"Thanks," she said, knowing full well that she would take her own car. "Sounds like fun."

Of course later, as they were having their fried chicken with mashed potatoes and gravy without a single vegetable on the plate—despite the bounty of squash Margie had brought over—neither of them thought it would be much fun.

"I know," she said. "But they're your cousins."

"So?"

"So…that's why we moved out here. So you could be around Grandma Margie and Paw Paw Dennis," she said. "And whatever other relatives popped in."

"But I don't even know them," he complained.

"I don't either. But Nathan was your dad's cousin," she said, hoping that explained it. James and Nathan were close in age and grew up together. Once they'd left home, however, they hadn't really kept in touch. Regardless, they would go to the party and try to connect with James's family. That was the main reason they'd moved here.

Jack bit into a drumstick and immediately followed that up with a fork full of mashed potatoes. His cheeks bulged as he chewed. He looked adorable.

"Are you lonely?" she asked him.

He looked at her, blinking his eyes several times. "Not anymore," he said, potatoes showing as he talked.

She knew what he meant by that comment so she ignored it, continuing on with her train of thought. "You and me...we should do something, don't you think?"

He shrugged. "You've been busy."

"Yes, I have. I'm trying to get this place looking like home for us. I'm nearly finished, though. I want to plant some flowers. What do you say?"

He shrugged again. "Okay."

"You want to go with me? Margie says the Ranch Outpost in Utopia sells flowers and stuff. We can go tomorrow. Maybe have lunch there...get a burger or something."

He shook his head. "I'm supposed to meet Lindsey. Can we go early in the morning instead?"

She stared at him. How in the world could she compete with a made-up friend? Should she be worried? Should she suggest a therapist? She blew out her breath. James would tell her she was overreacting. James would tell her to chill out.

"Okay. We'll go early then," she conceded.

She was rewarded with a nod and smile as he shoved more mashed potatoes into his mouth.

CHAPTER NINE

Lindsey sat in the shade, watching as Jack tossed his line into the creek. He was barefoot, walking carefully across the rocks, trying to get out of the sun.

"It's hot," he said. "I wish we could go swimming."

"Yeah, me too. I guess your mom would be plenty mad, though."

"Yeah, she would." He squatted down, sitting on a small rock. It was hot enough for Max and Barney to forego their normal chasing. Both dogs were lying half in, half out of the creek, chewing on sticks. "We went to a party on Saturday."

"Oh. I was wondering why you weren't around. Was it fun?"

He shook his head. "Cousins. They didn't talk to me much. They thought I was a little kid."

"How old are they?"

"One was eleven and one thirteen. He was an asshole," Jack said, then he looked at her quickly. "I can say that because my mom's not around, but that's what she called him."

She laughed. "Yeah…thirteen…he probably thinks he's hot shit, I guess."

He giggled, then splashed water at her. She splashed it back. After a few minutes, his smile faded.

"They were talking about my daddy. They thought I wasn't listening. My grandma said that he was in a better place now." He looked over at her. "What does that mean? What could be better than with me and Mom?"

Lindsey snorted. "That's bullshit," she said.

His eyes widened.

"Sorry. That's crap," she said instead.

He laughed and so did she. Again, his smile faded. "You don't think he's with Jesus, do you?"

She shook her head slowly. "Oh, kid…I'm not the one to ask. I don't think that there's a Jesus or a God or anything like that." She lay down against the rocks, staring up into the clear blue sky. "I lost my whole family," she said.

"All of them?"

"Yeah…all of them. My grandparents. My mom and dad. My brother Shane and his wife Jessica. Their three kids. My sister Lorrie and her husband Dale." She swallowed. "And their two kids."

He was quiet for a moment, then he laid his fishing pole down and came over to her, sitting down beside her.

"What happened?" he asked in a whisper.

She turned her head slightly, meeting his blue eyes. "We… we had this annual trip we took. Every year. Every February. We went skiing in Colorado for ten days." She turned away from him, looking up into the sky again. "My grandfather was a pilot. He had a plane, an old Gulfstream…kept it over at the small airport in Uvalde. They were supposed to fly to Dallas and pick me up, like always." She closed her eyes. "I had a client change a design at the last minute. I'm a…I *was*…an architect." She swallowed and cleared her throat. "Anyway, I had…I had some changes to make and I couldn't get away. I told them to go on without me and I'd get a flight out in the next day or two." She opened her eyes again, seeing far into the heavens above her, not a single cloud in sight. "So my grandparents left here and went to San Antonio to pick up my parents and brother and sister and then, instead of flying to Dallas to get me, they headed to…to Colorado."

She felt tears running out of her eyes and she couldn't stop them. Her friends back in Dallas, her colleagues, they all knew what had happened—her family was killed in a plane crash. But this was the first time she'd said it out loud, the first time she'd recounted it in detail…and all of this to a nine-year-old kid. To her surprise, Jack laid down beside her and took her hand, his tiny fingers entwining with hers. Her tears turned to sobs.

"What happened?" he whispered.

"They…they didn't make it. The plane…the plane went down in New Mexico," she cried. "They…they were all gone. All of them. Gone." She tried to stop her tears but couldn't. He squeezed her hand tightly and she squeezed it back. "I was supposed to be with them, Jack. And I wasn't. Now I'm the only one still here."

Jack didn't say anything. Hell…he was nine years old, what was he going to say? They lay there on the rocks, her crying and him holding her hand. Max came over, his wet tongue wiping at her cheeks as he usually did when she cried. She gave a half-hearted laugh and pushed him away.

"Thanks, Max."

She finally sat up and bent over the creek, splashing her face with water. She used her shirt to dry her face, her eyes. Jack was still lying back, looking up into the sky. He turned his head and she was surprised to see tears in his eyes.

"That's why you look so sad sometimes," he said.

She nodded. "Yeah. Like you miss your daddy…I miss them."

He stared at her intently. "Do you have any friends, Lindsey?"

She slowly shook her head. "Just you."

He nodded in understanding. "Me neither. Just you."

CHAPTER TEN

Jack was sitting on the floor, putting on the filthy pair of Adidas he wore every day. Hannah glanced at the clock. Each day, he was going earlier and earlier to the creek and coming back dirtier and dirtier. What in the world was he getting into? She slowly shook her head. Was she being a terrible mother for letting him go out alone? In her defense, she'd asked him just yesterday if she could go with him, but he had said no, that he was fine.

Well, her unpacking and rearranging of the house was finished—finally—and she had time on her hands. So over breakfast, she'd offered to take him to the state park that was downstream on the Frio River and see if he wanted to go swimming. She thought he'd jump all over it. But no. He wasn't interested.

She tilted her head, watching him tie his shoes. "Jack?"

He looked up. "Uh-huh."

"What do you do down at the creek?"

He shrugged. "Stuff."

"Stuff? What kind of stuff?"

He shrugged again. "We fish. We talk. We put our feet in the water."

"We?"

He nodded. "Me and Lindsey. The dogs play in the water."

"Barney's…friend?"

"Yeah. Max. Sometimes Lindsey brings me a sandwich." The he grinned. "She brings me a Coke too. And a beer for her."

Hannah's eyes widened. How old was this imaginary friend of his, anyway? Well, enough was enough. She had to put an end to this. Other than forbidding him to go to the creek and dragging him—against his will—to the river for a day of swimming, her only option was to expose this so-called friend.

"Jack…how about I meet this friend that you say you have?"

He looked at her, his blue eyes blinking back at her. "I don't know. She might not want to meet you. She's kinda…private."

"I see." She put her hands on her hips in her best imitation of her own mother. "Well, I want to meet her. In fact, I insist on it."

He shrugged. "Okay," he said easily. "I'll ask her."

He then ran for the door, Barney at his heels. "Be back later," he said as the door slammed shut.

She watched through the window as he hurried down the hill with his fishing pole. She admitted he did look happier. A lot happier. And she couldn't recall the last time she'd seen him cry. That should count for something. But still…she felt like she'd abandoned him, forced him to invent a friend to play with. Not only that, he'd also made up a friend for Barney. How sad was that?

She was now more worried than before. Not only was his imaginary friend a girl…she was apparently old enough to drink beer. Where in the world would that have come from?

Should she tell Margie about it? Oh, God…as soon as that thought popped into her head, she pushed it aside.

"Don't be crazy," she murmured. Instead, she grabbed her phone and called her mother.

"Great minds think alike. I was just about to call you," came her mother's familiar voice. "How are you, honey?"

"Worried," she admitted. "About Jack," she clarified.

"What's wrong? I thought you said he seemed to be more like his old self."

"Yeah, but it's the *reason* for that that's got me worried. He has this…this friend," she said.

"What's wrong with that? Wasn't that why you moved there? So Jack could get a fresh start?"

She heard her mother pour a cup of coffee and she eyed her own pot, seeing that there was enough left for another cup.

"Well, this friend comes complete with a friend for Barney too. Oh, did I mention she's a she?" she asked as she poured the last of it into her cup.

"What are you talking about?"

"I left him alone, on his own. When we got to this house, I thought I'd been thrown back into the 1950s or something. I told you the condition of the house. Did I tell you about the wallpaper in the kitchen?" She glanced at the wall that was now bare of the offending paper, ready for paint instead.

"You did. What has this to do with Jack?"

"He seemed to be content going off to the creek by himself. I put some boundaries down there."

Her mother laughed. "Yes, you told me you cut up one of Mrs. Larson's old dresses."

Hannah laughed too. "It was forty years old, if it was a day!" Her smile faded. "Anyway, I left him alone too much, I guess. He's made up this friend, Mom. And he's made up a friend for Barney too. Not only has he made up a friend, it's a *girl* and she drinks beer! And he'd rather be with this…this person than go with me to the park where we could go swimming. You know how much he likes to swim. *That's* why I'm worried."

"Oh, honey, kids make up imaginary friends all the time. I'm sure it's nothing to worry about."

"Yeah, *kids*. Jack isn't a kid. He's mature for his age to begin with, not to mention he'll be ten in November."

"I think you're overreacting."

She sighed. "James would say the same thing."

"That's because James never worried about a thing. You did enough of that for the both of you." Her mother paused. "So how are *you* doing?"

Hannah looked out the window, seeing the empty space where Jack had been. "I'm lonely too," she admitted. "Margie is my only outlet for conversation. You can imagine how that goes."

"How was the family party last Saturday?"

"Oh, about like I expected. Jack and I felt out of place. And Nathan's kids, well, they picked on Jack constantly and the parents didn't do a thing. I wanted to wring their little necks."

"Having second thoughts on moving?"

"I'm way past second," she said with a laugh. "Once school starts, well, I'll become involved in that."

"Are you considering teaching again?"

"Mom, I've been out of the classroom for nine years. I barely remember the two years I did teach. So no. I am going to talk to the principal, though, and see about volunteering or something. There's also a small public library in town. I thought I might go by there and see if I could volunteer a few hours there too."

"Well, you make friends easily, honey. I'm sure once you meet people, things will get better," her mother said.

"I suppose. In the meantime…are you and Dad up for a visit some weekend? I know you're going to San Diego soon. Maybe when you're back from your trip?"

"Of course. We would love for you and Jack to visit. And once you get everything squared away there, we want to come see your new place."

"Yes, I remember. I'm afraid I haven't gotten to the spare bedroom yet."

"We're not picky."

"I know. I've just crammed all the unwanted stuff in there for now," she said with a laugh. "Well, I suppose I should let you go. I've got paint samples to go over."

"Okay, honey. And don't worry about Jack and his new friend. It'll blow over on its own."

"Well, it might be over very soon. I told Jack I wanted to meet his friend. I'm sure he'll have a good excuse as to why I can't. I'll just keep after him."

"Like you said, he's mature for his age. You could always ask him."

"I know…but I don't want to embarrass him. I'd rather this go away quietly and we never talk about it again."

CHAPTER ELEVEN

Lindsey sat down on the rock that Jack normally used when he waited for her. He was usually there before her, and she wondered if maybe his mom had something for him to do today. She tossed the rock she was holding into the creek and looked over her shoulder. Max was half-in, half-out of the water, already chewing on a stick.

She admitted that it was a little weird—this friendship that she and Jack had struck up. She wasn't entirely sure how healthy it was either. She knew that Jack wasn't her nephew. Of course she knew that. But the void she had in her life was huge, and he helped fill a small part of it. She actually looked forward to the days now instead of dreading them. And earlier, after breakfast, she and Max had gone down to the river. She'd taken the lane down to her parents' cabin. Yeah…her heart had lodged in her throat and she hadn't been able to stop there, but she'd taken the Mule past the house, down to the river. The old rope swing was there, dangling lazily from the cypress branch that her brother—years and years ago—had climbed up on to hang it.

She'd gone with the intent of getting in the river and she'd dressed appropriately...river shorts and water sandals. Unfortunately, she'd forgotten a swim top so she'd simply pulled her T-shirt over her head and tossed it down, her sports bra sufficing. She'd gone out to the pier and taken the rope in her hands, listening for the sounds of laughter, of clapping and cheering. Listening for the voice of her youngest niece, begging to swing out with her.

It was unusually quiet, though. A lone cardinal, bright red against the soft green of the cypress branch, landed next to her. He, too, was silent. Then his sharp, metallic sound rang out... crystal clear in the silence. He tilted his head, watching her, then once more his song echoed through the trees. To her, he sounded lonesome. Was he all alone? Then she heard it. Upstream, an answering call resonated and the cardinal flew off toward it. She watched the bird until it disappeared from sight, then, without much ceremony, she took a tighter hold of the rope, pushing off the pier like she'd done hundreds of times before.

She'd landed with a splash in the cold, clear river, surfacing with a loud "whoa" as the cold water surrounded her. She floated there for a second. It was a very lonely sound...the absence of laughter.

Then Max barked. And barked again. He walked to the edge of the pier, looking at her in the water. He tilted his head, then barked again.

"Well, come on in."

He was a Lab...a water dog, yet he hadn't been swimming. She waded over to the edge, coaxing him off the pier. He came around to the bank, walking across the cypress knees, just out of her reach...as if he knew what she'd planned.

"Come on, boy."

She'd finally grabbed him and pulled him into the water, his paws moving wildly as if swimming even before he touched down. She walked him out into deeper water, then let him go. He headed straight back toward the bank, stopping when he touched bottom. She did that three times before he finally took his first swim, moving past her into the deeper water, then back around her in a circle.

Her quick trip to the river turned into an hour-long play session with Max. And she'd had a blast. So had he.

She looked over at him now. She couldn't stop herself from smiling as he contentedly chewed on the stick. He looked up, ears alert, and she turned, following his gaze. Jack and Barney were coming down the trail. Max got to his feet and ran up to greet them.

"You beat me," Jack said.

"Sure did."

He pointed at her shorts. "Those are different."

"River shorts," she said. "For swimming. They dry in, like, five minutes."

By silent consent, they walked past the marker and to their little fishing hole.

"You told me yourself that the hole we fish in isn't even over my head. I don't think you'll fit."

"No? Well, maybe I'll just hop in and cool off."

"No! You'll chase away all the fish!"

She reached out and ruffled his hair. "Aren't you tired of catching the same little sunfish over and over?"

"No…it's fun."

"What's fun is fishing the river and catching a big bass or something. Or throwing lines out at night and catching blue cats," she said.

"What's that?"

"Catfish."

They got to their spot and she handed him a plastic bag of corn, and he went about the routine of baiting his hook.

"I went over to the river this morning," she said.

"You did? Were you okay?"

She nodded. "I didn't stop at their house. I went down to our old swimming hole." She pointed at her shorts. "I got in. That's the reason for these."

He nodded. "My momma asked me to go swimming with her. Over at the state park."

"Garner? Yeah, that's nice but crowded. During the summer, you can hardly get in the place." She sat down beside him. "Why didn't you go?"

He shrugged. "I wanted to come down here with you."

"It's hot. You should go with her. We can do this anytime."

"I know…but…"

She bumped his shoulder affectionately. "I like spending time with you too," she said quietly.

He smiled up at her, then turned his attention back to his bobber, which hadn't moved. After a few minutes, he turned to her.

"She wants to meet you."

Her eyebrows shot up. "She does? You told her about me?"

"Kinda. I don't think she thinks you're real."

"What do you mean?"

"The way she looks when I mention you…like I made you up." He kicked at a rock. "Like I'm some little kid or something."

"Oh," she said. "Like an imaginary playmate?"

"Uh-huh."

She nodded. Well, she knew this day would come sooner or later. It was probably past time that she met his mother. If they met and she saw that Lindsey wasn't some wacko or something, maybe she'd let Jack go fishing with her. Real fishing, at the river. And maybe swimming too.

And maybe she'd take him out to the pond. She wanted to go there, but she didn't want to go alone. If she was going to go with anybody, she wanted it to be Jack. So yeah, maybe it was time to meet his mom.

It was hot. Hotter than usual and the fish weren't biting. They'd given up fishing and had simply walked in the creek, splashing around to keep cool. Jack was barefoot, carrying his shoes with him as they walked.

"You need to get some sandals like this," she told him.

He nodded. "I'll ask Mom."

When they got back to their usual meeting place, she motioned up the hill. "You want me to walk home with you and meet your mom now?"

He looked at her and smiled. "Would you?"

"Sure. It'll put her mind at ease, at least. And maybe if she likes me, she might let you go fishing with me."

His eyes lit up. "At the river?"

"Yeah." She grinned too. "And maybe swimming."

"Oh, that'd be so cool, Lindsey! And Barney could come too, right?"

"Of course. Max and Barney are buddies, just like you and me."

"Yeah…buddies like us."

Jack sat down and quickly put his shoes back on, then led the way up the hill. Barney ran around him with Max following. She brought up the rear.

"So what's your mom like?"

He shrugged. "She's just Mom. Kinda old, I guess."

Old? Well, the kid was nine, almost ten. She thought his mother could be anywhere between thirty and forty. Lindsey didn't really have an image of her in her mind. She hadn't given his mother much thought, really. Would she look like Jack? Blond hair and blue eyes? Or was Jack a replica of his dad?

When the house came into sight, it brought back an old memory that she hadn't thought of in years. She and Shane— pre-teens at the time—had crossed the creek onto the Larson's property and had crept up the hill, hoping to catch Old Lady Larson outside. They had hidden behind some young cedars, the house—this house—looking huge and sinister to their eyes. Sure enough, Old Lady Larson was hanging clothes out on the line. They'd lost their nerve to run up and scare her, though. They had broken into a fit of giggles at the thought, however, and she had heard them. To their surprise, she was still quite nimble on her feet and she chased them through the woods and back across the creek, screaming at them the whole time. By the time they'd made it back to their grandparents' house, she had already called, telling them to keep those "hoodlum" kids off her property. Her grandmother's words still rang in her ears today: "She's a mean old biddy. Best leave her alone. If she catches you, we're likely to never get you back."

She smiled at the memory. That scene only reinforced the warnings that they'd heard most of their young lives…warnings to stay away from the Larson place.

Now, here she was, some seventeen years later, walking up to that very same house, the house that Jack now lived in. She wondered what had happened to Old Lady Larson and if she was still alive.

"Jack...you said this was your great-grandmother's house?"

"Uh-huh."

"Where is she? Does she live with you?"

"No. She's really old. She's in...what do they call it? A home?"

"Nursing home?"

"Yeah. There. So Grandma Margie said we could live here." He stopped walking. "She had so much old junk in there, we didn't have anywhere to put our stuff. That's what my mom's been doing...cleaning it." His voice lowered. "Grandma Margie isn't real happy with the change."

Lindsey smiled at him and nodded. "Change is hard." Her smile disappeared as quickly as it had come. Yeah, she should know. Change was very hard. Of course, Jack would know that too.

The dogs romping by the back porch must have caused enough racket for Jack's mother to hear. The back door opened slowly and a woman came out. An attractive young woman, perhaps only a few years older than herself. And no, she wasn't blond like Jack. Her hair was light brown, cut short like her own, barely covering her ears on the side. She walked out onto the porch, and even from this distance, Lindsey could see the shock on her face. Jack had been right. His mother thought she was only a figment of his imagination.

As she and Jack walked closer, the woman looked between the two of them, then her gaze darted to the dogs, then back to Jack. Jack jerked his thumb at Lindsey.

"Well, you wanted to meet her. Here she is. And that's Max."

She was clearly shaken so Lindsey walked to the porch, smiling, hoping to put her at ease. "I'm Lindsey McDermott," she said.

The woman's eyes were brown, not blue. "Hannah... Hannah Larson," she said. "I'm—"

"Jack's mom," Lindsey finished for her. "Nice to meet you."

Hannah Larson stared her up and down, apparently still not sure what to make of her. Lindsey stood there, shifting a bit nervously as Hannah inspected her. Hannah finally gave her a hesitant smile.

"Come in, please," she said, motioning to the back door. "Jack...why don't you stay outside with the dogs."

He smirked. "I know you want to talk about me. It's okay."

At that, Hannah Larson smiled. "Quit being such a smarty-pants."

Lindsey winked conspiratorially at Jack, getting an exaggerated wink in return. She was smiling as she followed his mother inside, the coolness of the house a welcome change from the heat outside.

"Excuse the mess," Hannah said, waving at the newspapers spread out on the floor. "I'm just starting to paint." She pointed to a bare wall. "The most godawful wallpaper I've ever seen in my life was there."

Lindsey nodded politely. "I can imagine."

Hannah looked at her directly. "So...you're real."

Lindsey smiled at that. "Yeah, I'm real. Not an imaginary friend."

Hannah raised her eyebrows. "He knew I thought that?"

"Yeah. He's a pretty smart kid." She shoved her hands into the pockets of her shorts. "I live across the creek. That's all my...my grandparents' property over there. I stumbled across Jack one day." She shrugged, almost embarrassed by their friendship. She was twenty years older than Jack. "I needed a fishing partner," she said, hoping that explained it.

"Well, I don't know what to say. I feel like I've had a babysitter these last few weeks and I didn't even know it." She moved to the fridge. "Can I offer you something to drink?"

"I'm okay," she said, thinking of the cooler she'd left down at the creek. That cold beer sure would be good right about now. "I should probably get going anyway. Jack just said you wanted to meet me."

"Yes. I was worried about him, actually. His father...he—"

"Died," she supplied. "Brain tumor. I'm very sorry for your loss," she said automatically.

"He told you? I'm surprised. He doesn't ever talk about it."

"Well…yeah, we've talked about it. Listen…I hope you don't mind Jack hanging out with me. The kid likes to fish."

"Apparently."

Lindsey laughed. "The creek is not exactly the best place. He's caught a few sunfish and a couple of perch. He probably catches the same ones over and over."

"I know it's shallow. That's the only reason I let him go down there alone."

"Yeah, it is. But…I was thinking, if you didn't mind, I could take him out and do some real fishing."

"Real fishing?"

"Yeah. Our property borders the Frio. There are some great fishing holes." She brushed at the hair on her forehead nervously. "I…when I was growing up, I practically lived out here during the summer months."

"And you want to take him fishing?"

Lindsey met her gaze. "Yeah. I think he'd have fun."

Hannah looked at her suspiciously. "And what are *you* getting out of it?"

How did she answer that question? She didn't even know the answer herself. What *was* she getting out of it? Company? Sure, that went without saying. It was more than that, though. Jack gave her a purpose…a reason to get up each day. He helped fill a little bit of the emptiness that surrounded her. He brought a little bit of light into her dark world. But how did she tell his mother that? How did she tell Hannah Larson that her son—without even knowing it—was helping to heal her broken heart?

"I'm staying here all summer…by myself." She gave a slight shrug. "With my grandparents gone," she said evasively, "it's a little lonely out there. Jack's been great company." She smiled. "And Max and Barney have become inseparable. So…if you think it'd be okay, I'd love to take him fishing to the river." It was her turn to look at Hannah with a questionable gaze.

"Well, I'm sure he would enjoy that. I just don't want him to monopolize your time."

"He's not." She pointed to the bare wall. "You seem to be busy with painting. I'd be happy to take him off your hands for a few hours."

"Okay, no offense, Lindsey, but—and while you seem like a very nice person—I don't even know you. I mean—"

"How is Mrs. Larson? Lilly, I believe is her name. I haven't seen her in years."

Hannah looked surprised. "You know Lilly?"

"Well, she used to run us out of the creek when we were kids," she said with a laugh. "Jack said she was in a nursing home."

Hannah nodded. "They moved her there a few months ago. She's ninety-two, I think."

"Wow." She headed to the door. "I should get going. It was nice to meet you." She paused at the door. "If you'd like to exchange phone numbers…you know, in case—"

"In case I decide to let Jack go fishing with you?"

She nodded. "Yeah. I hope you will. Because even though you don't know *me*, I know the Larsons. Like I said, I spent every summer out here."

"Well, I suppose it wouldn't hurt to exchange numbers."

When she went back outside, Jack was throwing a ball to the dogs. She was pleased that Max seemed to be winning at this game. Maybe her evening sessions with him were paying off.

"So? How did it go?" Jack asked quietly.

"I'm not sure yet. I think she's still in shock that I'm real," she said with a smile. She ruffled his head. "Your mom is pretty cute. You probably shouldn't call her old. She'd be pissed," she teased.

He rolled his eyes.

"I should go."

"Okay," he said, his smile fading.

She paused, then tapped his head playfully. "See you later, buddy."

CHAPTER TWELVE

Hannah was literally speechless as she watched Lindsey and Jack. An affectionate ruffle of his hair, the dejected look on Jack's face as Lindsey walked away…she noticed all of it. So yes, there really was a friend. She felt a twinge of guilt for doubting him. But what did it mean? Why was this woman hanging around her son? It was odd. Very odd.

She stood at the window long after Lindsey McDermott had left, still watching as Jack sat on the porch, his legs swinging idly, his gaze on the woods and the creek beyond that. Yes…it was odd. And she had no clue as to what to say to him.

She finally pushed the door open and went outside. He glanced at her, offering a tiny smile as she sat down beside him.

"So that's your Lindsey, huh?"

"Uh-huh." He got right to the point. "Can I go fishing with her? *Please*," he begged.

"I don't know, Jack. I don't even know her."

"But I know her," he said. "She's…she needs a friend." His voice was quiet and she thought he was trying not to cry.

"And you need a friend?" she asked softly.

He nodded. Yes, he was trying very hard not to cry. She didn't have the heart to disappoint him.

"Okay...you can go with her."

He flew into her arms, nearly knocking them off onto their backs.

"Thank you!"

She hugged him tightly, hoping she wasn't making a mistake...hoping that Lindsey McDermott was as trustworthy as she seemed.

"Okay...go get cleaned up. Let's drive into Leaky. I've got some shopping to do. Then we'll get an early dinner. How about Mexican food?"

"Yay!"

He ran into the house with Barney at his heels. The lone Mexican food restaurant in the area was up in Leaky, forty-five minutes away. It wasn't great, by any means, but it would do. Living in San Antonio, she was spoiled by all the choices. Here? The twenty-minute drive into Utopia would get her to a very modest grocery store and an old, dated hardware store. There was exactly one place to eat—the café, which served decent enough burgers. There was one beauty shop which she dreaded having to go to when it came time for a trim. There was a lone gas station and convenience store with a laundry and car wash. There were five churches. *Five.* And three antique shops. Two liquor stores. Her favorite spot so far was the Utopia General Store. They sold a little bit of everything, and they even had a few groceries, along with a meat market and a deli.

She could make do. Still...moving from a vibrant, thriving city to the remote Hill Country northwest of San Antonio would be an adjustment for her. An adjustment she'd been willing to make. As she'd told her mother, once Jack started school, once she got out and actually met people, they would surely feel more comfortable out here. But for now...it was just the two of them...she and Jack.

And, of course, Lindsey McDermott.

She finally got up from her spot on the porch, glancing once at the woods the woman had disappeared into. Who was

Lindsey McDermott? If she had to guess, she would say Lindsey was thirtyish. An attractive woman, her dark hair cut in a cute, sporty style. She appeared to be well-mannered and perfectly normal. And she'd given Jack permission to go fishing with her, but who *was* she? Well, she had no choice but to ask Margie about her. Margie hadn't been by the house today, which meant she'd definitely be by tomorrow to see what color she'd picked out for the kitchen.

She went inside, glancing at the bare wall. She'd tackle it first thing in the morning, she decided. And maybe with a little persuasion—like pancakes—she'd get Jack to help. She paused, looking around the room. It was beginning to look more like her own kitchen, but she wondered if she'd ever feel like it was truly hers. Margie—despite her insistence that the house was hers to do with as she wanted—never failed to make a comment about how Lilly would be "devastated" to see all the changes. The changes were minimal, in her opinion. Even ripping off the hideous wallpaper was minor. If she *really* felt like this was her house, there were countless other changes she would make. If they made the year and decided to stay on, then she would insist on them. Now, however, she didn't have the will to fight with Margie over it. That had always been James's duty...to stand up to his mother. It had been a constant battle and over the years, their visits had gotten shorter—day trips mostly— and less frequent. When James got sick, they stopped coming altogether. Margie and Dennis made the drive into San Antonio to see them. At the end, Margie stayed for nearly two weeks. Hannah couldn't deny her that...her wish to be there when "the Lord called him home." But when Margie tried to change the funeral plans, plans that James had set up himself, Hannah had had enough. They both said things that they probably shouldn't have, but she made her point and Margie had left, only coming back for the day of the service. Because of that, she'd been as shocked as anyone when Margie had proposed that she and Jack move to their place here near Utopia.

She blew out her breath and looked around the kitchen once again. No, even with her familiar things out, it still didn't feel like home. She wondered if it ever would.

CHAPTER THIRTEEN

"This is so cool!"

Lindsey smiled at Jack's exuberance. The Mule was bouncing along the trail, the dogs running behind them. After picking Jack up at the creek, she decided to take the long way around to the river. They climbed up the rocky trail, going higher up the mountain where the view looked down toward Concan and the Frio River on one side and then east, toward Utopia. The mountains in the Texas Hill Country didn't rival the Rockies by any means, but they were a beautiful sight nonetheless, some rising over three thousand feet. Granite and craggy limestone outcrops, wooded canyons and of course, the fertile river valley—she had a little of it all here...the river, the creek, and the wooded hills. No wonder her grandmother called it their little slice of paradise.

She stopped the Mule at the pullout on Antler Peak—her grandfather's name for it—and paused to take in the views.

"You can see forever up here," Jack said in awe. "Look! There's some deer running."

"Yeah. I should have brought the binoculars."

"Do you shoot deer?"

"Me? No." She shook her head. Years and years ago, when they'd first bought the property, her grandfather had hunted, and when her father was young, he'd also hunted. Over the years, that tradition had stopped—thankfully. By the time she came around, the deer feeder had been moved closer to the house so they could watch the deer, not shoot them.

"We have deer come right up to the porch," Jack said. "Barney barks at them. Mom says they're coming up to eat the shrubs."

"Yeah, they'll eat just about anything. I've got a feeder at the house, but there's no corn in it. I've seen them go to my grandmother's vegetable garden but..."

Jack met her eyes. "There's nothing in it?"

"No. Not this year."

He looked at her thoughtfully. "Maybe next year."

She smiled at him affectionately. "Yeah...maybe next year I'll try my hand at gardening."

Before starting out again, she put the tired puppies on the back. Max had ridden with her before, but this was a first for Barney. With tails wagging, they hung their heads over the side as she headed down to the river trail. When she passed the cutoff that would take her to the back side of the pond, she had a sudden urge to visit it instead of the river. She looked over at Jack.

"So...it's kinda late already. Hot."

He nodded.

"Want to go swimming instead of fishing?"

He grinned. "Oh, yeah!" Then his smile faltered a little. "I didn't bring anything to swim in."

"Well...we'll run by my place. My nephews...well, they kept stuff there."

His smile faded altogether. "Are you sure?"

She nodded. "I'm sure."

She'd done little more than stick her head into the spare bedrooms that her brother and sister had used for their families.

The master bedroom, where her grandparents had slept, had been converted into her own room. Their clothes had been boxed, but so far she hadn't had the heart to give anything away. Same with the other rooms. Mostly summer clothes—river clothes—and a few odds and ends. She needed to box everything up, clean it up, but she'd been in no hurry.

"Wow," Jack said when they turned into the lane that would take them to the house. "This is pretty."

The lane was lined with pecan trees, eight on each side, their branches reaching across, making a canopy overhead. When they pulled up to the house, he uttered another "wow."

"This is bigger than our house," he said.

"I don't know. I think it's the decks and porches that make it look big. Three bedrooms, that's all." She lifted the dogs off the back. "That's why my parents had the little river cabin. There wasn't room for all of us here."

Max and Barney took off around the side, chasing after a squirrel that had apparently come to check the bird feeder. The empty, neglected bird feeder. She had a sudden vision of her grandmother carrying the old blue bucket she used, scooping out seed with a coffee can and filling the feeders.

She walked over to them now, conscious of Jack beside her. The area was nestled between four small oaks. The birdbath, complete with a mister hanging from a branch, was dry as a bone. The three feeders—two box and one cylinder—hung from branches, the seed long gone. Spiderwebs dangled from them now, and she wiped them away. Her grandmother would be disappointed in her. Hell, *she* was disappointed in her. She'd abandoned the things that her grandmother loved the most— the garden, the deer and bird feeders. She'd neglected them, not giving them a thought really. She was too caught up in her own grief to pay them any attention. But like her uncle said, *this* was where the laughter was, this was where the love was. If she was going to get that back...try to get that back...then she needed to bring back some of the things that her grandmother loved.

"Are you okay, Lindsey?"

Jack's words were barely more than a whisper. She pulled her gaze from the empty, lonely feeders, giving him a quick smile.

"Yeah. I was thinking about how much my grandmother liked to watch the birds. And how I'd neglected this area." She walked over to the edge where the faucet was and turned it on. The mister came to life, spraying a fine mist of water over the birdbath and the once vibrant ferns that were around it. She mentally added birdseed and deer corn to her shopping list.

"Okay, come on. Let's see if we can find you something to swim in."

* * *

"He went *where*?"

"Fishing," Hannah said again.

Margie frowned so sharply her eyebrows were meeting between her eyes. "With a *McDermott*?"

"Yes. Lindsey. Do you know her?"

"The McDermotts were killed," she said. "A terrible accident. The whole family," she said with a shake of her head. "I tell you, he was too old to still be flying that plane, but they always thought they were better than everyone else."

"What kind of accident?"

"Some ski trip," she said with a wave of her hand. "The plane crashed. I don't know all of the details, just what we heard in town. Lilly said the whole family was nothing but hoodlums. Always were. Crazy people, she called them."

Hannah frowned. *Hoodlums*? "So...this Lindsey is...who then?"

"I think she's their granddaughter, but I'd heard the whole family had perished. I didn't think anyone was living over there."

"I don't know anything about that."

"Then why on God's green earth would you let Jack go off with her? Why...she could abduct him. Next thing you know, we'll have to file an Amber Alert or something," she said, her hands waving wildly in the air.

She didn't want to just dismiss Margie's fears...it's something she'd already thought of herself. But as James would say, they were overreacting.

"Jack has apparently been spending time with her...down at the creek. She seemed perfectly normal, nice. I don't think we have anything to worry about," she said, hoping to ease her own fears as well.

"Nowadays you can't trust people, Hannah."

She put her paintbrush down and glanced at the clock. It hadn't even been an hour since Jack had left. Was it too soon to call and check up on him? Yes, of course it was. Lindsey had promised to take good care of him. Jack had been so excited he was practically dancing in the kitchen when Hannah had called her, telling Lindsey that he could go fishing. So no, she wasn't going to buy into Margie's assertion that Lindsey McDermott was a "hoodlum." As she'd thought earlier, Lindsey was nice and appeared to be perfectly normal. She would trust her own instincts.

"I think it'll be fine," she said to Margie. "If you can't trust your neighbors, then our society is in very sad shape."

"*Is* she a neighbor? Did she move here? Is she here for the summer? What? What do you know about her?"

"I don't know...I don't know anything." Truthfully, she knew absolutely zero about Lindsey McDermott. And as soon as Jack was returned home safely, she would be a little more diligent in finding out about her. Especially if Jack wanted to make this fishing excursion a common occurrence.

CHAPTER FOURTEEN

"Okay…remember, this is a secret," she said as they turned onto the trail that would take them to the pond.

"How'd you find it?"

She grinned. "Can't tell you. It wouldn't be a secret then. I should really blindfold you, you know."

He laughed. "I won't tell anyone. I don't even know where we are."

"Yeah, it's confusing. The trail I picked you up on…by the creek…that used to be an old Jeep road. My grandfather stopped using the Jeep when they came out with these utility vehicles, like this Mule."

"Do you still have it?"

She shook her head. "Not his, no. He got rid of it a few years ago. He always used this when riding around out here." She nudged him with her arm. "There's a four-wheeler at the pond, though."

"Oh, cool! Can we ride it?"

"I don't even know if it'll start. It hadn't been used since last summer, I guess. And…your mother would probably kill me if she found out. It's bad enough I'm sneaking you off to go swimming."

Yeah, the adult in her knew that this probably wasn't the smartest move she'd ever made. She was going on Jack's word that he knew how to swim. The pond was deep. But there were water toys there that the kids had used…the tubes, the noodles, and her favorite—the fanny floaters. She assumed everything would be like they'd left it. Labor Day weekend was the last time they'd swum in the pond.

"So what kind of a pond is this?"

"It's paradise," she said, using her grandmother's word. "It was formed when an underground spring collapsed. Well, the ground on top of it collapsed. It's this big limestone pool, really. It's got a little waterfall and everything."

"Oh, cool!"

His grin was contagious and she returned it. It disappeared from her face, however, when the pond came into sight. She pulled the Mule to the side, next to the lean-to. Like everything else, the place looked neglected. Tree branches were scattered about and leaves still covered the canvas tarp that was draped over the four-wheeler.

Jack was sitting in awe, though, his mouth slightly open as he stared. The dogs were whimpering on the back, wanting to get out.

"Wow," he whispered. "It's…it's magical."

"Yeah…I know," she said quietly, her gaze taking in the pond and waterfall. The waterfall was small by most standards—ten feet high at most. It dropped in a nice cascade into the pond, adding icy cold spring water by the gallons.

"It looks like a picture or something," Jack said. "How did you find it?" he asked again.

"This pond was here long before we were," she said. "When my great-grandfather bought this land, he found it. My grandfather learned to swim in this very pond. So did my father."

"And then you."

"Yep."

His face turned solemn. "And your brother and sister?"

She nodded. "Lorrie was the oldest, then Shane." She swallowed. "Their kids all learned to swim here too." She took a deep breath, pushing down the grief that threatened to show itself.

She went around to the back of the Mule and dropped the tailgate, letting the dogs hop off.

With Max's newfound love of swimming, he led the way and splashed into the pond. Barney, however, held back, walking in only enough to get his feet wet.

She laughed. "Yeah…finally something Max can do that Barney can't."

Jack got out of the Mule, seemingly taking it all in. He watched the dogs, then glanced at the pier, then the lean-to, then back to the pier.

He walked out onto it and stood there, his gaze going to the waterfall that plunged into the pond. It was still flowing pretty good, she noted. Some years when it was hot and dry, the flow was nothing more than a trickle. The pier had been there forever, but her grandfather had added the little deck on the side of the pond within the last five years. Her father had wanted to put a larger deck next to the lean-to, but her grandfather wouldn't hear of it. He wanted it to remain primitive. Even so, the little deck got its use. While the kids were playing in the water, the adults would sit there, drinking beer from the cooler he'd packed. Lindsey would alternate between playing with the kids…and joining the adults on the pier with a cold beer. She smiled now, thinking of those long, lazy summer days. She looked about, hating that she'd let it get to this condition. Her grandfather always had the pond and the surrounding area looking pristine. Now…it looked neglected, as it had been.

"When you were little, did you swim in the river too?"

She turned her attention to Jack, pushing her memories aside. "We weren't allowed to go into the river until we could prove that we could swim across the pond."

The pond itself, while deep in the middle, wasn't extremely wide. She'd guess forty feet across at its farthest point and perhaps fifteen feet deep in the middle. Away from the waterfall, where the pier was, it was only thirty feet across, if that. The limestone bottom made for a crystal clear pool, the hue of the water changing from blue to green, depending on the angle of the sun. The ferns that grew along and under the rim, however, made it look like something from a tropical paradise and not the Hill Country. Unlike the river and creek, there were no cypress trees here. Oaks, maples and the ever-present juniper—cedar— dominated the terrain.

She walked over to the lean-to and opened up one of the two metal footlockers there. Inside were the water toys she'd remembered. She pulled out a noddle and tossed it to Jack, who caught it between his hands. She smiled as she found her favorite fanny floater.

"Okay…so you swear you won't drown, right?"

He laughed. "I swear."

Max and Barney were splashing in the water on the far end of the pond where the overflow trickled down to form an unnamed creek that eventually found its way into little Buffalo Creek.

"I'll warn you now, it's cold," she said. "I always found it best to just jump in and get it over with."

She pulled her tank top off and tossed it on the pier. She'd at least remembered her top this time so she wasn't just in a sports bra. She looked down at herself, thinking the bra covered more than this little bikini top did. She walked out to the end of the pier, holding the fanny floater in her arms and…after looking around the empty pond, she turned to look at Jack, meeting his gaze. No, it wasn't empty. Jack was here. He smiled at her and she smiled back, then she took a couple of running steps and plunged into the cold water.

"Oh…yeah!" she yelled as she surfaced. She shook her hair, slicking it away from her face, then climbed into the fanny floater, sinking down into the water, the float keeping only her arms and torso above water. "Okay, kid…your turn."

Jack did his version of a Tarzan yell as he ran down the pier and jumped in. The noodle he carried flew out ahead of him and when he surfaced, she had a moment of panic. But he grinned at her and swam over to the noodle, resting one arm across it.

"It's not that cold," he said.

"No?"

He grinned. "Okay…a little." He dogpaddled over toward her, holding on to her float with one hand and his noodle with the other.

With them both out in the water, the dogs were getting anxious. After a little coaxing, Max jumped in and swam toward them, getting close enough for a rub on the head before heading back to shore. Barney whimpered and pawed at the water but refused to get in.

"Why won't he swim? He gets in the creek."

"Well, he's still a pup," she said. "The creek is shallow. He can walk across it."

"Max isn't scared."

"It took me three or four tries before Max would swim on his own. Don't worry, Barney will come in."

She'd no sooner spoke the words and he lunged into the water as Max swam back to him. Down he went, his big feet splashing as he tried to swim. He headed back into shallow water, standing near the shore as Max swam back out.

"You used to come here a lot?"

"We went to the river more, I guess. My parents' house was right there so we had everything. Here, there's no electricity, no drinking water, no bathrooms."

"But this is like a swimming pool."

"Yeah, but the river has a big rope swing in one of the cypress trees. Now that's fun," she said with a grin. "We'll do that too."

He pushed off of her, swimming toward the shore and the dogs, leaving his noodle behind. He got out of the water, his bare feet slipping on the rocks as he climbed back to the pier. He held his arms up, then took off running, leaping high in the air and landing with a splash into the water. Again, she had a moment of panic, only releasing her breath when his head popped above water. She shoved the noodle in his direction and he draped his arms over it, kicking his feet to float over toward her.

"So whose swim shorts am I wearing?" he asked, surprising her with the question.

"Those were Jett's. He was my brother's oldest child. He would have been ten this summer…in August."

"Like me. I'll be ten in November."

She nodded. "Yeah…like you." She met his gaze. "You…you remind me of him. Well, actually, you remind me of Eli, his little brother, but he was only seven." She paused. "I don't know if that's a good thing or not. I know you're not him…yet…"

"That's okay, Lindsey. You remind me of my dad. I know you're not him, but you do stuff with me, take me fishing." He smiled. "Now swimming."

She splashed water at him playfully. "Your dad, huh? You probably shouldn't tell your mother that."

He splashed water back at her, then ducked under and swam for shore. She smiled as she watched him get out and climb back on the pier, giving another Tarzan yell as he jumped once again into the pond.

CHAPTER FIFTEEN

Hannah couldn't help but notice the change in Jack the last few weeks. He was as happy as she'd ever seen him. The summer so far—at least for him—was turning out how she'd wanted...him carefree and enjoying his time out here where his dad grew up. But for her? She looked at the freshly painted kitchen. That had been her so-called fun. She'd done about as much to the place as she could without Margie having a stroke. Most of Lilly's things were boxed up and put away. Her and Jack's things were now out. The kitchen was pretty much all hers, the unpacking was done, the cleaning was finished.

She now had time on her hands. Unfortunately, her son was nowhere to be found. She'd practically abandoned him the first four weeks they'd been here. She'd left him on his own while she tended to the house. Since he'd found a friend, it seemed that he was now abandoning *her*.

Here she sat—alone—waiting on him to return from yet another fun outing with Lindsey McDermott.

God, she hoped the woman wasn't doing anything...anything *bad* to her son. She shook her head. Don't be ridiculous, she told herself. Jack was happy. Jack practically danced when he was leaving here, running down the trail to the creek with Barney... running to meet Lindsey.

Okay, so was she jealous that he had a friend? Did she feel like someone was taking her place? She nibbled on her lower lip. Yes, maybe a little of both, she admitted. She wasn't really worried, she told herself. Not really. Lindsey usually texted her if they were going to be late. Like yesterday when they'd been fishing. She glanced at the clock. There'd been no text today so she assumed Jack would be back any minute now. She'd made a cheesy, gooey casserole for dinner, one of his favorite meals. All she had to do was bake it. That was how she'd spent her afternoon—cooking—while he'd been out playing.

She leaned back in her chair. God, how depressing. If James were here, he'd tell her that she was digging herself in deeper and deeper into her pool of misery. He would tell her to get out and do something. Of course, if James were here, they wouldn't be *here*.

She brushed away a tear, surprised that it had formed. The tears she had now...were they still for James? Or were they for herself and the sad state she found herself in? How selfish of her if the tears were for the latter. It was her own fault. There were plenty of ways to meet people, to make new friends. She simply hadn't been in the right frame of mind. Was she now? Could she make another two months of this, waiting on school to start?

No. She couldn't. She had to get out. She had to *do* something and she'd drag Jack along—kicking and screaming—if she had to. Of course, that brought to mind a scene from the other day when she'd once again asked if Jack wanted to go to the state park. His answer had been quick and decisive—no. He already had plans with Lindsey.

Which again made her wonder just what it was that they did together. She squeezed her eyes shut for a moment, hoping that Lindsey wasn't hurting him, hoping she wasn't...well, doing unthinkable things with him.

Stop it! No! Jack was happy. There were absolutely no signs whatsoever that Lindsey was doing anything inappropriate. Still, he was nine years old, for god's sake. Just a child.

No, the problem was, Jack shared very little about what they did. His answers were always evasive, vague. Well, to put her mind at ease, she would ask him directly today what in the hell it was that they did all day long!

It was only a few moments later that she saw him emerge from the woods, using the trail he and Barney had made. As she watched him, she noted the smile on his face. She also noted what appeared to be a skinned knee. Had he fallen? Then she frowned. Where was his fishing pole? Hadn't he taken it with him?

He burst into the back door of the kitchen, Barney at his heels.

"Hey, Mom," he said.

"Hey, yourself," she answered. She stopped him when he would have walked on past. "What happened to you?"

"What do you mean?"

"Your knee."

"Oh." He held his leg out and looked down at his injury. "I fell on the rocks."

"I see. And…where is your fishing pole?"

"Lindsey has it."

She got up and walked around him, turning him to face her. "Jack…what is it that you and Lindsey do all day?"

He shrugged. "Fishing…and stuff."

"What kind of stuff?"

"Just…stuff," he said.

"Jack…no, that answer is not going to fly this time," she said as she put her hands on her hips. "I want to know what you do."

He bit his lip nervously and shifted in front of her, refusing to meet her gaze.

"Jack?"

"It's…it's a secret," he said quietly.

She felt her heart jump into her throat. A secret? What did that mean? What was Lindsey doing with him—to him—that warranted it be kept a secret from her? Was she brainwashing him? Manipulating him? She tried very hard to keep her expression even.

"Jack…a secret?"

He nodded. "I can't tell you."

"Jack…you need to tell me right now what she's doing to you."

He shook his head. "I can't. It's our secret."

Oh, God…

She took his shoulders and squeezed them. "Jack…tell me right now."

"Mom…you'll get mad."

Oh, my God. Oh, my God. Oh, my God. What was this woman doing to him? She tried to push back her fear, hoping it wasn't showing on her face.

"No, I promise I won't get mad, Jack. You have to tell me, okay?"

"You won't get mad?"

"I promise," she said again.

He looked away from her, his head hung down. "We've… we've been going…swimming," he said quietly.

She frowned. "Swimming?"

"Yeah."

She released the hold she had on him and stood up straight. "*Swimming?*" she asked with raised eyebrows.

"You said you wouldn't get mad."

She took a deep breath. "Okay. Swimming." *Thank you!* She paused. "Where?"

"Well, sometimes in the river."

"The *river?*"

"We have floats and stuff. And sometimes we go…well, I can't tell you. It's a secret."

She grabbed the bridge of her nose and squeezed it. "Jack… you're nine years old. I know you know how to swim but—"

"I'm almost ten."

"Okay. Okay…let's say you're ten. You're still too young to be out by yourself, swimming in the *river*, for god's sake!"

"I'm not by myself. Lindsey's with me. She's a good swimmer. She's taught me to do the backstroke and everything."

Great…some strange woman is teaching my son the backstroke. She rubbed her forehead, surprised that her head hadn't already exploded. "So where else do you go besides the river?"

He shook his head. "I can't tell you. It's a secret."

She stared at him. "Okay, you're really starting to piss me off, Jack."

He stared back at her, his big blue eyes serious. "You shouldn't use words like that in front of me."

Okay, so this was going nowhere. Well, if Jack wouldn't tell her, then she'd just have to ask Lindsey where the hell they went that was such a big secret.

"Go take a bath," she said abruptly, pointing to the door. "I'll get dinner going."

"What are we having?"

"Liver and onions."

His eyes widened. "Oh, gross, Mom."

"Yes, indeed." She rolled her eyes. "You know very well that it's not liver and onions. Had I known that you were going to be keeping secrets from me, I wouldn't have made your favorite."

"Spaghetti and meatballs?"

"Your other favorite."

"The triple-cheese hamburger casserole?"

"That's the one."

He clapped his hands. "Oh, goody!" he yelled before running from the kitchen.

Well, at least I did something right, she thought as she turned the oven on.

* * *

After dinner, while Jack was playing with his game, she took her phone out to the back porch and called Lindsey McDermott.

"Yes, this is Hannah Larson. Jack's mom."

"Okay, sure. Hi, Hannah." A slight pause. "Is everything okay?"

"I think...I think we need to talk," she said.

"Is something wrong?"

"I don't know. Is there?"

"Is...is Jack okay?"

She looked up into the sky. "Yes, he's fine. It's...it's me, mostly."

"I don't understand."

Maybe calling wasn't such a good idea, she thought. "I feel like I've abandoned my son. And now...I can't get him back."

"Oh. I see." There was another pause. "So you...you don't want me to see Jack anymore?"

Hannah ignored the pain she heard in Lindsey's voice. "I think...well, for the time being, I think I need to spend some time with him. Not you. I'd like you to stay away."

Lindsey cleared her throat before speaking. "I understand."

The call ended without goodbyes, and Hannah wondered if she'd done the right thing or not. Lindsey was clearly upset. She could tell that by the sound of her voice...by the silence. She held the phone tightly in her hand. Yes, of course it was the right thing to do. But how in the world was she going to tell Jack?

CHAPTER SIXTEEN

After a restless night's sleep—the first one she'd had in weeks—Lindsey made herself fix breakfast. She had to keep things as normal as possible...whatever normal was. She tried not to think about the phone call last night, even though it was still fresh in her mind. Part of her wasn't really surprised by the call. She'd been wondering how long Hannah Larson would allow Jack to spend his days with her. If things were reversed... well, if Jack were her son, she probably wouldn't have let him out of her sight. She'd lost her husband...Jack was her only child. She imagined that, yes, she did want to spend time with him.

She took her coffee and the plain scrambled egg and toast out to the deck. Max took his normal spot beside her chair. She took a couple of bites, then put the fork down. Max waited patiently as she tore off a piece of toast. He'd gotten better about snatching food out of her hands, but he still swallowed whatever she gave him in one bite.

The day suddenly loomed long and empty. They'd planned on going to the pond first for Jack's swimming lesson, then they were going to go upstream of her parents' cabin to do some fishing. The river there was well shaded and she knew of several deep pools where she'd caught bass before.

Without Jack around, the pond would be a lonely place. And fishing? No.

She looked across to where her grandmother's garden was. She still hadn't gotten around to cleaning it out. Today would be a good day for that, she supposed. She took another bite of her eggs, her glance going to the bird feeders. Jack had helped her fill them yesterday. There were two cardinals there now.

She pushed her plate away. Surely when Hannah Larson said that she needed to spend some time with Jack, she didn't mean that Lindsey couldn't *ever* see Jack again. She didn't know what purpose that would serve.

No. If in a day or two, if there wasn't any word from them, she'd go over to their house. She had to. The thought of never seeing Jack again…well, she didn't even want to think about it.

* * *

Hannah was washing the dishes from their lunch when she saw Jack hurrying toward the house. When he said he was going down to the creek—like always—she simply hadn't had the heart to tell him that Lindsey wouldn't be there today. He'd been so happy, she didn't want to chase his smile away. So she let him go, knowing that he'd be back. Her plan was to take him to the state park for a swim, then stop in Concan for pizza and perhaps rent a couple of movies.

When he opened the back door, his young face was etched with worry.

"Something's wrong," he said.

She raised her eyebrows. "What?"

"I waited and waited, but Lindsey didn't come."

"Well, honey, maybe she had something to do today."

"No! You call her. Something's wrong. She might be hurt."

"Jack, I'm sure she's fine."

Tears welled up in his eyes. "No...you've got to call her, Mom. What if she's hurt or something?"

At that moment, Hannah felt like...well, like an ass. Like a selfish ass. She hadn't considered how Jack would feel if Lindsey stayed away.

"Okay, I'll—"

"Hannah?"

"Jesus...why does she think she can just come in unannounced?" she murmured as Margie came in through the front door. Margie was going to force her to start locking the damn door.

"There you are," Margie said.

"Hi, Margie, I didn't even hear you knock," she said, hoping Margie would get the hint.

Margie waved her hands dismissively. "Oh, I never think about it. We're all family here." She pulled out a chair and sat down. "Hi, Jack. Why the sour look on your face?"

Jack ignored his grandmother and turned back to her with pleading eyes. "Mom...please?"

"Okay, honey. Why don't you go outside."

Jack's shoulders sagged, and he turned away, dragging his feet as he went back onto the porch where Barney was waiting.

"What's wrong with him?"

She rubbed her temples with both hands. "Lindsey didn't show up at the creek today."

"Are you still allowing him to see her? I thought you were going to put a stop to that?"

"Yes, well..."

"It's just not natural, I'm telling you that. She acts like Jack is her son or something. She could kidnap him and take him away, Hannah. We don't know this woman."

Hannah held her hand up. "Okay, Margie, no, you're freaking me out here. She's not going to kidnap him."

"You don't know! She's a McDermott! They're crazy people."

"Well, crazy or not, I called her last night. I told her...well, I told her that I should be the one spending time with Jack, not her. I asked her to stay away."

"Well, good for you. It's about time. That woman has no place in Jack's life."

Hannah jerked her head up, surprised to find Jack standing in the doorway leading to the living room. Apparently he'd snuck back in the front door and was listening to their conversation. The tears in his eyes told her he'd heard every word.

He looked at her accusingly. "She's my friend," he said around his tears. He tapped his chest. "*My* friend. You can't make her stay away. You can't! She *needs* me!"

Before she could even reply, he darted past her, out the kitchen door once again. She ran after him, barely catching a glimpse as he and Barney disappeared into the woods.

"Jack! *Jack!*" she yelled as she ran after him. When she got to the creek, he was nowhere in sight. "Oh, God…what have I done?" She stared down both directions of the creek, looking for him, looking for Barney. "Jack!" she screamed.

On the other side of the creek, she could see a trail. Was that Lindsey's trail? Was that where she came from when she came to see Jack? Is this where Jack sat as he waited for Lindsey? Like today…waited and waited, but she never came.

She reached into the pocket of her shorts, only to find it empty. She'd left her phone on the kitchen counter. "Shit," she murmured before turning and running back to the house.

Margie was standing on the porch, her hands held out questioningly. "Well?"

"I couldn't find him."

Margie followed her into the kitchen. "Should I call Dennis? Should we call the sheriff?" She pointed her finger at Hannah. "I *told* you this woman was going to be trouble! I told you—"

"This is my fault, not Lindsey's," Hannah said as she grabbed her phone from the counter. "And no, you don't need to call the sheriff." *At least not yet*, she added silently.

"Who are you calling?"

"I'm calling Lindsey." She held her hand up when Margie would have spoken. "I've got this handled, Margie. Why don't you go on home? I'll call you later, after Jack comes back."

"I can't possibly leave when my only grandchild has run away from home! Who knows where—"

"He did not run away from home." She held her head in her hands. "Please, Margie…just go. I can handle this."

Margie squared her shoulders. "Well…I never…" she mumbled, letting her voice trail away. "I hope you'll at least let us know if you need help."

"You'll be the first one I call," she said as she walked back onto the porch, leaving Margie in the kitchen.

For all her brave words that she had a handle on this, that Jack hadn't run away from home…her heart was still pounding nervously as the phone rang in her ear. What if Lindsey didn't answer? What if—

"Hello."

She felt relief wash over her at the sound of Lindsey's voice. "It's Hannah Larson…Jack's—"

"I know who you are, Hannah."

Yes, Lindsey's voice was oddly cool, short. That, too, was her fault. She felt tears well in her eyes. "It's…it's—"

"What's wrong?" Concern replaced the coolness immediately.

"It's Jack…"

"Is he okay? What happened?" she asked, her voice urgent.

"He…he ran way," she blurted out. "Sort of."

"What the hell does that mean?"

"I'm sorry…it's all my fault. He…he overhead me talking to Margie—that's his grandmother—about you. He was…he was heartbroken when you didn't come today, and he thought something might have happened to you." She wiped at the tears on her cheek. "I was telling Margie that I had called you, that I'd…well, you know."

"That you told me to stay away."

"Yes. So he ran out the door with Barney, down to the creek. I followed him but I couldn't find him. He was gone and I don't know where he goes, where y'all go when you're together. I just—"

"I'll find him."

"I'm sorry, Lindsey. I overreacted. I—"

"I'll find him," Lindsey said again.

The phone went dead, and she slipped it into her pocket, her gaze following the path to the creek. How many days... weeks, now...had she watched Jack make that solitary trek down there, just him and his dog.

Yes, this most definitely was all her fault.

CHAPTER SEVENTEEN

Lindsey told herself not to panic. She told herself she knew where he'd go. But hell, the kid was nine years old. He was used to riding in the Mule, not walking the trails. He could so easily get lost.

No, he couldn't. The main trail, the one by the creek that was the old Jeep road, made a loop around the property. If he missed the upper trail to the pond, he'd just keep on walking. He'd eventually get to the pullout where she'd showed him the view on both sides of the mountain. If he stayed on that trail, he'd eventually make it to her grandparents' house.

She shook her head. He was nine freakin' years old. Did she really expect him to walk across the whole damn mountain, over nearly fifteen hundred acres?

The logical thing for her to do was to go to the creek and follow the Jeep trail from there. She'd come upon him sooner or later. And if Hannah had called her immediately, she didn't think Jack would have had enough time to make it to the pond, not unless he ran most of the way. Yeah…he's a nine-year-old kid. She could almost *see* him running up the trail, Barney at his heels.

"Hang on, Max," she said as she pushed the Mule, going faster than she should. She gripped the steering wheel tightly, bouncing over rocks as she practically flew down the trail. When she got to the spot where she usually parked the Mule to head down to the creek, she stopped, even though Hannah had said there'd been no sign of him down there. She left a whimpering Max on the back and she jogged down the trail, finding their spot at the creek. The water gurgled over the rocks lazily, a chickadee sang from the branch of an oak tree and two deer startled her as they ducked under a cedar not more than fifty feet away. Jack, however, was nowhere in sight.

She retraced her steps to the Mule and hopped in, taking the trail as it climbed up the hill. She slowed now, the rocks too large to bounce over as she'd done down below. When she got to the cutoff that would take her to the pond, she stopped, glancing up ahead in case Jack had missed the turn. Even though they usually took the trail from the other side, by the house, they'd come this way before. Surely Jack would know the way by now. *Again…he's nine years old!*

Well, she went with her gut and her gut told her she'd find him at the pond, so she turned left, taking the old trail that wound through the trees. As she got closer, she could see the water glistening in the sunshine. It was cooler down here, the trees making a canopy over the trail. She slowed as she came around the side, her heart jumping wildly when she saw him. He was sitting cross-legged on the pier, Barney at his side. Jack's head jerked up when he heard the Mule approach. Barney barked and ran toward her. Max returned his bark as his big paws hung over the side as if he was about to jump.

Jack got to his feet, watching her. Then he, much like Barney had done, took off running. She'd barely gotten out of the Mule before he flung himself at her, nearly knocking them both down. He was crying—sobbing—and she squeezed him tight.

"It's okay…I've got you," she said. "It's okay."

"She…she said that we—"

"I know, buddy. She called me last night." She let him slide out of her arms and back to the ground. His eyes were red from crying and his cheeks were tear-stained. She wiped at the tears, then ran her hand across his hair. "Come on. Let's talk."

Max's high-pitched bark told her she'd forgotten him on the back of the Mule. She let the tailgate down, and he hopped off, circling around Barney with a wagging tail before heading toward the pond. She put her arm around Jack's shoulders, and they went to the pier and sat down. Jack wiped his nose with his T-shirt.

"I probably shouldn't have run away," he said, his voice quiet and small.

"No...probably not. You scared your mom."

"When you didn't come, I...I thought maybe you were hurt or something. I asked her to call you." Tears started flowing again. "I overheard them talking. She said she'd told you to stay away."

"I think she wants to spend some time with you too," she said.

"I'm with her all the time," he said as he again wiped his nose with his shirt. "My grandmother doesn't like you. Why?"

"I don't know. I don't think I've ever met her."

"She said the McDermotts were crazy people."

Lindsey laughed. "Well, she probably heard that from Lilly. She and my grandparents...well, they were complete opposites. I don't think they got along very well."

He leaned closer to her, resting his head against her shoulder. "I don't want you to stay away."

"Me either." She patted his leg. "So you know what that means, don't you?"

He looked at her. "What?"

"That means that we've got to start including your mom."

"What do you mean?"

"When we go fishing, when we go swimming...we need to invite her along. That way, she can spend time with you and I can spend time you...and you can spend time with both of us."

"Do you think she'll go?"

"I don't know. What do you think? Does she like to swim?"

He nodded. "My grandparents have a pool at their house. In San Antonio. We used to go over there all the time."

"Well, see. She'd probably like going with us." She nudged his shoulder. "While we've been out here having fun, she's been at home by herself. I think maybe it was lonely for her."

"She was cleaning and painting and stuff," he said.

"Yeah. But she's probably through now, huh?"

He nodded. "I guess."

"So what do you say? Tomorrow we'll go to the river. We'll show her how you can swing off the rope."

He smiled. "Yeah...that'd be good." He pointed out at the water. "What about here?"

"I don't know yet. This is kinda our secret place."

He smiled broader. "Yeah, this is our place. We'll need to wait a while before we bring her here."

Lindsey laughed, then drew him closer in a hug. "You got that right."

He looked up at her, his blue eyes blinking at her. "Was she mad?"

"Scared," she corrected. "Now...when you get back home safe and sound, *then* she'll probably be mad." She reached into her pocket and took out her phone. "I guess I should call her and let her know you're okay."

"Can we still go swimming?" he asked hopefully.

"I think you're pushing your luck, kid. I better take you back home before she's mad at *both* of us."

His smile faded. "Yeah...I guess."

"But tomorrow...you ask your mom to go with us, okay?"

He bit his lip. "Why don't *you* ask her?"

CHAPTER EIGHTEEN

Hannah only barely resisted the urge to run toward Jack when he and Lindsey came walking up the trail. As before, the dogs beat them to the house, but Hannah didn't need them to alert her. She'd been sitting on the porch, waiting. She was torn between beating the crap out of Jack for running away and hugging him to death. As soon as she saw him, however, thoughts of punishment vanished and she only wanted to squeeze him tight.

He looked at her a bit guiltily when they got to the porch. "You're mad, I guess."

She raised her eyebrow. "You think so?"

He nodded and took a step closer to Lindsey, as if she might protect him from the scolding he thought he deserved.

"Why don't you go on in the house and let me talk to Lindsey." It wasn't a request and he knew it. He looked up at Lindsey, who smiled down at him and squeezed his shoulder.

"I'll see you later," Lindsey said.

"Okay."

He walked off silently and alone. Barney—normally at his heels—was wrestling with Max over a stick.

Hannah walked down the steps and moved away from the house, in case Jack was at the door listening. Lindsey followed along beside her.

"Thank you again for finding him."

"He was afraid you wouldn't let him see me anymore."

Hannah nodded. "Yes. I handled that poorly. I let Margie's concerns get to me, I'm afraid." She turned to her. "Can you blame me, though? I mean, I don't know you, yet Jack apparently thinks you hung the moon. He would rather be with you than me."

Lindsey smiled at her, and Hannah again noted how attractive she was. How young and fresh and outdoorsy Lindsey was compared to her. Her dark brown hair was nicely layered, feathering back from her face, brushing the tops of her shoulders in the back. She wondered if her guess at her age was correct.

"Come with us."

She raised her eyebrows. "What?"

"Tomorrow…come with us," Lindsey said again. "You said you wanted to spend time with Jack. Come with us…get to know me. Let's have a…a picnic or something. We'll go swimming."

"Swimming? That's right…Jack said you'd been taking him swimming. That's really what started this whole thing. He's only nine years old. He shouldn't—"

"He swims like a fish," Lindsey countered. "And I watch him like a hawk." She shoved her hands in her pockets. "You're right, though. I should have asked permission."

"I would have said no."

"Yeah…that's what Jack said."

"So he's been sneaking his swimming trunks out with him?"

"No. My…my nephew left some…left some behind." The easy smile Lindsey had been sporting left her face. "So? You want to?"

Lindsey had apparently forgotten their phone conversation the other night. Last night. Was it only last night that she'd called her and told her that *she* was the one who should be spending time with Jack, not Lindsey? A picnic did sound nice though. And it had been blistering hot the last few days. A swim sounded even better.

"How old are you?"

Lindsey's smile returned. "Are you wondering if I'm old enough to be trusted with Jack or too old to be hanging out with him?"

"Neither. I was just curious, that's all."

"Twenty-nine." She laughed. "Barely hanging on to it, actually."

"When is the big day?"

"September first."

Hannah smiled, remembering when she'd turned thirty. They had talked—briefly—about having another child. She told James thirty was her cutoff. The day had come and gone and she remembered celebrating it with both regret and jubilation. That was four years ago.

"Okay...I'll go with you. Honestly, I'm going stir-crazy being here at the house."

"No doubt."

"I tried to get Jack to go to the state park, but..."

"This'll be better than the state park. Same river but no crowd." Lindsey tapped her thigh, beckoning the dogs over. "I should get going. I've got stuff for sandwiches, unless there's something you'd rather have."

"Sandwiches sound good. I'll put together some snacks or something too."

"Great. About eleven?"

"Where should we meet you?"

Lindsey pointed through the woods. "Jack knows the place. I'll pick you up in the Mule."

"The *what*?"

Lindsey just smiled and took off walking toward the trail Jack used. When Barney went to follow, Hannah grabbed his collar, holding him. She watched until Lindsey disappeared, then headed back to the house.

"Come on, boy. Let's go inside."

Jack was waiting in the kitchen, watching from the window. When she closed the door, they stood there looking at each other.

"Are you going to spank me?"

She rolled her eyes. "Yeah, right. When's the last time that happened?"

"I was four."

"You were three and I'm sure you don't remember." She walked over to him, bringing him into a hug. "You run away from me like that again and I'll beat the crap out of you."

"I'm sorry," he mumbled against her.

"No...I'm sorry," she said. "We should have talked about it. I should have told you my concerns."

"Lindsey said that you were lonely."

"She said that, huh? Well, yeah, that's true. I'm here all alone while you're out having fun."

"But you said you had stuff to do," he reminded her. "You told me to play at the creek with Barney."

"I did. But my work's all done now."

"So...I can't go with Lindsey anymore?" he asked, his voice cracking with unshed tears.

She hugged him quickly. "We're having a picnic tomorrow. And swimming. She's picking us up at eleven."

His grin was contagious, and he did an exaggerated fist pump. "Yay!"

"I take it you approve?"

"I can't wait to show you the rope swing! You ought to see how far I can swing out!"

Her eyes widened. "You jump off a rope swing? Into the *river*?"

"Uh-huh." He backed away from her slowly. "I'm going to go take a bath now."

They made eye contact, then he turned and ran from the room. She managed to hold her laughter in until he was out of sight. The kid was too damn cute for his own good.

But a rope swing? Was that safe? He was only nine years old. Did Lindsey know anything about the limitations of nine-year-olds? Well, she supposed she would find out tomorrow.

CHAPTER NINETEEN

"Mom…come *on*. We're going to be late!"

"I'm pretty sure she'll wait for us if we are."

"She might think we're not coming."

"We have fifteen minutes." She slapped at his hand when he tried to steal a cookie. "They're for the picnic."

"Lindsey makes really good sandwiches."

"She does, huh."

"Uh-huh. Turkey and a big slice of cheese." He made a face. "Sometimes lettuce too, but that's okay."

She laughed. "Yeah…hate for you to get too many veggies."

The chocolate chip and pecan cookies were Jack's favorites, and she'd baked them that morning. When she'd told Lindsey she'd pack some snacks, she didn't realize how bare her pantry was. Besides the cookies, there was a bag of potato chips that they'd opened the other night when she'd made sloppy joes. As Jack had said, they sure tasted better than the steamed broccoli she'd served. They must have, they'd eaten half the bag.

"Where are your swim shorts?" she asked him.

"Oh, yeah. I'm not used to taking them from here." He ran from the room and hurried back to his bedroom.

No, he was used to sneaking off and wearing someone else's. She looked down at her own attire. She felt a bit self-conscious in the bikini top, but when she'd pulled out the one-piece suit that she normally wore, Jack had shook his head. "Lindsey wears swim shorts and sandals." Well, she didn't have any swim shorts and the only sandals she had were brushed leather. Obviously, she wasn't prepared for a day on the river. She'd donned the bikini instead, slipping on blue jean shorts over it and a white tank top. Flip-flops would have to suffice in lieu of sandals.

Jack came back wearing his red and black swim shorts and swinging his T-shirt in his hands. As usual, his feet were clad in his dirty Adidas.

"What do you wear in the water?"

"I go barefoot. But maybe the next time we go shopping, you could buy me some sandals like Lindsey has. The rocks get slippery and...you know...I fell," he said, pointing at his knee.

"Yes. Maybe we could both get some."

He literally skipped to the door, a huge smile on his face. "Come on, Mom."

She returned his smile, glad that she was getting to participate in his outing today. It had been pretty selfish of her to try to keep him away from Lindsey. Despite Margie's assertion that the McDermotts were "crazy," she had no such qualms. She was just happy to be getting out of the house for what she hoped would be a fun-filled day in the water.

She followed Jack and Barney down the trail to the creek. Lindsey wasn't there yet, and Jack sat down on a large rock at the water's edge. Barney splashed into the creek and went across to the other side, as if waiting for his friend Max to show up. It was only then that she saw the trail of rocks in the water and she wondered if Jack and Lindsey had put them there to help them cross the creek.

"Lindsey usually sits over there," he said, pointing to another rock that was half in, half out of the water.

"I guess I'll just stand," she said. Her flip-flops weren't exactly the best choice, she realized. Maybe they'd drive into

Uvalde tomorrow morning and do some shopping. For that matter, they could simply go into San Antonio for real shopping. Her parents were in San Diego, but maybe her sister could meet them for lunch. She was about to suggest that to Jack when Barney barked and took off up the hill.

Jack jumped up off his perch and walked across the rock bridge, hands held out to his side to balance.

"Come on, Mom," he said. "It's easy."

Considering she was in flip-flops and the water was barely over a foot deep, she didn't anticipate any problems. Three steps in, however, she lost her balance. Fearing she would fall and drench her picnic bag, she simply walked off the rock bridge and into the water.

"Yeah...that's always my solution too," came an amused voice from the other side.

Hannah smiled at Lindsey as she desperately tried to keep her flip-flops on her feet in the rocky creek. "I've been told I don't have the proper footwear," she said.

"Yeah...they make those dorky water shoes, but I prefer a sports sandal," Lindsey said as she stepped forward and offered a hand.

Hannah took it with relief and let herself be pulled up onto dry land. Jack was laughing at her, of course.

"You almost fell. That would have been so funny, Mom!"

She pinched his cheek when she got to him. "Sorry to disappoint you."

Jack and the dogs led the way up the trail and Hannah found herself following behind Lindsey. She was wearing navy blue shorts and a white tank top like she was. There was a navy and white bikini top underneath it, so she assumed the blue shorts were her swim shorts. Her sports sandals were also a shade of blue. Judging by her tan, Lindsey spent many hours outdoors. Of course, Jack's skin too had turned a pretty golden brown. She, on the other hand, looked like she'd spent her summer indoors, which had been the case so far.

They came to a clearing and she realized they were on a narrow road. Parked there was a dark green vehicle, open and doorless with nothing but a roof over roll bars—the Kawasaki

Mule. The dogs went to the back and Jack lowered the tailgate. Lindsey went around to hoist the dogs up. Jack then closed the tailgate. Hannah assumed this was their normal routine. The Mule had only one bench seat and Jack scooted toward the middle, giving her room.

"Did you make sandwiches?" Jack asked.

Lindsey nodded. "I did. They're at the cabin."

His eyes widened. "You went inside?" he asked quietly.

Lindsey nodded again.

"Were you...okay?"

Hannah watched this exchange, a bit puzzled by Jack's questions.

"Yeah...I was okay. The fridge needed a little work but I got it all cleaned out."

Hannah frowned as Jack placed his small hand on Lindsey's thigh and patted it gently. What in the world was going on with them?

"We'll take the long way around, give your mom a tour, if that's okay?" The question was directed at Jack, but Lindsey looked at her over the top of Jack's head. Hannah nodded.

She held on as the Mule jerked forward, and they started climbing up the hill. The views were spectacular, and she wondered how much land Lindsey's family owned on this side of the creek. The Larsons owned about six hundred acres, but they didn't have the large hills like those that were on this side. Most of their land was for grazing, although her father-in-law only kept about a hundred head of cattle now. The rest of the land he leased out to other ranchers in the area.

"Do you have cattle?" she asked.

Lindsey shook her head. "My grandfather used to, but he sold all of his about ten years ago, I think. The best grazing is down along the river, and the cows became more of a nuisance than anything. Plus, he was...he was getting older and it was a lot for him to keep up with."

Lindsey's expression had changed slightly, and she remembered Margie telling her that the McDermotts were killed in a plane crash. She wondered how long ago that had been. Maybe it was recently. Well, she wouldn't pry but she was a little curious.

"How much land do you have?" she asked.

"About fifteen hundred acres," she said. "It's pretty, but most of it's not very usable."

"It's beautiful up here. On the Larsons' side, it's rather flat compared to this."

Lindsey stopped and pulled the Mule off the side.

"Mom...this is called Antler Peak," Jack said importantly. "You can see for miles and miles."

"That way is Utopia," Lindsey said, pointing to their right. "This side looks toward the river and Concan. Great spot for both a sunrise and sunset."

The view was indeed nice...very pretty, actually, but she was more intrigued by Jack. He was sitting between them, but she noticed that he was closer to Lindsey than to herself. He also appeared to be very familiar with his surroundings. She wondered again what all he and Lindsey did when they were together. Obviously, not just fishing. Or swimming, as she'd found out they'd been sneaking off to do. They seemed... emotionally close. She wasn't sure if that bothered her or not. And if it did, she wasn't sure *why* it bothered her.

* * *

Lindsey slowed when a small cabin came into view. Hannah wondered if this was where she lived. If so, it seemed an awfully long way from the creek where she'd picked them up. How was it that she stumbled upon Jack?

"Be right back," Lindsey said as she jogged up the steps and went inside.

"This was her parents' cabin," Jack said quietly.

"Oh." A pause. "Was?"

He nodded somberly but said nothing else. Before she could question him, Lindsey returned carrying a picnic basket. To Hannah's surprise, Lindsey placed it on her lap, and she moved her own bag out of the way.

She said nothing, just offered a quick smile before getting back in. The Mule lurched forward again.

"The river is within walking distance," Lindsey explained, "but it'd be kinda hard to carry everything. I've got a cooler with drinks on the back."

She'd no sooner said the words when the river came into view. Hannah had only glimpsed the Frio from a few spots along the road to Concan. It didn't appear to be much wider than the creek, but judging by the flow, it was much deeper. And to think that her nine-year-old son had been swimming in it.

She pushed down her apprehension. Lindsey was an adult. She would know the risks. And yes, she said she watched Jack like a hawk. But still…

"There's the rope swing, Mom," Jack said excitedly, pointing to a deck that had been built along the shore. A cypress tree shaded it, and a thick rope hung down from one of the branches. It was swaying lazily in the light breeze, and she noted several knots tied at the bottom. Hand grips, she assumed.

"So this is where you swing into the river?" she asked, eyebrows raised.

He grinned. "Uh-huh. It's so much fun!"

She smiled back at him. "I'll take your word for it."

"No, Mom…you can jump off too. Lindsey does."

Hannah glanced at Lindsey, who nodded. "It's fun. Makes you feel like a kid again."

Lindsey parked the Mule off to the side, away from the deck. The dogs were clamoring to get off the back. Hannah got out and Jack went around and lowered the tailgate. The dogs didn't wait for Lindsey to lift them out. They both jumped and headed to the water. She was shocked to see Barney follow Max in.

"He can swim?"

"Oh, yeah. He was scared at first, but we were all in the water so he finally got in too," Jack said.

Hannah stood by as Lindsey took the cooler off the back and placed it on the deck in the shade. Jack went to the side of the deck and opened a metal container. It looked like a large footlocker. Inside were a couple of tubes and some noodles. He then pulled something else out…a seat of some sort.

"That's Lindsey's," he explained as he tossed it on the deck. "She calls it a fanny floater."

"I should have brought some lawn chairs down," Lindsey said. "I hope you don't mind sitting on the deck while we have lunch."

"No, that's fine."

Jack tossed her a towel, then handed one to Lindsey.

"The water is crystal clear," she said as she finally walked over to inspect it. "And deep."

"Deep in spots," Lindsey said. "It's deep here. That's why we put the rope swing up. You can float downstream about twenty yards or so and it's only four foot deep in places."

"Watch, Mom!" Jack said as he took hold of the rope. "Watch me!"

"Be careful," she said automatically, noting that he'd dropped his T-shirt and it was half on, half off the deck.

He backed up with the rope, then took a running start, his little hands holding tightly to the knot. She found herself holding her breath as he swung out. He let go of the rope and landed with a splash. She didn't breathe again until his head popped out of the water. Barney barked and swam out toward him while Jack swam back to shore.

"Did you see? Was it good?"

"Yes…it was really good," she said with a smile. "I see you've been practicing it a lot."

Lindsey laughed quietly beside her. "I practically have to drag him to the Mule. He always wants just one more swing."

Jack pushed his blond hair away from his eyes and climbed back up on the deck. "You want to go?"

"Don't you want to have lunch?"

"In a minute," he said. He dripped water on her towel when he walked past and took hold of the rope again.

"So this is a daily thing, huh?" she asked Lindsey.

"It's too hot to fish. We need to get out at daybreak sometime. Or late evening."

Hannah stared as Lindsey pulled her shirt over her head, leaving her in only a bikini top. Well, it looked like a bikini from the front. The straps on the back were crossed, looking more like a sports bra. Lindsey's skin was a lovely golden brown and her gaze was drawn to her breasts as Lindsey bent over to lay out a towel. Embarrassed for staring, Hannah turned her head when Lindsey straightened up.

"Since he's not ready to eat, I guess I'll join him in the water for a bit," Lindsey said. "You want to get in and float around a little?"

It was why she came, she told herself...to swim. Yet she was feeling a bit self-conscious. Lindsey was obviously very comfortable in what she was wearing. Hannah wished she could be as confident. *I should have worn the one-piece.* Well, she had nothing to be ashamed of. Hadn't James always told her she had a beautiful body? Was it true or had he been lying? No... she took pride in her appearance. Only, her exercise routine had suffered once James got sick. When she used to join Avery and Jennifer five days a week for their four-mile run, she'd cut back to three days...then two...then finally giving up altogether. James had encouraged her to keep going. It was an outlet for her, at least. It was the only time James's illness wasn't at the forefront of her mind. Toward the end, though, James needed her at home. She couldn't possibly leave him.

Lindsey was looking at her expectantly, and she realized she hadn't answered her question. So she nodded.

"Sure. It'll be nice to cool off."

Lindsey tossed a tube and a noodle into the water, which Jack swam over to retrieve. Then she tossed in the fanny floater. The dogs were still splashing in the water, but nearer the bank. Max looked up as Lindsey took hold of the rope and, like Jack, backed up a few feet before running to the edge. She let out a playful yell as she splashed into the water and Max immediately jumped in and swam toward her.

"Oh, yeah...that feels good," Lindsey said as she maneuvered into the fanny floater.

"Come on, Mom! Your turn!"

With both of them staring at her, she pulled her tank top over her head, trying not to compare her rather pale skin with

Lindsey's. Give her a week or two in the sun and she'd catch up with her. She hesitated, however, when she unbuttoned her shorts. Damn, but why didn't she wear the one-piece? Oh, well. She was thirty-four years old. And she happened to think she looked pretty damn good for her age!

But as she stepped out of her shorts—standing there in nothing more than her black bikini—she'd never felt more insecure in her entire life. Two sets of eyes were watching her. Jack was smiling, waiting on her to take the rope swing. Lindsey, however, quickly averted her gaze when Hannah looked her way. Was Lindsey embarrassed to look at her? Was her thirty-four-year-old body *that* hard to look at? Hannah had to resist the urge to pull her shorts back on and somewhat cover herself.

"Come on, Mom! Jump in!"

Hannah pushed all of her insecurities aside, telling herself she would simply ignore Lindsey McDermott. She was younger, she was obviously more fit, she had a fabulous tan and a very nice body—but there was absolutely no reason for her to feel intimidated by any of those things.

Right.

So she grabbed the rope swing and held on tight, praying she wouldn't fall and further embarrass herself. As she was swinging over the water, two thoughts popped into her mind. One, they were going shopping in the morning to buy some water shorts. And two...what in the *hell* was she doing? She slipped from the rope, her arms no longer able to support her. She landed in the water with a clumsy splash, conscious enough to hear laughter coming from her son.

When she slicked the hair from her eyes, Lindsey pushed a tube in her direction and she held on to it. For a second, their eyes met, and Hannah smiled her thanks.

"Yeah...we'll need to work on your landing," Lindsey teased.

"That was great, Mom!" He laughed again. "You should have seen your face!"

Hannah splashed water in his direction. "I'm old. I can't help it."

With as much grace as she could manage, she got into the tube, finally relaxing as she leaned back, her face turned up to the sun. The water felt wonderful on such a hot day. She turned her head as Jack swam past her, heading back to the deck and another swing on the rope. He looked strong swimming and she wondered how much credit Lindsey deserved for that.

She looked over at her now, finding Lindsey's gaze on her. "I understand you're teaching him the backstroke."

Lindsey nodded. "As well as I can. I'm not very good at it myself, but as a kid, I had to learn all the strokes. I thought if Jack was going to be out here in the river, he could stand a few lessons."

"Watch, Mom!"

She turned, nodding, as he took a running leap with the rope, landing far out in the river. He popped up, a huge grin on his face.

"That's my best jump yet!"

He swam back over to his noodle and wrapped an arm around it, grinning at Lindsey. She looked over at Lindsey, who was smiling back at Jack. Yes, they were close. She'd have to be blind not to see the bond between them.

CHAPTER TWENTY

Lindsey wasn't sure of the reason—maybe because she'd lived in such a vacuum the last few months—but the sight of Hannah Larson in a bikini nearly caused her to tip out of her fanny floater. She tried to look away. It was totally inappropriate, after all. It reminded her of the time she had a crush on her friend Mattie's mother, Mrs. Simmons. They lived down the street from them. She had been probably twelve or thirteen at the time…too young to know what the crush meant, but she'd get completely tongue-tied around the woman. When she'd picked roses from her mother's flowerbed to take to Mrs. Simmons, however, her mother had finally sat her down and they'd had a talk. She was so embarrassed afterward that she stayed away from Mattie's house for nearly a month.

She glanced at Hannah now, who was sitting cross-legged on the deck, her towel tossed casually across her legs—to cover herself perhaps? That was a pity, she thought as she handed out sandwiches.

"Extra cheese for you," she said to Jack.

"Goody," he said as he snatched it out of her hand.

"I see you're contributing to his cheese addiction," Hannah said as she took the sandwich Lindsey offered her.

"I had no choice. He informed me after the first one that it would taste 'way better' if it had two slices on it."

"Yes, he tries that with me too. It doesn't work."

Lindsey looked over at Jack, who was giving her a sly smile. "Looks like you're busted, kid."

He grinned and took a huge bite of his sandwich. Mayo mixed with mustard wedged in the corner of his mouth as he chewed. Hannah handed him a napkin and pointed to his mouth, however Barney—with one quick lick of his tongue—cleaned it up.

Hannah shook her head. "You do remember that he is a dog, right?"

Jack laughed. "He doesn't think so."

Lindsey sat down between them, then scooted the cooler closer. Her family had been beer drinkers, especially out here at the river. While she rarely drank anything when she lived in Dallas, she found herself following the tradition here. She pulled out a Coke for Jack and handed it to him. For her, she took a can of beer out and slipped it into one of the koozies she kept in the side pocket of the cooler.

She looked over at Hannah. "I've got beer, Coke, or bottled water."

"I'll take a beer."

Lindsey was surprised. She would have bet a hundred bucks that Hannah would choose the water.

"So you've been living out here since the end of May, huh?"

Hannah nodded. "As soon as school was out. Dennis—that's my father-in-law—drove the rental truck. We didn't bring very much furniture as the house was already well furnished but... well, I wish we had now."

"Old stuff?"

"Old and worn, yes. And Lilly is in the nursing home and not coming back, but Margie thinks it would be disrespectful to get rid of her things."

"She's really old," Jack offered. "We went to see her. She didn't even know us."

"Dementia?" Lindsey guessed.

"She had a stroke. Or a mini-stroke, as Margie called it. She had memory issues after that. She was easily confused, and they didn't trust her living alone."

"Well, she must be old. When I was a kid, we called her Old Lady Larson even back then," Lindsey admitted. "She was… well, to quote my grandmother, a mean old biddy."

Hannah laughed. "Yes, that describes her perfectly. James was afraid of her when he was young." Her smile faded slightly. "I'm afraid some of her personality rubbed off on Margie." She looked quickly at Jack. "Don't you repeat that," she threatened as she pointed a finger at him.

"What's an old biddy?" he asked innocently.

Lindsey laughed at the look on Hannah's face.

"You don't need to know, and don't you *ever* say that to your grandmother," Hannah said. She looked back at Lindsey. "Margie is a bit of a nag."

"And the queen of guilt."

Hannah glared at him. "Do you have to repeat *everything* I say?"

He shrugged.

"She's very condescending, and when she's lecturing me about something, she can make me feel like a teenager sometimes," Hannah explained to Lindsey. "She's not impressed by my parenting skills."

"If you don't mind my asking, why did you move here?"

Hannah chewed her sandwich slowly, as if thinking of an appropriate answer to the question. She took a sip of beer, then shrugged her shoulders slightly.

"It seemed like the right thing to do at the time. Mostly. And like Jack said, Margie could make even an immoral man quiver with guilt. James was her only child. Jack is her only grandchild."

"Ah. I see."

"And…we needed a change. After James died…well, we needed a change," she said again.

Lindsey waited, assuming Hannah would ask her the same question. Their eyes met and Lindsey saw numerous questions floating in Hannah's gaze. But before she could ask any of them, Jack got up and stood in front of them.

"Hurry up and finish," he said. "We're gonna try to teach the dogs to jump off the deck, remember?"

Lindsey nodded. "I remember. I even brought a tennis ball."

His blond hair was dry again and it blew into his eyes. He impatiently wiped it away. He was a cute kid—too damn cute—and Lindsey could imagine the girls chasing after him in a few years.

"Do you want a cookie?" Hannah asked him.

"Oh, yeah. I forgot."

He stuck his hand into the zippered plastic bag and brought out two, grinning as he shoved one into his mouth, then ran to the Mule, presumably to get the tennis ball.

Lindsey had been ignoring Max, but a large paw on her thigh made her look at him. His gaze, however, was locked on what remained of her sandwich. She took one more bite, then handed him the rest, which he devoured in one chomp.

"You didn't even taste it," she told him. He tilted his head. Yeah, he probably recognized the words, she said them often enough.

"Max is as spoiled as Barney, I see."

"Yeah, but Barney is a little more polite with his eating. Max hasn't mastered the art of chewing yet, I'm afraid."

She got up, conscious of Hannah watching her. She resisted the urge to turn and look back at her. Instead, she turned her attention to Jack as he ran back over with the ball, causing the dogs to jump up excitedly.

"So how do we do it?"

"Well, I think first, we get them to chase the ball from the bank," she said.

The dogs proved to be harder to entice off the deck than she'd imagined. They splashed in happily from the bank to retrieve the ball but refused to jump from the deck. By the time they gave up, both she and Jack were waterlogged and exhausted from the many jumps they'd made. Hannah apparently enjoyed the show as she floated in her tube, laughing at their attempts to cajole the stubborn puppies into the water.

"Maybe they're too young," Hannah offered. "They just learned to swim, didn't they?"

"Yeah…I sometimes forget they're still puppies," she said as she got back in her fanny floater.

Jack hung on his noodle, floating between them. The dogs were apparently tired from their swimming, and both of them were on the deck, lying in the shade. Lindsey leaned her head back, looking up into the sky. She'd been a little apprehensive about Jack's mother joining them, afraid things would be different. It was unwarranted, though. It had been a fun day, and Hannah hadn't gotten in the way. In fact, it was kinda nice to talk to an adult. Since she'd moved here, besides Jack, her only other conversations were when she went grocery shopping and made idle chitchat with the clerk.

She looked over, watching Hannah as she relaxed in her tube, her eyes closed, one hand hanging lazily in the water, the other resting on her stomach. She assumed Hannah was five or six years older than she was, but still, she looked really good in a bikini. Really good. Her gaze lingered on Hannah's breasts, then she quickly looked away. This was Jack's *mother*, for god's sake!

"What are we going to do tomorrow?" Jack asked, his voice breaking the silence.

Hannah opened her eyes. "We're going shopping. Water shoes and shorts."

"Oh, Mom," he complained. "I *hate* shopping."

"I thought you wanted some water sandals like I have," Lindsey reminded him.

"Yeah, I do," he conceded.

"If we leave early, we can be back in time for an afternoon swim," Hannah said. She glanced over at her. "That is, if Lindsey wants to."

Jack looked at her. "Can we?" he asked hopefully.

She smiled at him. "Of course. In fact, we can make it late afternoon, and then, if you want," she said, addressing Hannah, "you can stay for dinner. I'll put something on the grill."

Jack grinned and looked at his mom. "Well? Can we?"

Hannah spun around in her tube, facing her. "I...I don't want to monopolize your time, Lindsey. You'll be sick of us before too long."

"No, she won't," Jack said quickly.

Lindsey smiled at him, then splashed water in his direction. "I wouldn't have offered if I didn't want your company," she said to Hannah. "It would sure be better than eating alone."

Hannah studied her for a long moment, then nodded. "Okay. We'd love to have dinner with you."

"Yay!" Jack yelled.

CHAPTER TWENTY-ONE

Jack helped her bring in their loot from their shopping trip. It had been a quick trip to San Antonio. So quick, in fact, that she hadn't called her sister to see if she'd want to meet up for lunch. Jack had been too antsy to get back. Not knowing what Lindsey planned for dinner, she hadn't wanted to eat burgers in case that was going to be on the menu so she pulled into a Taco Bell—at Jack's request—for tacos. Actually, what she hoped Lindsey had planned was steak. She hadn't had a good one in more months than she could recall. James always handled that and…well… he hadn't had an appetite for much of anything toward the end. Before they sold the house—and the gas grill—she'd attempted to cook one for her and Jack. While Jack claimed that it was good and he ate his entire portion, she knew it had been terribly overcooked. She should have kept the gas grill, she realized. The only thing here was an ancient charcoal grill with a rusted grate. On the occasions that they had burgers, she always fried them or broiled them in the oven. Jack didn't seem to mind, as long as he could put "extra" cheese on his.

"Did you call her yet?"

"We just got back. And it's not exactly late afternoon, you know."

"But—"

"Honey, if we're going to have dinner with her, we don't need to take up her whole afternoon too. I'll call her about three and ask when she'd like to pick us up. I would imagine four would be the earliest."

"Four?" he complained with a whine. "That's hours yet. Lindsey won't mind if we come over."

"That's only two hours. Surely you can entertain yourself for that long."

He huffed off to his room and she shook her head. What, exactly, was his infatuation with Lindsey? Did he view her as a new friend, despite their age difference? Did he have a crush on her like he might for a teacher? They were close, she could tell that. And they were comfortable, familiar with each other. That was obvious. Still…Lindsey was twenty years older than he was. She could see Jack's attachment, but what about Lindsey? What was Lindsey getting out of it?

Was she, perhaps, lonely too? When Margie had said the whole family had perished, who all did that mean? Obviously, the grandparents. Who else?

She went back to her bedroom, intending to sort out the new clothes she'd bought and decide on what to wear. Instead, she stopped at Jack's room. The door was ajar and she pushed it open, finding him on top of his bed, playing on his iPad. Barney was also on the bed, sprawled out like he did most nights. Margie would have a stroke if she saw this, she mused.

"Jack?"

He looked up but said nothing.

"Has Lindsey…has she mentioned much about her family?" she asked.

He nodded. "Yeah." He said nothing else and returned to his game.

"Well?"

"Well, what?"

God, he was so difficult sometimes. "What did she say about them?"

He looked back at her. "They died," he said, his voice quiet.

"Her grandparents?"

"Yes. All of them."

"All of them?"

He nodded. "Her parents, her brother and sister. Their kids too. I used to wear her nephew's swim trunks," he said.

"Did they...did they all live here?"

"No."

He knew more, she could tell. But he was being guarded with his answers. Why? Protecting Lindsey? Protecting her privacy? No...he was too young to know anything about that. Yet...she could tell he was only giving her the minor details, nothing more.

She walked closer and sat down beside him, nudging him over. "You've talked about it? About what happened?"

He nodded. "She cried," he said, his young voice only a whisper.

"And...you told her about your dad?"

He nodded again, then turned once more to his game.

Well, if she wanted to know more, she'd obviously have to ask Lindsey. Of course, it wasn't really any of her business. And apparently, if she'd told Jack about it...and cried while doing so, then Hannah certainly didn't want to bring it up voluntarily. If the subject came up, if Lindsey felt like sharing, so be it. The same was true of her. Going over all of the horrid details of James's death wasn't something she wanted to do. She had finally gotten to the point where James—and his illness—wasn't constantly on her mind. She wasn't ready to rehash it all over again. No doubt, neither was Lindsey.

She stood up, only then noticing that he already had on his new swim shorts and sandals. He was clearly ready to go see Lindsey. Even though she'd said she would wait until three, she decided to go ahead and call her now.

* * *

Lindsey averted her eyes when Hannah pulled off her tank top, surprised at her disappointment when she realized that she had indeed bought water shorts. There would be no bikini today. Then she mentally rolled her eyes. Jack's mom, she reminded herself once again. This was Jack's mom. This wasn't some woman she'd met in Dallas—another lesbian—who might be interested in her. Oh hell...like she had something to offer someone anyway.

Wasn't that why Teri stopped coming around? Yeah, it was. Teri had tried to talk to her, had tried to console her, but Lindsey hadn't been receptive to it. She and Teri were...well, they'd been dating for a while, but Teri had never met her family. That right there should have told her something. She had had little desire to introduce Teri to them and Teri had never pushed. After the accident, well, Teri had apparently grown tired of trying to reach her. Little by little, she'd simply stopped coming around, stopped calling. And at first, she hadn't even missed her. She tilted her head slightly. Had she *ever* really missed her?

When she heard a splash, she turned back around, finding Hannah in the river with Jack. They were both smiling which in turn made Lindsey smile. Hannah was attractive...cute. And she looked like a goddess in a bikini, she admitted. And she was also Jack's mom—a very *straight* woman—and they were becoming friends. It would be nice to have a friend...an adult friend. When she'd moved out here that had been the least of her concerns. The friends she'd left behind in Dallas had stopped calling, had stopped trying to contact her, much like Teri had done. She simply hadn't had the energy or desire to maintain those relationships.

Now? Well, Jack had wormed his way into her heart and time spent with him was as satisfying as any relationship she'd left behind. And now Hannah? While Jack may have been a carbon copy of his father when it came to looks, his personality certainly seemed to be like his mother's. Hannah was game for pretty much anything they'd suggested. A swift smile could light her face, much like Jack. Yet her eyes turned serious just as quickly…again, much like Jack.

"You coming in?"

The question was from Hannah, not Jack. Lindsey let her eyes drift over to meet hers, seeing the questions in them. She smiled and nodded.

"Yeah…just lost in thought there for a minute," she said truthfully.

She took her shirt off and tossed it on the deck next to Hannah's. She then took ahold of the rope and swung out into the river to join them. Jack was already getting out and hurrying back to the deck to take another swing on the rope. She swam over to Hannah who was holding her fanny floater, and she got in, resting her arms on the sides of it as her body was submerged.

"Where did you get that? I kinda like it," Hannah said.

"Oh, I don't even remember. Ordered it online a few years ago. But we've got two others," she offered. "Well, not here." No, they were at the pond, the pond that Hannah didn't know existed. "I'll bring one for you the next time, if you want."

"If it wouldn't be too much trouble, I'd like to try it."

"Mom…watch!"

Hannah, with her hands, moved her tube out of the way as Jack did a Tarzan yell and landed a few feet away, splashing them with water.

Lindsey splashed him back, causing him to laugh. She turned back to Hannah. "You can try mine, if you'd like. I'll take the tube." She could tell Hannah was about to refuse, so she slipped out into the water and held on to Hannah's tube. "I don't mind. Give it a try."

"Okay."

Hannah rolled out of her tube and disappeared under water for a moment, coming up with a smile on her face. She placed her hand on it next to Lindsey's, wiping the hair out of her eyes with her other hand.

"The water feels great."

Lindsey nodded. "I'm glad you called when you did. Later in the afternoon, by five, this is all in the shade."

"See," Jack said. "I told you."

Lindsey raised her eyebrows. "What?"

"She wanted to wait," he said. "She said—"

"Jack," Hannah said quickly. "Must you repeat *everything* I say?"

He laughed. "It's just Lindsey."

Lindsey looked at her. "You said what?"

Hannah gave her a quick smile. "I don't want us to become pests," she said. "I told him if we were going to have dinner with you, we shouldn't take up your whole afternoon too."

Lindsey pushed the fanny floater in Hannah's direction. She took it and slipped onto the seat.

"Oh, yeah…this is great," she said with a grin. "No wonder you like it best."

"Yeah. I'll bring another down here."

She climbed on top of the tube, but it wasn't effortless like the fanny floater. She found Hannah and Jack watching her as she settled on top, her feet dangling in the water, as were her hands.

"I don't have a lot of things to occupy my time, so I was happy you called when you did," she admitted. "I already had everything set up for dinner. I was just waiting around for your call anyway."

"What are we having?" Jack asked. "Burgers?"

"Well, your mother and I are having steaks. You can have a burger if you'd like but I bought a small steak, in case you want that."

He tilted his head thoughtfully. "I don't know yet. I'll let you know." He left his noodle behind and swam toward shore. "What will the dogs eat?" he called when he got to shore.

"Whatever you don't, I guess." She looked at Hannah. "Steak is okay, right?"

Hannah smiled and nodded. "Oh, yeah. I haven't had a good steak since…well, since James was still able to cook." Her smile faded completely. "More months than I can recall, really."

"I'm sorry," she said automatically.

Hannah waved her apology away. "I wouldn't dare say this in front of Jack, but it was almost a relief when it was over with.

James had been in so much pain, and there was nothing I could do for him. The last month had been…well, horrible really." She looked at Jack who was taking hold of the rope. "About two weeks before the end, when James was still somewhat coherent, he begged me to…to…well, we had morphine."

Hannah stopped talking and without thinking, Lindsey reached over and touched her hand. Hannah looked at her, meeting her gaze.

"I wish I'd been strong enough to do it," she said in a whisper as Jack landed in the water close to them.

Lindsey said nothing as Jack swam over, holding on to her tube with his elbows. His eyes were sharp though, as he watched them.

"What's wrong?"

Lindsey removed her hand from Hannah's quickly. "Nothing, buddy," she said. She splashed at him playfully. "You want to try something different?"

"Sure. What?"

She wiggled her eyebrows at him. "We both go off the rope at the same time."

"Oh…cool!"

He was already swimming back to shore before she could even get out of the tube. After several long strokes, she almost caught up with him, but he felt her gaining and as soon as he touched bottom, he ran through the water laughing, causing Barney and Max to run into the water to meet him.

Lindsey scooped him up in her arms, causing him to squeal with laughter. She put him right back down, then beat him to the deck by two steps.

He was still laughing as he leaned against her, catching his breath. Both dogs were up on the deck with them. Lindsey paused to glance at Hannah, who was smiling at them. She grinned back, then took the rope with her hands, holding it higher than she normally did.

"When we get over the water, you've got to let loose first or else I'll land on top of you, okay?"

"Okay."

She pulled the rope back, holding it high. His small hands grabbed above the last knot. She looked down at him.

"Ready?"

"Ready."

"One…two…three!" she yelled, taking a running start. She pushed off, feeling the weight of Jack on the rope, trying to get far enough out into the deep water. "Jump!"

He let go and then she did too, landing several yards past him. When she surfaced, she glanced to the deck just in time. Both dogs, led by Max, jumped off the deck and splashed out into the river, swimming fast toward them. Jack was clapping as he bobbed in the water, then Hannah shoved his noodle toward him, just seconds before the dogs got there.

"They did it! They did it!"

She swam over to her tube, not getting in but using it as a float. Max swam near her, and she patted his head as he turned and headed back to shore.

"Good dog."

"I can't believe they did that," Hannah said. "Not after their refusal yesterday."

"I guess they thought they were missing out on the fun."

"Can we do it again?" Jack asked.

"You've started something now," Hannah murmured with a smile.

Lindsey arched an eyebrow. "You want to take a turn?"

"No, no. I'll watch."

The dogs were ready this time. They started running as soon as Lindsey did and she was afraid that either Jack would land on them or vice versa. Unwarranted fear, it turned out. Without them already in the water, the dogs did little more than fall off the deck. Jack landed well away from them and Lindsey followed.

She finally climbed back inside her tube, signaling an end to the jumping. She eyed the cooler, wondering if Hannah would mind if she sent Jack over to get a beer. Hannah must have read her mind.

"Yeah, a beer sounds good and I haven't even done anything." Hannah turned to Jack. "Would you be a sweetheart and get two beers for us from the cooler?"

He grinned. "Only if I can have a Coke."

"I suppose you've earned it."

CHAPTER TWENTY-TWO

To say Hannah loved the deck would be an understatement. It was a massive three-level affair with the second level being the cooking deck. Bench seats were built against the railings and several chairs were also placed about. The table—a table that could easily hold twelve people—was up on the main deck nearer the house. The third level was smaller, wrapping around the second. She wondered if it was used for anything other than a walkway. There were no chairs there.

Large oaks shaded the area, blocking out the late afternoon sun. Jack was sitting in the shade, playing on his iPad. The dogs were lying near him, both asleep. Lindsey was still inside, showering and changing into dry clothes. Hannah had planned only to change, but Lindsey had offered her a shower as well and she'd accepted. Jack, however, had simply changed into dry shorts and a clean T-shirt, leaving his feet bare. When she'd gone back outside, he was already perched where he was now, having found his iPad in her bag.

"Do you come over here much?" she asked him.

He looked up and nodded. "Sometimes. I help her fill the bird feeders and the deer feeders." He pointed between a couple of smaller oaks. "I haven't seen them, but Lindsey says the deer come to eat right before dark."

Hannah followed his gaze, seeing the feeder up on a tripod. Bird feeders hung from the low branches of the trees, and she spotted several cardinals at them. It was a very inviting scene, and she wondered why she hadn't thought to put up bird feeders at their house. Probably because she'd been trying so hard to turn the inside into their house, she hadn't given the outside much thought, other than to make sure the grass was mowed. Lindsey, like them, had a very small yard as the natural landscape crept close to the house.

She walked around to the other side of the deck, taking in the house itself. It appeared to be about the same size as theirs— three bedrooms—but this one looked like it had been remodeled recently as the interior was much more modern than their own. Through the windows, she saw movement and watched as Lindsey went back into the kitchen. She was in shorts and flip-flops now and instead of a tank top, which is what she usually wore whenever Hannah had seen her, she was wearing a dark T-shirt. Hannah walked back over toward Jack when she saw Lindsey coming back out.

"Hannah?"

"Over here," she said.

"You want wine?"

"I would love some. Can I help with anything?"

Lindsey nodded. "Sure. You can scrub the potatoes and get them in the oven. I've got a marinade chilling, and I need to get that on the steaks." She looked over at Jack. "Did you decide what you want?"

"I guess a steak. Mom can make me a burger anytime."

"Okay. Barney and Max get the burger then."

Hannah followed her inside to the kitchen. It, too, was large like her own. The appliances were new compared to the ancient ones she used.

"Recently remodeled?"

Lindsey nodded. "Four or five years ago, I guess. My grandmother was a big cook so she was lost without her kitchen for the few weeks it was torn apart." She motioned out to the deck. "The grill got a lot of use during that time."

Hannah watched her for a moment, noting the shadow that crossed her face. Then Lindsey pushed it away and she smiled. "Potatoes are by the sink. Scrub brush should be in the second drawer."

Hannah found it and went about the business of washing and scrubbing the russets. They were huge, and she knew she'd never be able to eat the whole thing. She and Jack could probably share one. When Lindsey spoke, Hannah wondered if she could read her mind.

"I know they're big, but Max thinks it's quite a treat to get my leftover potato. With Barney here too, I figured they wouldn't go to waste."

"They get spoiled quickly, don't they?"

"I'll say."

Lindsey placed a glass of wine next to her, a deep red. Hannah put the potato down and picked up the glass, swirling the liquid slowly before taking a sip. "Mmm. Very good," she murmured. "Thank you."

It didn't take long to wash the three potatoes. She wondered how Lindsey normally prepared them. Again, as if reading her mind...

"I usually just stab them with a fork and toss them in the oven," Lindsey said. "But if you do something different...like put them in foil and add olive oil or something, feel free. I'm not picky in the least."

"Yes, I do them like that sometimes, but I actually like them better just baked on the rack."

So as Lindsey poured a delicious smelling marinade over three thick steaks—one only slightly smaller than the other two—she pierced the potatoes with a fork and set them on the rack before turning the oven on. Lindsey left the steaks on the counter, then topped off their wineglasses before leading the way back outside.

"Jack says you feed the deer."

"Yeah. They'll be out before too long. At first, they were pretty shy. I think it was because of Max. My grandparents didn't have a dog. But after a while, they got used to us being out here and they came right up." Lindsey pulled two chairs over to the side of the deck. "You can see them best from over here," she said. "Jack? You want something to drink?"

He looked at Hannah instead of Lindsey. "Can I have another Coke?" he asked hopefully.

"I've got some juice," Lindsey offered.

He wrinkled up his nose, and Lindsey laughed, turning to her. "So a Coke?"

"I guess." She turned to him and winked. "Don't get spoiled, mister."

He grinned and hurried into the house, presumably to get his Coke. Hannah turned to Lindsey, who had settled in the chair next to her.

"I take it he's familiar with your house?"

"Well…he's been here a few times," Lindsey said vaguely.

She reached over and touched her arm quickly. "I wasn't asking because it upsets me," she explained. "It's just…well, I've got some catching up to do with you two."

Lindsey nodded. "Okay…well, then yeah, he's been over here a handful of times." She smiled. "He's pretty handy with filling bird feeders."

"I saw some cardinals at yours," she said. "I was just thinking that I need to put one up myself."

"Birdwatching…it was one of my grandmother's passions," Lindsey said, her eyes drawn to the feeders. "Along with gardening. I'm afraid I've neglected her vegetable garden, though. If I don't do something with it this fall, I'll definitely try to plant something in the spring."

Jack came back and resumed his spot on the deck, knees drawn up and his iPad resting against them. Curiosity got the best of her.

"Margie said that your…that your grandparents were in an accident," she said quietly.

Lindsey nodded and Hannah could see the sadness on her face, even as the early evening shadows lengthened. Lindsey finally turned her head, meeting her gaze.

"My grandfather was a pilot." She said no more for the longest time, then Hannah saw her swallow. "There was a... there was a crash. They—"

"Look! Deer!"

Jack's excited voice interrupted them, and Hannah wondered at his enthusiasm. They had deer milling around their house all the time. But she followed his gaze and her eyes widened. A buck, a huge buck, was under the feeder eating corn. Next to him was a doe and another smaller buck.

"Wow," she whispered. "He's beautiful."

"Yeah. He doesn't come every day, though," Lindsey said. "But the other one, the little six-pointer, he comes almost every evening. I call him Little Bucky."

Hannah smiled. "But you haven't named that monster yet? What is he? At least a ten?"

"Yeah. And there'll be more. Last evening there were twelve deer total." Lindsey paused. "You grew up in the city?"

Hannah nodded. "I did. When James and I first married, we came out here to visit several times a year. But...well, his mother—Margie—can be difficult to get along with, like I said. Our visits dwindled to a couple of times a year. Even with Jack, we still didn't come here much."

"I like it here," Jack chimed in, letting her know he was listening to their conversation.

"Now you do. And I would guess it has more to do with Lindsey and less to do with your grandparents," she told him. She turned to Lindsey. "Margie invites us at least once a week to have dinner with them. We've gone a few times. That's the extent of us seeing Dennis. He never comes to the house. Margie, on the other hand, pops over several times a week."

"Well, you said she doesn't like me. Does she know you've been out with me?"

Hannah shook her head. "No. Actually, I haven't seen her since the day...well," she lowered her voice. "Since the day Jack disappeared on me." She met Lindsey's eyes. "Since I told you to—"

"Stay away from him," Lindsey finished for her, but there was a smile on her face. "I'm sorry that didn't work out."

Hannah laughed. "No...I'm sorry." Her smile faded. "I... well, I..."

"It's okay," Lindsey said. "It's all good now, huh?"

Hannah nodded. "Yes. It's been a wonderful day. Yesterday too. Now I know why Jack was always so anxious to see you. You've made it fun." She glanced at Lindsey quickly. "It hasn't been fun in so long," she said, her voice lowering to a whisper, hoping Jack hadn't heard her.

Lindsey nodded sadly. "I know what you mean."

Of course she would, Hannah thought. How insensitive of her to assume it was only her and Jack lacking in the fun department. They hadn't lost their entire family. The sadness in Lindsey's eyes nearly broke her heart. Before she could say something, offer some words of comfort, Lindsey got up and headed back into the house. It was just as well. As far as Lindsey knew, Hannah wasn't aware of her loss. Lindsey had only mentioned her grandparents. Unless, of course, Lindsey assumed that Jack had told her.

She looked over at Jack, who was again engrossed in his game. When she stood, he looked up at her.

"I'm going inside to help Lindsey with dinner," she said. "Be right back."

"Okay."

She found Lindsey in the kitchen, leaning against the counter, a tomato held in her hand. When she heard Hannah, she looked up, then quickly turned, picking up a knife.

"Salad okay?" Lindsey asked. "I've got some squash too. I could—"

"Salad is fine." She moved up next to her, waiting until Lindsey looked at her. "You want to talk?"

Lindsey let out a heavy sigh. "I suppose Jack told you."

"Only with a little prodding, and at that, he told me very little. He seems very protective of you."

Lindsey smiled. "Yeah. He's a great kid, but I guess you already know that."

"Thank you. He's more mature than he should be at nine, but I guess I should be thankful for that." She touched Lindsey's arm. "Margie is the one who told me about your grandparents. She said your family had perished. I didn't really know what all that entailed."

Lindsey put the knife down and turned to her. "It happened in early February. And yes, my whole family." She swallowed. "But I don't want to ruin the evening...or dinner, by talking about it," she said quietly. Lindsey squared her shoulders. "For the most part, I'm dealing with it." A small smile touched her face. "Jack...Jack has helped a lot."

Hannah nodded, finally understanding the depth of their relationship. It made sense now how upset Jack had been when Lindsey hadn't shown up that day...when Hannah had told her to stay away. Jack had been worried something had happened to Lindsey, worried that she was hurt. And his words came back to her now.

"She's my friend. You can't make her stay away. You can't! She needs me!"

She cleared her throat slightly. "Lindsey...I'm very, very sorry for what I said to you on the phone that night. I was feeling a bit...well, insecure, I guess. And lonely," she added. "And Jack...Jack is my lifeline. Only it seemed he would rather be with you than with me." When Lindsey would have spoken, she held her hand up, stopping her. "I'm only saying this because I didn't realize the extent of your relationship with him." She paused. "Or his with you. I'm sorry."

Lindsey nodded and their eyes held for a moment. "Like I said, he's a good kid." She smiled. "Too damn smart for his own good." She laughed lightly. "Too damn *cute* for his own good."

"That he is," she agreed. Then she gently moved Lindsey out of the way. "I'm great with salads. Let me."

"Okay. I guess I'll get the grill going." Lindsey walked away, then stopped and turned back around. "Thanks, Hannah." At Hannah's raised eyebrows, she explained. "For offering to talk.

Listen. My emotions are still sometimes very raw. I may…well, I may take you up on it sometime." She paused. "And it goes both ways. I mean, with your husband and all…if you want to talk."

She nodded. "Thank you."

CHAPTER TWENTY-THREE

After Lindsey had dropped Jack and Hannah off at the creek—after she'd walked them across it and up to their house using her flashlight—she'd taken the long way home, climbing up the mountain to Antler Peak. It was a crystal clear night, the sky filled with stars. The moon, still a week from full, was already creeping higher in the sky.

She stopped at the top and got out. Max was riding in the front with her, but he was too tired and sleepy to follow her. He sprawled out, watching her as she leaned against the side, her gaze turned up into the heavens.

It had been a good day, she told herself. A really good day. She'd had a moment there when, sitting on her grandparents' deck, she'd been nearly overwhelmed by the past. It was the first time she'd had company...the first time she'd entertained, if you could call it that. The first time the deck had someone on it other than herself...and her family. As they'd sat there, watching the evening, watching the deer come up...she'd looked around, almost expecting to see her parents, her brother,

her sister…the kids. Sadness had settled and if Hannah and Jack hadn't been there, she feared she would have slipped back into the early stages of her grief.

Hannah had apparently understood. She'd come in search of her, had offered to talk. That had surprised her. But why should it? Hannah had her own grief. Of course she understood what Lindsey was going through.

So Lindsey had pushed her grief away. Instead of living in the past, she lived in the moment. She'd teased with Jack, she'd cooked their steaks, and she'd chatted with Hannah. The evening had ended on a good note. She'd enjoyed herself, and she thought that Hannah had too. By the time dinner was over and they'd sat out to finish off their wine, Jack had sunk down onto one of the chairs and had fallen asleep.

She and Hannah had talked quietly, not touching on anything too personal, just enjoying the conversation. As Hannah had told her, Jack—and Margie—wasn't her only outlet. For Lindsey, Jack, too, was her only outlet. Perhaps it was good that she and Hannah got along as well as they did. It would be nice to have someone to talk to. Not necessarily about her family, about her grief…just nice to have a friend. And she thought she and Hannah could become friends, despite the obvious differences between them. They got along well enough. She lifted a corner of her mouth in a half smile. Well, after they got past the initial meeting that is and Hannah telling her to stay away. They were past that now.

She took a deep breath and shifted, her gaze following the progress of the moon overhead. She supposed she should get back to the house. It would be an early day tomorrow. She had promised Jack she'd take him fishing in the morning. Hannah hadn't yet decided if she would join them or not. Whether she did or didn't, it would still be a short outing. Hannah and Jack had plans in the afternoon. Hannah had told her that Margie and Dennis were having a Saturday get-together with family. Jack had moaned in protest.

"I'd rather go swimming with Lindsey."

Hannah had smiled and nodded. "Yes, I'm certain I would too."

Lindsey had felt a twinge of jealousy that they actually *had* family, but she knew it wasn't the same. These were in-laws. These were her husband's people, not theirs. She had learned enough from Jack and Hannah to know that they weren't close to this side of the family. But still, it had made her miss what she knew she'd never have again—a family gathering.

No...because there was no more family left to gather. Only her.

And just like that...grief settled upon her shoulders, weighing them down. She felt alone...and lonely. Out here, under the night sky, where there were no sights or sounds of other people, she felt very alone indeed. It was as if everyone had deserted her, left her behind to fend for herself...as if she were the only person left in this world.

She felt a moment of panic...felt like the dark night was swallowing her up. She could hear her heart beating in her ears, and she looked around, feeling frightened. Then Max shifted on the seat and she relaxed again. She listened, hearing other night sounds...familiar sounds that had faded to the background. She heard the shrill, rolling sound of a screech owl down below in the canyon. And later, she heard a sound that made her smile. Whip-poor-will. No, she corrected herself. Common poorwill, her grandmother had said. Their calls were similar, though, and she listened to the haunting sound as it echoed across the rocks and through the trees. She tilted her head, finally hearing an answering call.

No. She wasn't alone after all. She blew out another breath, then got back inside the Mule. Max moved over a little, then lay back down, his head resting on her thigh. She rubbed his head lightly, letting her fingers caress his ear several times before turning the key. The Mule's engine broke the silence, drowning out the night sounds...the night sounds that had changed from lonely to peaceful in a matter of seconds.

CHAPTER TWENTY-FOUR

Hannah had originally planned to let Jack go with Lindsey by himself. For one, she wasn't exactly a fan of fishing. In fact, she had been once before and that was before James got sick. They'd taken Jack out to a catfish farm one day. And two…she'd promised Margie she'd make a side dish to bring to the party that afternoon.

Despite that, here she sat in the shade, watching as Lindsey helped Jack bait his hook. Not a pole today. No, it was a rod and reel that Lindsey said she'd found up at the house. It looked new and unused so she wasn't sure if that was the case or not. Maybe it was. It didn't really matter, she thought. Jack had been so excited to use something other than a "boring old pole."

She wrinkled up her nose as they impaled a poor worm on the hook. A slimy, disgusting worm. Lindsey must have seen her face and she laughed.

"Sure you don't want to join us?"

"No, no. I'm fine over here with the dogs." Her job assignment was to keep Barney and Max out of the water. That was proving harder to do than she thought.

Lindsey had shown Jack how to cast the rod before they put the worm on. Now, Lindsey stood back, offering tips to him as he held the rod over his shoulder, then flung it out. The hook and bobber landed only a foot from the riverbank.

"Release your thumb a little earlier," Lindsey instructed.

Jack reeled the line back in and tried it again with the same result.

"You do it," Jack said, handing it to Lindsey.

"Watch me."

Hannah's eyes were on Lindsey as were Jack's. She was tall and graceful, and with only a flick of her wrist, the worm—and hook—and bobber landed far out in the river. She reeled it in a little, then handed it to Jack.

"It's in a nice, deep hole there," she said. "Just let it sit for a while and see if you get a bite."

"What are you hoping to catch?" Hannah asked.

Lindsey walked over and sat down beside her. "There are some nice bass in here," she said. "And catfish. Although I have better luck with catfish in late evenings."

"You fish a lot?"

"I used to. When…well, when the family was here, my nephews loved to fish. We would get up early, before dawn, and come out here," Lindsey said. "Some mornings, all we'd hit were perch but as Jack will tell you, they're fun to catch too."

"Yes, you caught perch in the creek," she said. "Using corn?"

"Yeah. They'll hit on just about anything."

"My bobber's moving!"

Lindsey got back up and went over to him. "Hold it steady, don't jerk it." Before she could answer, the bobber disappeared under water. "Okay…pop it up!"

Jack jerked on the rod but wasn't turning the reel. The tip of the rod bent and he held it up to Lindsey.

"Take it!"

Lindsey grabbed the rod and began reeling the line back in. Hannah sat up excitedly as she saw a fish struggling on the end of the line. Jack jumped up and down beside Lindsey as she pulled the fish on shore. Hannah clapped as Lindsey held it up.

It wasn't as large as she'd imagined it would be, but Jack was beaming.

"I caught one! I caught one!"

"Here...hold him up like this," Lindsey instructed. "I'll get a picture."

She pulled her cell phone out and captured a smiling little boy as he held his prize. Hannah watched their interaction, again noting how close they seemed to be. Jack and Lindsey were completely at ease with each other, evidence of how much time they'd spent together this summer. Her eyes were drawn to Lindsey's hands as she carefully unhooked the fish from the line, then gently put him back in the water. She was surprised that Jack didn't protest, wanting to keep his catch, but it was as if he already knew that Lindsey would release it.

Again, they baited a hook, and this time, when Jack attempted to throw the line, it went out a little farther than his earlier attempts. Apparently, not far enough, though, because Lindsey instructed him to reel it in and try again. The next attempt was much better, and Lindsey tousled the hair on his head affectionately before coming back to join her.

"He's getting the hang of it."

"You're very patient," Hannah said.

Lindsey shrugged. "Had lots of practice."

Hannah's expression softened. "The rod and reel...did it belong to one of your nephews?"

Lindsey looked over at her, meeting her gaze. "Yeah. I had gotten it for Eli—he was seven—for Christmas." Sadness settled over Lindsey's face. "He never got to use it," she said quietly.

An "I'm sorry" was about to spring to Hannah's lips, but she kept it inside. It would be meaningless. Lindsey seemed to sense her hesitation.

"I'm really glad Jack is getting to use it."

Hannah smiled at her. "Me too." She looked at Jack now, who was sitting on a rock, his gaze fixed on the bobber. "After his dad died...well, he kinda withdrew, became very quiet. Introverted, almost. I didn't know what I was expecting, really, when we moved here. Like I said before, we needed a change."

She looked at Lindsey. "I had thought his solitary outings to the creek were helping him. He became more like his old self." She smiled. "I now know that it was *you* who was helping him."

Lindsey gave her an almost apologetic look. "Jack was helping *me*."

"Lindsey...nothing's happening," Jack called.

Lindsey got up. "Okay. Reel it in. Let's try a different spot."

They spent over an hour moving slowly along the river. Jack caught three more fish, but they were all smaller than the first one. The last was a little perch that Jack took off the hook by himself. The sun was higher and it was getting warmer by the minute. When Lindsey asked if they were ready for a swim, Hannah readily agreed.

They put the fishing stuff up and walked back to the Mule, then drove along the river, back toward the cabin—her parents' place—and the deck. The dogs were happy to be allowed back in the water, and as soon as Jack lowered the tailgate on the Mule, they jumped off and splashed in.

As before, Jack opened up the metal case and pulled out a noodle, then he paused.

"There are two of them," he said, holding up a fanny floater.

"Yeah...I brought one down for your mom," Lindsey said before looking at her. "Unless you'd rather have a tube."

Hannah smiled. "Thank you. No, I'll use the fanny floater."

Jack tossed all three items into the water, then was the first to strip off his shirt and grab the rope. In an instant, he was flying over the river before splashing into the water with a childlike yell.

Lindsey's T-shirt followed his, and she caught the rope as it swung back to the deck. Hannah wondered if this was a ritual for getting into the river or if it would be allowed to just walk in. Her gaze followed Lindsey as she mimicked Jack, yelling out before she hit the water. Hannah stood there, a smile on her face as Lindsey playfully chased after Jack. His swimming skills had definitely improved since last summer, and she knew she had Lindsey to thank for that.

Feeling quite relaxed and, dare she say happy…she pulled her tank top over her head and dropped it on top of Lindsey's shirt. She caught the gently swaying rope and pulled it back, taking a few running steps before swinging out over the water as they had done. She did, however, contain a scream as she fell into the river. When she surfaced, Lindsey had already pushed the fanny floater over toward her, and she took only a few strokes to reach it.

"This is absolutely wonderful," she said as she settled in. With the fanny floater, only her upper torso was above water. Much cooler than being on top of the water in a tube.

"When do you have to get back?"

Hannah sighed. "We're supposed to be at Margie's by three," she said. "But I still have to make a dish."

Lindsey nodded. "What kind of party?"

"Margie said barbecue. Dennis likes to do briskets, so I'm sure he's had his smoker going since early this morning. There'll be some aunts and uncles there."

"Do we *have* to go?" Jack whined.

She splashed water in his direction. "You know we do."

"Do you get along with Dennis?"

She nodded. "Better than Margie," she admitted. "Dennis is pretty laid back, which is shocking considering his mother." She smiled. "Margie could be Lilly's daughter. That's how similar they are."

"I take it your husband was more like his father."

"Yes. If James had been anything like his mother, we would have never gotten married." At Lindsey's raised eyebrows, she continued. "We met in college and got married about a year before we graduated. Jack came along three years later."

"Stay-at-home mom?"

"Schoolteacher by trade," she explained. "I taught until he was born, then stayed home. I was actually contemplating going back when…when James got sick." She looked over at Lindsey, aware that Jack was listening to their conversation. "I may still go back. Depends on how things work out here. My plan right now is to volunteer, either at the library or the elementary school."

"Got cabin fever?" Lindsey guessed.

"Well...not so much right now," she said with a laugh as she dangled her hands in the water. "Last week I was going stir-crazy."

"When do I have to go back to school?" Jack asked.

"Not until the third week of August. There's still plenty of summer left," she told him, even though July was right around the corner. In fact, the Fourth was only nine days away. She was about to ask Lindsey what she normally did on the holiday, but she kept her question to herself. No doubt it involved her family and she didn't want to upset her.

"Maybe the next time, we could do a float trip," Lindsey said.

"Like you said y'all used to do?" Jack asked solemnly.

"Yeah." She glanced over at Hannah. "You game?"

"Sure. What do you do?"

"We'll take tubes upstream in the Mule." She smiled. "A cooler of beer and some snacks too. Then we'll float back down here. Takes a couple of hours. It's a lazy trip," she said. "There's one spot where it's pretty shallow. That's where we normally got out and had lunch. And played in the rapids."

Hannah noticed the reflective look on Lindsey's face and knew that she was mentally going back to that time and place when her family was still alive. She wished Lindsey would talk to her about it. She wished she could better understand the magnitude of what Lindsey felt. She tried to imagine what it would be like to lose her parents, her sister...the kids. She couldn't even fathom it.

"Can we go tomorrow?" Jack asked excitedly.

"If you want to," Lindsey said.

"If you don't set some ground rules," Hannah warned, "he'll want to be over here every day."

"And I wouldn't mind in the least," Lindsey said easily. "I'll do sandwiches again."

"Can we, Mom?"

Hannah looked between the two of them, seeing almost identical expressions on their faces. How could she possibly deny those looks? So, she smiled and nodded.

"Sounds like fun."

"Yay!"

CHAPTER TWENTY-FIVE

"Fishing?"

"Uh-huh. And I caught four!"

Margie's question was directed at her, not Jack. "And where did you go? To the creek?"

"We...we went to the river," she said with a smile. "Lindsey took us."

Margie's brow furrowed. "Lindsey McDermott? I thought you—"

"She's very nice," Hannah interrupted her. "Jack, take these out to the table for me, please," she said, giving him the plate of deviled eggs. By the time they'd gotten back from their swim she simply hadn't the energy to whip up a side dish for dinner. As soon as Jack was out of sight, Margie turned to her.

"Hannah...really," she said. "I told you, the McDermotts are nothing but trouble. I thought you were going to put an end to this? Especially after Jack ran away."

She held her hand up. "He did not run away," she said. "I've spent some time with her. Like I said, she's very nice. We're... we're becoming friends."

"With a McDermott?" She gave a condescending laugh. "That will never happen."

"Look, whatever issues you have with the McDermotts, they're not *my* issues," she said pointedly. "She's only a few years younger than I am and Jack simply adores her."

"She's a stranger, Hannah. You know nothing about her. Why, she could—"

"Margie, it's fine. She's no longer a stranger. In fact, we had dinner with her the other night." As soon as she said the words, she wanted to take them back.

"Dinner?" Margie's lips pursed. "Yet you can't find the time to join *us* for dinner?"

"It was…well, an impromptu dinner," she said lamely, thankful that Jack had come back inside.

Margie eyed her, changing the subject. "You've gotten some sun. Are you finally through rearranging Lilly's house?"

She nodded. "The last thing was the kitchen. You've seen it since I've finished painting, so…"

"Yes. Lilly would hate that color."

Hannah silently groaned as she flicked her eyes at Jack. The teasing face he made at her reminded her so much of James that she almost started laughing. She had to turn away from Margie to hide her smile.

"Is there something else we can help you with?"

"You can take the pitcher of tea out if you like."

"I'd be happy to," she said quickly, willing to do anything to get away from her.

She sat in a lawn chair outside…close enough to the group to be sociable yet far enough away to have her own space. Jack was playing with two boys, both younger than he was. The family gathered today was mostly from Margie's side and Hannah didn't know them. A few, she'd seen at the funeral, but she didn't recall speaking with them. The only two she knew were Dennis's sister Darlene and her husband. She'd visited with them earlier in the summer when their son, Nathan and his family had come down. Nathan—James's cousin—and his two bratty boys who had picked on Jack, she reminded herself.

Oh, well. It was good that Jack was being exposed to James's family a little more. These cousins just lived over in Vanderpool, east of Utopia. And even though Jack seemed to be having fun, he'd met her eyes a few times. She wondered if he, like her, wished they were back at their own house. Most likely, he was wishing he was in the river with Lindsey. She had to admit, she wished she was too. It wasn't blistering hot, not like it would be in July and August, but she would still prefer the cool, clear water of the Frio River to this. She smiled to herself. Or maybe it was Lindsey's company that she would prefer.

* * *

Barney jumped all over Jack as if they'd been gone for days instead of hours. She laughed as Barney finally got the best of Jack, knocking him down on the kitchen floor.

"I told you we should have taken him along," Jack said as he ruffled Barney's fur.

"And I told you your grandmother would have had a stroke."

He got up and went to the fridge, staring inside. "Can I have a Coke?"

She was about to say no, it was late, but she spied the wine bottle on the counter, the one she'd opened two nights ago. She wouldn't mind relaxing with a glass. He looked at her thoughtfully and she nodded. She handed him a glass and he added ice, then popped the top on the can, pouring the Coke and watching as it fizzed, nearly spilling over. She pulled the cork out of the wine and filled a wineglass, then put the bottle back.

"What do you think Lindsey did tonight?" Jack asked as he took a swallow of his Coke.

"I don't know."

"You think she cooks dinner just for herself?"

Hannah stared at him, wondering at his questions. Was he worried about her?

"We should ask her over here for dinner," he continued. "You could make that triple-cheese hamburger casserole! I bet she'd like that!"

"I just made that. You'll have to wait at least a month before you get that again."

"What about spaghetti?"

"We had that not too long ago too," she reminded him.

"I love spaghetti and meatballs."

"Yes, I know you do."

"So?"

"So, what?"

"Can we?"

She sipped from her wine. "Can we invite her over or can we have spaghetti and meatballs?"

He grinned. "Both."

"How can you even think about food? I saw how much you put on your plate."

"Paw Paw Dennis gave me an extra rib too." He leaned against the counter, much like she was doing. "So? Can we?"

She studied him. "Are you worried about her?" she asked quietly.

He shrugged but said nothing.

"Does she help you not miss your dad so much?" she asked gently.

He nodded.

"And you help her not miss her nephews so much?"

He nodded again. "That's okay, isn't it?"

"Of course, honey. I'm sorry that I didn't understand before. I'm sorry that I tried to keep you apart."

She was surprised to see a tear in his eye, and he wiped it away. "So?" he asked again. "Can we?"

She smiled. "Sure. If she wants to."

He grinned. "She will." His smiled faded. "She probably gets lonely over there by herself."

Hannah nodded. She knew all about loneliness.

"You like her, don't you?"

She smiled at him. "Yes. Were you worried I wouldn't?"

He made a face. "Grandma Margie doesn't like her," he reminded her.

"Grandma Margie doesn't like her for no other reason than her last name."

"But why?"

"I don't know, honey. She's only repeating what Great-grandma Lilly has told her." She touched his head affectionately. "You don't need to worry about it. I'm not going to let Grandma Margie dictate who we make friends with."

He took a big sip of his Coke. "I can't wait for tomorrow," he said. "It's going to be so much fun."

With that, he left her alone in the kitchen, Barney following him back to his room.

"Bring your glass back before bed," she called after him.

Instead of finishing her wine where she stood, she went out to the back porch. It was a warm evening but still comfortable. Unlike Lindsey's deck, where ceiling fans turned to stir the air, there was nothing fancy about this small porch. She sat in one of the old rockers and she wondered how often Lilly had sat in it over the years. Her gaze was drawn toward the woods and the creek. Had Lilly sat here, keeping a watch for those "hoodlum" McDermotts?

She shook her head. Margie was sure adamant that they stay away from Lindsey McDermott. She knew it was only based on stories Lilly had told her over the years. Margie and Dennis had been married for over thirty-five years and had lived out here all of that time. She imagined Lilly had filled her head from the start.

It didn't matter. As she'd told Margie, Lindsey was nice. Normal. She felt like they were becoming friends. She hoped that was the case and that Lindsey felt the same way. Hannah suspected that Lindsey could use a friend, someone to talk to, someone other than Jack. She admitted she was very proud of Jack for understanding the reason that Lindsey had gravitated toward him. Of course, Jack had also been drawn to Lindsey. And Lindsey had kept him entertained, had taken him fishing, swimming. She knew now that their relationship was not one-sided, as she'd feared in the beginning. She smiled as she took a sip of wine. What she'd feared in the beginning was too embarrassing to even think about. She would never, *ever* tell Lindsey.

She let out a contented breath and pushed the rocker into motion. Yes, now she felt contentment. Early in the evening, not so much. Even though she'd wanted to leave the party as soon as they finished eating, she made herself stay a little longer, visiting with James's uncle a little and also sitting in a circle with Margie and some of her friends, listening to the stories they told. Jack had grown tired of playing and had pulled a chair up close to her. They communicated silently, both telling the other that they were ready to go. When there was a lull in the conversation, she finally stood, saying they were going to head home. Her announcement was met with protests—leaving so early?—mostly from Margie, but Jack gave an exaggerated yawn and Hannah had said she better get him to bed. They'd laughed about it on the short drive through the woods to their house.

The truth was, they were both looking forward to their outing with Lindsey tomorrow. And even though Lindsey said she would make sandwiches for their lunch, Hannah wanted to contribute something more than cookies and chips. She knew there was a link of summer sausage in the freezer. She'd picked it up at the meat market in Concan a few weeks ago. She also had cheddar cheese. She would slice the cheese and sausage up and bring a jar of Margie's dill pickles and some crackers. A perfect snack. Of course, she would also make cookies. Jack would feel slighted if she didn't.

She drank the last swallow of wine, then got up. She took one last look into the dark woods, then glanced up into the sky. It was only then that she realized her thoughts hadn't been filled with James. She also realized the heavy weight of sorrow—of loneliness—wasn't nearly as prevalent as it usually was.

She wasn't sure if that thought made her feel happy or sad.

CHAPTER TWENTY-SIX

"Oh, cool, Lindsey! You brought the four-wheeler down!"

"That I did."

"Can I drive it?"

Lindsey looked quickly at Hannah. "Even *I* wouldn't allow that," she said with a grin. "But Jack, if your mom will let you, I'll take you on a spin later."

Jack immediately tugged on his mom's arm. "Can I, Mom? Please?"

Hannah looked back at her. "Is it safe?"

Lindsey nodded. "Sure. I drive like a grandma," she lied. She'd actually had fun on the ride down, spinning out at every turn she came to.

Floating the river required two vehicles, unless you wanted to trek back upstream to retrieve the Mule. And after a float trip with a couple of beers, hiking a few miles wasn't at the top of her list. So, she and Max had gone out at daybreak and hiked to the pond. She wouldn't have been surprised if the four-wheeler hadn't started, but it took only a little coaxing on her part. She zipped it down to the river in no time.

"So can I?" Jack asked again.

"I suppose."

"I'll take you out too, if you like," she offered to Hannah. "I'll go slow. Promise."

Hannah smiled. "We'll see."

They drove past the deck and four-wheeler, going upstream like they'd done yesterday morning for fishing. Jack pointed out the spot where they'd been, but she kept going, deciding to take the long float trip. It was a nice, sunny day...and already hot. They had sandwiches and snacks and a cooler of drinks. If they took the long trip, they could stop at the little rapids and play for a while. She thought Jack would like that.

She found the spot that her grandfather had carved out of the rocks. It was well shaded and she parked the Mule there. Jack scrambled out and let the dogs off the back. They headed directly to the river with Jack following.

"The river looks wider here," Hannah noted.

"It is. Not quite as deep here, though," she said. "There are some flat rocks on the side. Easy to get in."

"Is this where...well, where you and your family would come?"

She nodded, smiling a little, glad the mention of her family didn't bring her down. "Yeah. My grandfather made this little parking area here. This used to be a huge rock pile. He brought the tractor down and cleared out this middle section." She took the cooler off the back. "We had two different put-in spots. This is the longer of the two. I hope you don't mind."

"Not at all."

Jack walked back over with two dripping wet dogs. "How long will it take to float it?"

"Two or three hours. Can you make it?" She reached up to untie the tubes from the top of the Mule.

"Sure."

"There's a spot about halfway down, got some little rapids there. It's a good place to stop for lunch. I'll show you how to go through the rapids without a tube."

His eyes widened. "Is it deep?"

"No, just rocky. But there's a little chute. It'll be fun."

"Okay." Then he looked at his mother for confirmation.

Hannah smiled at him. "If Lindsey thinks it's okay, sure."

They took their tubes to the water. Lindsey carried an extra one with a bottom—for the cooler. It was the same cooler that her dad had packed many times before, and the tube's bottom and sides had been custom made—by her grandfather—to fit the cooler and hold all the accessories, including a spot for the picnic basket.

Hannah laughed as she watched Lindsey secure the cooler inside the large tube. "So it's like a floating bar, huh?"

"Yep. Although when the whole family went, kids included, we had to have two coolers," she said. "My family wasn't shy about drinking beer."

Hannah smiled at her. "Sounds like a fun family."

At that, she felt a bit of a lump in her throat. "Yeah. Yeah, they were. There was always...laughter." She paused. "And singing. My grandfather was always singing."

Hannah came closer, touching her forearm, rubbing back and forth lightly. "Thank you for sharing this with us."

"I'm...I'm glad you're here."

Hannah gave her arm a gentle squeeze before taking her hand away. Lindsey felt an involuntary shiver travel across her skin where Hannah had touched. She had missed that, she realized. Missed the gentle touch of someone...the touch of another woman. She shook her head as if clearing her mind. This was Jack's *mother*, she reminded herself yet once again.

Yeah...Jack's mother. Regardless, she wasn't able to look away when Hannah pulled her tank over her head and tossed the shirt onto the seat of the Mule. The bikini top was a black and white striped fabric and she wondered if it was new. The other times, Hannah had worn a solid black top.

Before she could look away, Hannah turned, catching her staring. She smiled at her and adjusted the straps at her shoulders.

"I bought it the other day," Hannah explained. She turned her back to Lindsey, revealing the crossed straps. "I wanted one like yours...more sports bra than bikini." She smiled again. "Well, in the back anyway."

Lindsey nodded. "Much more comfortable when jumping off a rope swing."

She showed them where the rock ledge was and Jack was the first into the water. "What will the dogs do?"

"I'm sure they'll alternate between running on shore and swimming after us. But it's a slow-moving river. They can keep up."

Lindsey motioned for Hannah to sit in her tube. Lindsey bent over, giving her a gentle push and setting her in motion.

"Do you need help with the cooler?"

"I've got a rope," she said, holding it up. "I'll tie my tube to it."

She pushed the cooler and tube out into the river, then hopped on her own tube and followed. Max jumped in, and she pushed him away when his big feet made a splash as if he was trying to climb into her lap.

"No, you don't," she said. "Go with Barney."

"Don't get too far ahead," Hannah warned Jack as he floated away from them. Then she turned to Lindsey. "Or am I worrying too much?"

Lindsey smiled at her and nodded. "Yeah. There won't be any whitewater rapids or anything. It'll be a fairly tame float trip." She lowered her voice. "He'll probably be bored out of his mind."

* * *

Hannah couldn't remember the last time she felt this relaxed. Was it the beer she'd had? The sun? The gentle rocking of the tube? She rolled her head to the side, watching as Lindsey and Jack tossed a red rubber ball back and forth. Jack, of course, had spilled out of his tube several times, always scampering back into it without a problem. As Lindsey had said, the dogs kept up. They were in the water now, chasing after the ball Lindsey had tossed.

Jack laughed as he paddled as fast as he could, barely beating Max to the ball. He quickly tossed it back to Lindsey, and the dogs changed directions again.

"They'll sleep good tonight," Lindsey commented.

The dogs finally gave up their chase and headed to shore, their tongues hanging out as they plopped down on the rocks.

"Are they about the same age?"

"I think so. I got Max in March. Right before I moved out here," Lindsey said. "He was eight weeks old."

Hannah nodded. "We got Barney about a month...a month before James died," she said quietly, glancing quickly at Jack who met her gaze.

"Daddy died March third."

His voice was pretty matter-of-fact, but Hannah recognized the emotion there. March...nearly four months ago. Yet it seemed ages. She looked over at Lindsey, finding her eyes on her. Their gaze held for a long moment, then Lindsey gave her a comforting smile.

"Our lunch spot is coming up. Are y'all hungry?"

"I am!" Jack said with a wave of his hand.

Hannah shook her head. "You just ate four crackers with summer sausage and cheese."

"That was hours ago," he said with a grin. "I'm a growing boy."

He did a backward roll out of his tube and disappeared under the water, then popped his head up near her. She couldn't help but smile at him. He was too damn cute for his own good.

Cute, yeah. And happy. She couldn't deny that. She'd like to think that she had something to do with it, but she admitted it was mostly Lindsey. Well, maybe the fact that "Mom" was getting to tag along helped too. It certainly had done wonders for her own disposition.

Lindsey pulled out of the river right before they got to the small rapids she'd told them about. Jack, of course, wanted to ride them, but Lindsey talked him into waiting. The lunch spot was a series of flat, slab rocks—limestone, she said. They were shaded by cypress trees and they all piled their tubes together, out of the water. She went about distributing sandwiches while Lindsey passed out paper plates and napkins. Pickles and chips were passed around next, and Hannah frowned when she saw an extra sandwich, minus the lettuce and tomatoes of the others.

"Oh...say you didn't," she teased as she held it up. "Really?"

Lindsey laughed. "Well, it's their outing too."

"I didn't think Barney could get any more spoiled than he was. I see I was wrong."

While she and Lindsey ate at a normal pace, Jack and the dogs devoured their sandwiches. She didn't know if Jack was really that hungry or if he was anxious to try out the rapids. It didn't take long for her to get her answer.

"Can I go now?" His question was directed at Lindsey, not her.

"Okay. But when you go through the chute, you want to paddle to the left so you can come back this way," she said.

"Is it safe?" Hannah asked. "I mean..."

Lindsey gave a quick smile. "It is. Very tame rapids. Just enough for a little thrill." Then she pointed at Jack. "Don't fall out of your tube. I don't want to have to come rescue you."

"I won't. And later...we'll do it without tubes?"

"Yeah, we'll give it a try."

He shoved the last of his chips into his mouth, then got up and took his tube back out into the water. Since she and Lindsey were still eating, the dogs made no attempt to follow him.

"Go more toward the other bank," Lindsey called to him. "The chute is at an angle."

They watched him and Hannah realized she was holding her breath. He gave a little scream as he bounced over the rocks, but his tube made it through the chute unscathed. As instructed, he paddled to his left, into calmer water.

"It's shallow there," Lindsey called.

He stood up, the water just above his waist. He walked back upstream, pulling his tube behind him. "Can I go again?"

"Have at it," Lindsey said. She turned to Hannah. "He doesn't shy away from anything, does he?"

"I think you have something to do with that. He feels... secure with you."

"You think so?"

"Yes, I do." She waited until Lindsey met her eyes. "You've been very good for him."

Lindsey held her gaze. "He's been good for me."

Hannah tilted her head, studying Lindsey. "You're what? Twenty-nine?"

"Yes."

"Obviously not married," she said. "Seeing someone? Leave someone behind when you moved here?"

Lindsey shrugged. "Yeah, I was kinda seeing someone. But… well, she couldn't deal with me, couldn't handle my moods, my grief." She shrugged again. "So…no, I guess. I didn't really leave anyone behind."

Hannah stared at her, shocked. "She?"

"Yeah."

Hannah swallowed. "Oh. So…you're *gay*?"

Lindsey raised her eyebrows. "You didn't know?"

Hannah shook her head. "No. But…well…no. Honestly, I hadn't given it a thought one way or the other."

Lindsey met her gaze again. "Does it matter?"

"No. No…of course not." She lowered her voice. "Does Jack know?"

Lindsey smiled. "We've talked about a lot of things…but that subject has never come up, thank goodness." Lindsey paused. "You don't have any gay friends, do you?"

"Actually…well…no. I mean, my roommate in college was gay, but we kinda lost touch over the years. And then there's Bruce. He's cut my hair for the last…oh, I don't know…fifteen years."

Lindsey laughed. "You can't count your gay hairdresser."

"Why not? I know all about his life and he knows all about mine."

Lindsey ate one more chip. "Okay. I'll give you that."

Hannah handed the last of her sandwich to Barney. "So my roommate doesn't count?"

"Did she hit on you?"

Hannah laughed. "Yeah."

"Okay...then I guess you can count her." Lindsey got up. "I'm going to go play with Jack. It's been years since I rode the chute without a tube."

Hannah watched her get up, wondering why it hadn't occurred to her that Lindsey might be a lesbian. She had yet to see her with makeup on, not that that was a sign or anything. She was very *natural* in her appearance. No jewelry, other than a sports watch. Her hair wasn't overly short, even though that stereotype was surely outdated. She fingered her own hair, which was shorter than Lindsey's. No, you couldn't go by hairstyle, she told herself.

But there were other things about her...the way she carried herself, her athleticism, her grace, her confidence. Still, none of those things screamed gay. She turned her gaze to the river where Lindsey and Jack were. They had walked upstream where the water was only to Lindsey's thigh. She was holding Jack's hand, and Hannah smiled as she watched them. Lindsey was obviously instructing Jack on how to ride the rapids. She took a deep breath. Hopefully, she was telling him how to ride them without drowning.

She needn't have worried. Lindsey placed Jack in front of her, holding on to him as the current caught them. They shot through the chute quickly, bobbing above water, Jack laughing loudly as Lindsey stood and pulled him up with her.

"Oh, wow, Mom! That was so much fun!" he said excitedly as they came closer. "Much better than with the tube." He turned his smiling face back to Lindsey. "Can we go again?"

"Sure." Lindsey looked over at her. "You want to take a turn?"

"Oh, I don't know," she said hesitantly. "I might want to stick to the tube."

"It's fun, Mom! Ride it with Lindsey like I did."

Lindsey arched an eyebrow invitingly, and as their eyes held, Hannah wondered if she dared. Oh...what the hell. It did look like fun.

"Okay." She got up. "But please don't let me drown."

Lindsey laughed. "I wouldn't dream of it."

They walked out much like Lindsey and Jack had done. Lindsey had to shove Max away as he tried to follow, and Jack called him back.

"Now...do you want to sit on my lap like Jack did, or would you rather do it as a tandem?"

Her eyes flew to Lindsey's. *Sit on her lap?* "What's the advantage?"

"Well, if we go tandem, I'll go in the front and you'll hold on and ride behind me. You'll bounce on the rocks a little bit more."

"And...and your lap?"

"I take the brunt of the rocks. It'll be like you're on an underwater sleigh or something."

"That obviously sounds better for me," she said with a laugh. "Not sure about you, though."

Lindsey wiggled her eyebrows. "I doubt I'll complain."

Hannah looked away. Flirting? She was teasing, of course. Wasn't she? Now that Hannah knew she was gay, she could tease about stuff like that. Right?

Lindsey, however, made the choice for her. "On your first run, I'd recommend my lap. Then we'll do it tandem." Lindsey paused. "We used to...well, when the kids were here, we used to do it four and five at a time. Like a train. That was fun."

Hannah saw a shadow cross her face, and she couldn't stop herself from touching Lindsey's arm and squeezing it. Lindsey's teasing of earlier was just that. Hannah was almost embarrassed that she'd tried to turn it into something else.

"If I get the hang of it, maybe all three of us could go," she suggested.

"Yeah. Jack would like that."

So, she tried her best to ignore the hands at her waist that turned her around to face the rapids. She could feel the push of the water against her legs as they got closer to the chute.

"Okay, I'm going to pull you back," Lindsey said. "Don't tense up. Just relax. Let your legs go. It won't be over our heads."

She nodded, but her stare was on the fast approaching chute...and rocks. Again, she needn't have worried. Lindsey pulled her tight, and they sank into the water. She could feel Lindsey's legs under hers, and she held her hands out in front of her, feeling safe as Lindsey clutched her tightly. She was so focused on not hitting the rocks, she hardly had time to enjoy the ride. In no time at all, they shot through the chute and past the clutter of rocks and into stiller water.

Lindsey released her, and Hannah found the bottom, standing. They'd gone a little farther than Lindsey had done with Jack and the water was up to her waist. Without thinking, she took Lindsey's hand and let herself be pulled back into shallower water.

It was only then that she heard Jack clapping, and she glanced at him, grinning as much as he was.

"You did great, Mom!"

"That was fun," she admitted. "But it was over too fast."

"We can stay and play some," Lindsey said. "If you want to."

Play? When was the last time she'd played? Played just for the heck of it? Did she consider it play when she used to meet Avery and Jennifer for her daily run? No. That wasn't really playtime. Even so, that had ceased once James got sick. *Did* she ever play? She and James would play with Jack at the park. Did that count?

"Well?"

She looked at Lindsey, realizing she hadn't answered her. She nodded. "Yes, let's stay and play."

"Yay! My turn! My turn!"

She waited while Lindsey took Jack through the chute one more time, then waded out into the water.

"Are you getting tired?" she asked Lindsey.

"No, no. This is fun. Actually, it's been a while since I've taken the time to play like this."

"I know. I was thinking that very thing," she said.

"So? Want to try it tandem?"

"Actually, can we do it like before? I...well, it happened so fast, I don't think it even registered what I was doing."

"Sure," Lindsey said easily. "Don't worry about the rocks on the sides. You won't hit them."

As before, she let Lindsey guide her, feeling the hands at her waist tighten as they got closer.

"Ready?"

Hannah nodded, then relaxed as Lindsey pulled her back as they once again sank in the water. Unlike before, she was aware of her surroundings this time. She was aware of Lindsey's hands holding her, aware of their skin touching as she sat on Lindsey's lap. She was aware of their legs tangling as they shot through the chute, aware of arms pulling her tight as they bounced through the rapids. And aware as they slowed, aware of the arms loosening, the hands leaving her. Aware that her eyes were closed.

Aware that she was smiling.

She opened her eyes, finding Lindsey watching. Lindsey returned her smile, then headed to shore. Hannah sighed contentedly, then ducked her head under the water and slicked her hair back from her eyes.

Oh, yeah. What great fun.

Lindsey took Jack once more, then announced they would try it with all three linked together "like a train." Hannah hadn't yet done it in tandem, much less with three.

"What? Too soon?"

She shrugged. "You think it'll be okay?"

"Sure. I'll put Jack in front of me. You bring up the rear." Then Lindsey grinned. "You're going to get pretty wet though."

Jack laughed. "We're in the river. I guess so!"

"There's always a smartass in the group," Lindsey teased.

Jack pointed his finger at her. "Should you say that word in front of me?"

Hannah rolled her eyes. "Oh, please."

With all three of them in the river, they had a hard time keeping the dogs away, and they finally gave up. Barney was the first to get sucked through the rapids and into the chute. He had a panicked look on his face but made it through. Max followed, and they all laughed as his big paws pounded the water as he tried to swim upstream against the flow. Lindsey was about to go help him when he turned and rode the rapids, ending up in calmer water with Barney. They swam to shore, and this time they did not try to follow.

"I guess they've had enough," Lindsey said. She held onto Jack and guided him closer to the rapids. "Okay, you sit like before. I'm going to wrap my legs around you." She turned to Hannah. "You get behind me, wrap your legs around my waist." She grinned. "And hold on."

"Why again are we doing this?"

"Because it'll be fun."

"Yeah, Mom...it'll be fun!"

In Hannah's mind, their train of three looked like a disaster waiting to happen, but she would trust that Lindsey knew what she was doing.

"Okay...on three," Lindsey said.

Hannah got behind her and held on to her waist. Jack was bouncing in front of Lindsey, a mixture of excitement and fear on his face.

"One...two..."

Hannah's grip tightened as she felt Lindsey tense.

"Three!"

Hannah nearly panicked as she felt Lindsey and Jack slipping away from her. She wrapped her arms around Lindsey's waist as her legs folded around her too. Unlike before when she rode on Lindsey's lap, she was now sliding along the smooth rock bottom on her ass. The chute was upon them in no time, and she felt herself being whipped from side to side as she held on tightly to Lindsey. Jack's jubilant laughter rang out as they were flung out from the chute and into calmer—but deeper—water.

"Let's do it again!"

She was still holding on to Lindsey as she tried to stand, Jack's excitement bubbling over as he jumped up and down in the water.

"Well? What did you think?"

Hannah smiled at her. "It happened so fast, I'm not sure what to think. I swallowed a gallon of river water, I'm sure."

"Yeah...the one in the back gets the brunt of it."

"Can we go again?" Jack asked once more.

"Okay...one more time," Lindsey said. "Then we need to get going. We've still got about an hour of float time left." She glanced back at Hannah. "You want to go again or sit this one out?"

"I'll go again."

Yes, she'd swallowed a gallon of water. Yes, her ass had bounced along the bottom like a basketball. And yes, it had happened so fast, she hadn't had time to truly enjoy it.

But she wanted to do it again. Because she was playing, she told herself.

CHAPTER TWENTY-SEVEN

Lindsey leaned her shoulder against the edge of the deck frame, looking up into the nighttime sky. One more day until full—the moon was rising over the oaks behind the deer feeder. It cast enough light for her to make out three deer still eating.

She twisted the water bottle absently between her fingers, then moved out onto the deck, sitting down in the chair she normally used. Max was in the house, sprawled out on the kitchen floor and enjoying the coolness of the AC. She smiled as she watched him. Passed out was more like it. He'd nearly fallen asleep in his food bowl.

Yeah, she was pleasantly tired too. It had been an all-around great day. So much so that she hated to see it come to an end. She had assumed that their float trip—which had taken well over three hours by the time they'd stopped and played—would be the extent of their time together. Instead, Hannah had seemed in no hurry to leave, so they'd sat on the deck by the river and finished off the sausage, cheese, and crackers that Hannah had brought. Then they'd piled onto the four-wheeler—a four-wheeler meant for two, not three—and had driven back upstream to get the Mule. Despite protests that she had no idea what she was doing, Hannah had driven the Mule back, following slowly behind her and Jack on the four-wheeler.

Even then, they weren't ready to call it a day. She and Hannah had sat on the deck talking while Jack entertained them by attempting to do flips from the rope swing. He finally tired and joined them, stretching out on a towel as the sun started to sink lower. Eventually, though, their day came to an end, and they packed up the Mule and she drove them back to the creek. Jack was fighting yawns the whole way, but he still had enough energy to ask what they were going to do tomorrow.

"How about we take your mom to our secret place?"

He grinned. "Really?"

"Can we trust her?"

He grinned wider. "I don't know. We might have to blindfold her."

She laughed at his suggestion and had glanced at Hannah, who arched an eyebrow.

"Blindfold?"

"Well, you know, it's a secret."

She smiled as she looked up into the sky. Not only were they going to the pond, but Hannah had invited her for dinner tomorrow night. She warned, however, that it would most likely be Jack's favorite—spaghetti and meatballs.

So…it looked like she'd made a new friend. When she'd moved out here, making friends had been the least of her worries. She had simply been trying to make it through each day…each night. She didn't have anything to offer someone. She wondered if she did now.

She smiled as she pictured Hannah lying back on her tube, her skin beginning to turn a golden brown from their days in the sun. It would help if she didn't look so damn good in a bikini. She closed her eyes for a moment as she remembered their ride through the chute. How much fun had that been?

She shook her head. "You're very bad, Lindsey. Very bad."

* * *

Hannah relaxed in the rocker, sitting down with a tired sigh. Pleasantly tired, she thought. Jack had barely made it through dinner—reheated leftovers that Margie had sent home with them several days ago—and he hadn't even begged for ice cream afterward. He'd left her with a tired hug and a mumbled "It was a fun day, Mom" before he and Barney had scooted off to bed. She cleaned up dinner, then poured herself a glass of wine, taking it outside with her.

It was a warm evening, but a light breeze from the south stirred the air. She looked above the trees, watching the moon as it crept higher in the sky. Not full yet but plenty bright enough to chase some of the shadows away, enough for her to see the trees clearly.

What a fun day it had been. The kind of lazy, summer day that is usually reserved for kids, not adults. She felt like she'd played as much as Jack had. A slow smile formed as she remembered sitting on Lindsey's lap—of all things—to ride the rapids without tubes. Oh, it had been great fun, for sure. Lindsey had made it fun.

Her smile faltered a little. Lindsey was a lesbian. It didn't matter, of course. She was all for taking people at face value. Unlike Margie, who insisted they should avoid anyone with a last name of McDermott. Still…it didn't matter. She liked Lindsey. She was nice. She was fun. She was easy to be around. Easy. Yes. Their friendship, while still in the infancy stages, was almost effortless, despite the rocky start. Jack probably helped, she knew. Lindsey treated Jack like…well, like family.

Family. Sadness settled over her quickly. She'd lost a husband, but she still had family. She had Jack. She had her parents, her sister. She had in-laws. Lindsey? Did she have *anyone*? As far as she knew, no, there was no one. Did she maybe have cousins? Aunts? Uncles?

She decided she would ask her. Friends talked about that, didn't they? Of course, if she broached the subject, Lindsey might very well want to know about James. She hated to admit it, but she had a hard time recalling a time when James wasn't sick. The headaches had started long before he was diagnosed. It seemed like as soon as the word "cancer" was mentioned, he started slipping away from them. Fifteen long months later, he slipped away from them for good.

She closed her eyes for a moment, trying to recall his face without the constant pain that was etched on it. What popped into her head was an image of James and Jack at the neighborhood playground. James was sitting at the top of the slide with Jack in his lap. Jack probably wasn't much more than a year old, but they'd come buzzing down the slide in reckless fashion, Jack giggling and laughing when they'd landed in a heap on the sand below. If Jack had been talking then, she could imagine what he would have said.

"Can we go again?"

As Lindsey had said, Jack didn't shy away from anything. Did she have James to thank for that? Had James started to instill confidence in him, even at that young age?

She let out a heavy breath as she set the rocker in motion. If they hadn't met Lindsey—if *Jack* hadn't met Lindsey—would she be itching to leave here and go back to San Antonio? The loneliness that she'd lived with since James had died wasn't really hovering over her any longer. But if there was no Lindsey, what would she and Jack do every day? She shook her head with a smile. What in the hell had she been thinking when she'd moved them out here? Her mother had told her to wait, to not make a rash decision. Selling their home had been a rash decision, but it had been the right one. Neither she nor Jack could live with a ghost in the house. Guilt and grief had both contributed to the move out here, however. She admitted that only a few short weeks ago she'd been ready to throw in the towel and give up. Give up and head back home.

Now? Now she was having fun, she was playing. She wasn't lonely. She actually looked forward to the days now. Like tomorrow. *Blindfold?* What did Lindsey and Jack have planned? What secret place had they been talking about? Jack had refused to give it up, simply saying "it's our place" and leaving it at that. She supposed she would find out tomorrow.

She took a sip of her wine. Did that secret place involve water? She admitted, she was becoming quite comfortable wearing a bikini top all day. Like Lindsey, she always started out with a shirt or tank over her top, and like Lindsey, she always took it off as soon as they got to the river, not to put it back on again until the ride home. At first, yes, she was a little self-conscious. And who wouldn't be? Lindsey was still in her twenties. Her body was firm, athletic...young. Hannah was approaching thirty-five. Could she still say that about herself?

She smiled. Well, she had found Lindsey's gaze on her a time or two. Maybe she wasn't quite as *old* as she imagined. Although having a lesbian staring at her—was that something she should hail? She nodded in the darkness, the smile still on her face. It had been a long time since anyone had stared at her like that. She wondered if Lindsey knew she did that. Or if Lindsey knew that Hannah had caught her.

She leaned back in the rocker, her toe gently moving her back and forth. Yes, she was looking forward to tomorrow. She hoped it would prove to be another fun day.

CHAPTER TWENTY-EIGHT

Lindsey laughed as she swung the bandana in front of Hannah. Hannah held her hands up.

"Really? You were serious about the blindfold?"

"I told you, it's a secret place," Lindsey said, trying to keep the smile from her face. Having Jack giggling beside her didn't help.

"Okay, you two," Hannah said, wiggling a finger between them. "I'll play along." She stepped closer to Lindsey, her eyes teasing. "If anything fishy happens to me...paybacks are hell."

Lindsey grinned. "Fishy, huh? So I shouldn't toss you into the river?"

Hannah held her gaze. "At your own risk." She turned to Jack and pinched his cheek. "If you ever want triple-cheese hamburger casserole again, you'll make sure that Lindsey behaves."

He nodded seriously. "Okay. We won't throw you in the water." He glanced over at her. "Right?"

Lindsey nodded. "Right. Because whatever triple-cheese hamburger casserole is...it sounds really, really good."

Jack smiled and looked at his mom. "See! I told you she'd like it!"

Lindsey turned Hannah around, then folded the bandana and covered Hannah's eyes, securing it behind her head. She patted her shoulder.

"There. That ought to keep you from peeking."

"You know, I'm totally at your mercy."

"Yeah...how about that?" She laughed quietly. "And I'll try to behave."

She guided Hannah into the Mule, then let Jack get in between them. The dogs were already on the back and she drove up the trail toward Antler Peak—and the cutoff to the pond. This was the route she and Jack had taken the very first time she'd brought him to the pond. She glanced over, seeing Hannah holding on to the roll bar with one hand, but there was a smile on her face.

She never would have thought to use the blindfold if Jack hadn't brought it up. But it was a game and like Hannah had said, she'd play along. She nudged Jack with her elbow and winked at him. His grin was contagious.

She slowed and turned on the cutoff road. It wasn't as well used from this side of the property and it was quite rocky. Hannah was holding on with both hands now.

"Do you know how badly I want to take this damn blindfold off?"

She laughed. "All in good time."

When the pond came into view, she felt Jack sit up straighter in anticipation. Hannah must have felt it too, because she tilted her head as if listening for a clue as to where they were. She drove around the back and parked beside the lean-to. The dogs were clamoring to get off and she got out, letting Jack have the honors. Lindsey walked around the Mule to Hannah's side and took her arm, leading her out.

"Watch your step," she murmured.

"I wish I could."

Lindsey looked at Jack. "What do you think?" she asked. "Out there?" She pointed to the pier which jutted out toward the waterfall.

He nodded.

"Okay...this way," she told Hannah, still holding on to her elbow as she guided her onto the pier.

"I hear water."

Lindsey smiled. "Yeah. That'd be the dogs splashing around."

"It doesn't sound like the river, though."

"Nope."

She turned Hannah so that she was facing the waterfall, then stepped behind her to untie the bandana. When she took it away, she heard Hannah gasp in surprise.

"Oh, my God," she whispered. She turned quickly, meeting her gaze. "It's beautiful." Then she smiled. "What is it?"

"It's the pond," Jack supplied. "And it's a secret."

Hannah stared at him. "This is the secret place where you've been having swimming lessons?"

He nodded. "And it's really deep too."

"Okay, buddy, we probably shouldn't tell her that," Lindsey said as she ruffled his hair. She motioned behind her. "Go get the stuff."

He ran off the pier toward the footlocker and soon had his noodle and her fanny floater tossed in the pond.

"What is Mom going to use?"

"Can you throw that little rubber float in too? Thanks. I'll use that. Your mom can use the fanny floater."

Hannah touched her arm. "So what is this really?"

"A sinkhole, I guess. It's a spring. Limestone bottom." She shrugged. "We always just called it the pond."

"It's too beautiful for words. It's like something out of a magazine. No wonder you keep it a secret."

"Would you believe that you and Jack are the only two people to see it other than family?"

Again, a light touch on her arm and a gentle squeeze. "I'm honored. Thank you."

Jack ran past them and jumped off the end of the pier, sending water splashing around them.

"So how deep is it?"

"You don't want to know," she said. She stripped off her shirt and tossed it down. "But fair warning. It's a little colder than the river."

Instead of jumping in like Jack, Lindsey stood at the edge of the pier and dove in headfirst. Even though she was prepared, the cool water on her heated skin was a shock. She surfaced, then swam toward Jack, who was floating with an arm draped over his noodle.

"It's cold," she said. "I got used to the river, I think."

"What do you think Mom is going to do?" Jack whispered.

She grinned. "She's going to scream."

"What are you two whispering about?"

Jack giggled but said nothing. Lindsey watched as Hannah removed her tank. The black bikini top today. Her eyes traveled down to the flat stomach, the water shorts loose at Hannah's hips, hanging just below her navel. *God.* She looked away quickly before Hannah caught her staring.

Jack's mother, Jack's mother, Jack's mother.

Hannah took a few running steps and jumped into the pond much like Jack had done. When her head popped out of the water, she was grinning.

"Whoa," she said. "You weren't kidding. It's a lot colder than the river."

Lindsey pushed the fanny floater toward her and nodded. "It grows on you." She looked over at Jack. "Show your mom the backstroke."

"Okay. Mom...watch me."

Hannah got into the fanny floater, watching as Jack showed off his new swimming skill. Lindsey slid onto the thin rubber float, the float her sister used most often. She turned her attention to Jack. He'd gotten quite good, she admitted. Hannah seemed impressed too.

"Wow...you really have been working with him."

"He's a natural. Plus he loves it."

Jack swam back to them and Hannah clapped. "Very good!"

ovedlyarting over.

"I know. I'm getting real good." He left his noodle with them and went to shore. "I'm going to see if the dogs will jump off the pier with me."

Hannah smiled after him. "He's changed so much."

"How so?"

"He's happier. More sure of himself."

"He's getting older."

"I guess that has something to do with it, but…the last year, James didn't get to spend much time with him. Time like this, I mean. Outside, doing things." She smiled. "Playing."

"He doesn't seem to have suffered from it, though."

"He's better." Hannah looked at her. "You've helped so much, Lindsey. You've given him a purpose, I think."

"Y'all…watch! I think they're going to do it!"

They turned their attention to Jack and the two dogs, whose tails were wagging at record speed. He was clapping his hands and coaxing them to follow. He took off running, landing far out from the pier. The dogs ran after him, but only Max jumped off. Barney came to a screeching halt, and she and Hannah laughed as he almost tipped over into the water anyway.

"Oh…come on, Barney," Jack called. "Don't be a wimp!"

"Why do you think he'll jump off the deck at the river but not here?" Hannah asked.

"This is a little higher, I guess."

Max turned back to shore and Jack followed.

"This will keep him entertained for a while." Hannah then spun around in her fanny floater to face her. "Where did you move from?" she asked unexpectedly.

"Dallas."

"Was that where your family lived?"

Lindsey shook her head. "No. They all lived in San Antonio. Except my grandparents, of course." She arched an eyebrow. "Your family?"

"San Antonio. My parents. And I have a younger sister. She has two kids." She paused. "Why Dallas?"

Lindsey shrugged. "That's where my job was. I wanted to stay in this area, but…well, I couldn't turn down the job offer."

At Hannah's unasked question, she smiled. "I am...*was*...an architect. It was a fairly large firm. We did a lot of commercial projects." She glanced over as Jack jumped off the pier again, and again Barney refused to follow. "After the accident...I was pretty much worthless to them. I couldn't really function in my day-to-day life any longer."

"Did you move here with the intent of being close to them... or...?"

Lindsey sighed. "I'm not sure, really. I have an uncle. He lives in New York. He came down. He helped me with...well, with the arrangements. He's the one who finally convinced me to move out here. I was spending every day, every night inside my dark apartment—alone. I was—" She paused, wondering if she should be telling Hannah all this.

"Go on," Hannah said quietly. "You were what?"

"I was sinking into a deep, dark hole of depression," she admitted. "I didn't...want to live."

Hannah's eyes softened. "But you didn't want to die either?"

"Oh, I wanted to die," she said. "I just didn't have the courage."

"Oh, Lindsey...I'm so sorry."

"I don't know what I really expected when I moved out here. I quit my job, sold my car." She smiled. "Bought a Jeep and got a puppy." Her smiled faded. "It was hell the first month." She looked over at Hannah, meeting her eyes. "Actually, it was pretty much hell until I met Jack."

Hannah held her gaze. "I am so, so sorry that I tried to make you stay away from him."

Lindsey waved her apology away. "That was partly my fault. I shouldn't have been sneaking off with him. I should have come up to meet you sooner."

There was a huge splash, and they turned, finding that Max and Barney had both joined Jack on his jump into the pond.

"He did it! He did it!"

She and Hannah clapped and cheered, watching as Jack once again headed back to shore with two dogs hot on his trail.

"Lindsey...come throw me in!"

Lindsey flicked her eyes at Hannah. "You might not want to watch this."

* * *

Hannah stared with wide eyes as Lindsey grabbed Jack's wrists and started spinning him around like a pinwheel. He was laughing like crazy when Lindsey let go of him, flinging him far out into the pond. He popped up quickly, still grinning as he swam closer to her and his noodle.

"That is so much fun!"

"Aren't you dizzy?"

"Yeah! That's what makes it fun!"

She didn't go into the fact that being dizzy could make him disoriented, especially under water. This was obviously a game they'd played before. Maybe she should have taken Lindsey's advice and not watched.

She did watch, however, as Lindsey stood at the edge of the pier, preparing to dive in. At the last minute, Lindsey turned, meeting her gaze. A quick smile, then she pushed off, executing a perfect dive into the pond, barely rippling the surface as she went under.

"She's been teaching me to dive too," Jack announced. "But I'm not very good. I keep landing on my belly."

"Why don't you go try it for me?" she suggested.

"Okay. But don't laugh."

Lindsey swam over and got back on her float. "Lock your thumbs together," she said to him. "Keep your arms straight. Push off with your legs."

His first try was not a success. Neither was his second, and Hannah could tell he was getting discouraged.

"As good as he's been with everything else, he hasn't gotten the hang of this yet," Lindsey said quietly, keeping her gaze on Jack as he got out of the pond and went to try again. "Hang on, buddy. Let me come up there."

He seemed very stiff, almost like he was afraid. She didn't understand that. He'd been splashing in her parents' pool long before he even walked. He'd always been comfortable in the water. Lindsey stood beside him, urging him to mimic her stance.

"Bend your knees, like this."

"I am."

"Okay, look. When you run and jump in...you push off, right?"

"Right."

"When you're diving, you do the same thing. Watch."

Lindsey took several steps back on the pier, then ran forward, pushing off at the last second. Hannah's eyes were on her as her body split the water with barely a ripple. When she came up, she treaded water, bobbing up and down near Jack.

"If you try that, you're gonna bust your belly, though," she said with a smile. "So it's easier to learn by standing still. But you've got to push off. Lead with your hands, your arms. Your head will follow."

Jack was nodding while she talked, and Hannah wondered how many times Lindsey had recited those same words to him. She watched as Jack rubbed his hands together, his expression serious. He took a deep breath, then assumed his diving position. She could tell he was silently counting to three, then he pushed off...and fell into the water, knees first.

"Don't worry about it so much," Lindsey told him. "It'll come. Just takes practice."

She swam back over to her float and Jack found his noodle. The dogs were lying in the shade, each chewing on a stick. Hannah relaxed again, enjoying the cool water on her skin on such a hot day. But she knew they needed to end their playtime. She needed to get home and start on dinner. Making meatballs from scratch took a little time. Even though there was a package of frozen meatballs in the large chest freezer—which would suffice for Jack—she wanted to make her homemade ones. They were so much better and she thought Lindsey would appreciate that.

She glanced over at her now, finding her head back, her eyes closed. She turned to Jack, who was floating silently beside her.

"About time to go," she said.

His face scrunched up in a frown. "Already? We just got here."

"I'm sure we've been here well over an hour."

"Oh...*Mom*. I don't want to go yet."

"We're having company for dinner tonight," she reminded him. "Your room needs to be cleaned and it's your turn to vacuum."

The reminder that Lindsey was coming over seemed to appease him.

"Okay...but let me jump off the pier a few more times."

"It does seem like we just got here," Lindsey said when Jack swam off.

"You'll thank me later when you bite into one of my meatballs."

CHAPTER TWENTY-NINE

Hannah had just seasoned the ground meat—a combination of both beef and pork—and was about to plunge her hands in to mix it when she heard the front door open.

"Great," she murmured, knowing Margie was about to pop her head into the kitchen.

"Oh, I was trying to catch you before you started dinner."

"Hi, Margie," she said, eyeing the basket of veggies she carried.

"I just came from the garden. The squash are really coming in. And I have a bag of green beans," Margie said, holding one up. "I thought you could use some vegetables for dinner." She looked into the mixing bowl. "What are you mixing up?"

"Meatballs."

"Well, I really do love that you make your own meatballs from scratch, but spaghetti and meatballs isn't what I'd call a healthy meal."

"It's Jack's favorite," she said. "But I am making it a little differently tonight." She pointed to the sauce that was simmering. "I'm putting zucchini, mushrooms and spinach into the sauce." She smiled. "Don't tell Jack."

Margie held up a zucchini from her basket. "Then you can put this one to good use then." She sat the squash on the counter. "Where is Jack?"

"Cleaning his room, I hope." She debated whether to elaborate, then decided she wasn't going to hide her friendship with Lindsey. "I'm sure he'll want to show it to Lindsey later."

Margie eyed her sharply. "That woman is coming over? *Here?*"

"Yes. She's coming for dinner. Thus the vegetables in the sauce."

Margie let out an exaggerated sigh. "Lilly would have an absolute fit if she knew that a McDermott was in her house."

"Then I guess it's good that she doesn't know." Hannah washed her hands and dried them on a towel. "How is she doing anyway? Any change?"

"No. It's so sad to see her like that. Dennis refuses to go. She doesn't talk. She doesn't know that we're there."

"Yes, that is sad."

"I wish you could have gotten to know her. She was just the sweetest lady," Margie said wistfully. "I do miss her being here."

Hannah had to hold in her laughter. From what she'd learned over the years, Lilly was quite the opposite of sweet. James had even referred to her as the devil.

"Of course, if she was still here, you and Jack wouldn't be." Then her face hardened. "Not that we get to see that much of you. I don't know why you won't bring Jack around more."

"He's nine years old and wants to play. Nothing against you and Dennis, but he'd much rather be in the river with Lindsey than sitting around visiting," she said bluntly.

"I still think it was a mistake not to send him to church camp. He could have met some boys his own age. Now he'll be completely lost when he goes to school."

"I'm sure he'll be fine." She pointed out the kitchen door. "Why don't you go find him and say hello. I need to get my meatballs going." She paused. "And thank you for the vegetables."

Margie turned to go, then stopped. "What do you and Jack have planned for the Fourth?"

"Oh, I don't know yet. I'll probably take him somewhere to see fireworks. I read that Leaky has a celebration at the park in town."

"Yes, it's pretty good. But Dennis's sister invited us over to their place in Vanderpool. They're going to do burgers and hot dogs. Why don't you and Jack come with us? I know Darlene would be thrilled to see you."

Despite not being able to come up with an excuse as to why they couldn't join them, Hannah wasn't going to accept the invitation that easily.

"Thanks," she said with a shrug. "I'll let you know."

Margie stared at her for a long moment, as if she wanted to say more, but she finally nodded.

"Well...I'll go say hello to Jack."

Hannah blew out her breath as soon as Margie turned away. How could the woman—with only a stare—make her feel guilty? She shook her head. As James used to say, she was the Queen of Guilt. She plunged her hands into the meat mixture, trying to shake off the sense of obligation she felt. She again reminded herself that the main reason they'd moved here was so that Jack could connect with them. She paused in her task, staring at the wall without seeing it. That wasn't the *main* reason, she admitted. James's ghost was the real reason she'd wanted to leave San Antonio. In hindsight, yeah, she'd rushed into the move. She hadn't given herself and Jack much time to adjust to James being gone. If she had to do it over again, she would have simply bought a new house—probably close to her parents—and started over.

But that damn guilt that Margie could dish out. *That* was the real reason she was here and not at a new home in San Antonio.

Well, too late to lament it now. She'd been over this same scenario in her mind too many times to count. The outcome was always the same. She and Jack were living in her dead husband's grandmother's house...being watched closely by his mother. What in the *hell* had she been thinking?

As she absently began making the meatballs—rubbing the meat mixture into small balls in her palms—her thoughts drifted to Lindsey. If Lindsey wasn't here, if Jack had never met Lindsey, what would they be doing instead? What would fill their days? How could they possibly pass the time until school started?

"We could visit Margie and Dennis more," she mumbled to herself, the guilt starting to worm its way inside.

The problem with that…the only thing she had in common with Margie and Dennis was James. She wouldn't even count Jack. Jack only saw them once, sometimes twice a year before James got sick. Which should have been reason number one for *not* moving here, she told herself. Again…it was too late now. Besides, now that Lindsey and Jack were including her in their daily activities, she was having fun. Did she dare say she was even enjoying herself out here?

She smiled. Yes, she was. She felt almost normal again. She was glad Jack suggested they invite Lindsey over for dinner, even if it was a kid's meal of spaghetti and meatballs. Wine, of course, would turn it into an adult's meal as well.

"Mom?"

She looked up, finding Jack standing in the doorway.

"Why are you smiling?" he asked.

"Am I?" She shrugged. "Just thinking, I guess. Did your Grandma Margie leave?"

He nodded. "She says we're going to go with them over to Vanderpool for the Fourth of July."

She shook her head. "I did not agree to that yet." She rolled the last of the meat into a ball and placed it on the platter with the others. "What do you think? Do you want to go?"

He stood at the edge of the counter, resting one foot on top of the other. "Could Lindsey go with us?"

She laughed out loud at that. "Margie can barely tolerate the sound of her name. I really don't see that happening, Jack."

"But Lindsey's nice."

"I know, honey. Like I said before, the reason Margie doesn't like her has absolutely nothing to do with Lindsey."

"Then I don't want to go."

She put the empty bowl in the sink and filled it with hot water. "I was thinking we could go over to Leaky. They have a fireworks display at the park, by the river. Would you like that?"

"Can we invite Lindsey?"

Hannah smiled. "Sure. But she may already have plans," she said, knowing that probably wasn't the case. Who would she have plans with?

"We'll ask her tonight," he said.

"Okay, we'll ask her. Now…is your room clean?"

"Yes." He bit his lip. "Kinda."

She raised her eyebrows. "Kinda? Lindsey will want to see your room," she said. "Let's get it cleaner than 'kinda,' okay?"

His shoulders drooped as he walked away, his sign to her that he didn't approve of her request.

"And don't forget to vacuum," she called after him.

CHAPTER THIRTY

Lindsey eyed the rock bridge she and Jack had built, seeing one of the larger rocks misplaced. She smiled, remembering Hannah slipping off it just yesterday. She bent down and righted it—for at least the third time—then continued across. Wearing water sandals to dinner probably wasn't kosher, but it was perfect for crossing the shallow creek.

"If you get too wet, Hannah won't let you in the house," she warned as Max dipped his head in the water. She smiled. "Why do I talk to him like he understands?" She laughed. "And why are you talking to yourself?"

She paused on the other side of the creek, looking around at the familiar area, remembering all the days she and Jack had spent there. Well, not exactly here. No, they'd snuck off down the creek, past where Hannah had put her markers for Jack. That seemed like so long ago. Jack—and now Hannah—had chased away her loneliness, her grief. She didn't even want to think about what her days would be like if they weren't in them.

It didn't take much, however, to recall those long, dark, empty days of spring. She blew out her breath. No. She wasn't going to go there. Not now.

She turned, following Jack's trail. Max ran past her as if he knew where they were going. She had her small backpack slung over one shoulder. It contained a bottle of wine, a flashlight for tonight when they made the return trek across the creek, and a bag of dog food for Max. She took it off and put it on the other shoulder as she climbed the hill up to their house.

She found Jack and Barney on the back porch, waiting on them. Jack ran up to her and she smiled as he gave her a hug.

"Am I late?"

"No. But I wanted to ask you something."

She ruffled his hair and sat down on the porch. "Okay, ask away."

He sat down next to her, and they swung their legs back and forth over the edge. The dogs were wrestling over a stick that Max had found.

"Do you already have plans for the Fourth?"

She frowned. "The Fourth of July? I hadn't given it any thought, really." That was a lie, though. She'd intentionally blocked it from her mind. Like most holidays, her family always gathered here for the Fourth. It was a day she'd been dreading. Jack seemed to read her mind and he leaned closer to her.

"Mom wants to go to Leaky. They have fireworks," he said. "Would you go with us?"

Lindsey smiled over at him. "I think that sounds like fun. Thank you."

He nodded. "When...when your family was here, did y'all do stuff?"

"Yeah, we did." Her gaze landed on the dogs, and she watched their antics for a moment. "Food out on the deck. Burgers for the kids...ribs and chicken for the adults. A float trip on the river during the day. Fireworks out at the pond that evening." She turned to him. "When your dad was alive, what did you do?"

"We used to go to a park. They had a carnival with rides and stuff." He smiled. "Hot dogs and cotton candy. At dark, they had fireworks." The smile left his face. "Last year, though, we didn't go."

"He was already sick?"

Jack nodded. "We were supposed to go, but…well, he didn't feel too good."

Lindsey put her arm around him and pulled him close. "I'm sorry, buddy."

"But we'll have fun this year, right?"

"Yep. We'll have fun."

"Good." Then he grinned. "Because Grandma Margie came over today. She wants us to go with them. Mom said we didn't have to though."

"Where is your mom?"

"Cooking."

Lindsey turned, looking behind her, surprised to find Hannah standing at the window, watching them. She smiled as their gazes met, and Hannah returned it, then motioned her to come inside.

"I'm going to say hello to your mom," she said.

"Okay. Will you play catch with me?"

"Sure. Baseball?"

"Yeah. I have two gloves."

"Okay."

Jack beat her into the house and ran past Hannah without speaking. Hannah looked at her with raised eyebrows.

"Baseball," she explained. She pulled the bottle of red wine out of her pack. "Didn't know if you had anything for dinner."

"Nice," Hannah said as she inspected it. "I do have a bottle, but yours looks to be a little more expensive than mine." She grinned at her. "I knew there was a reason I liked you."

"I've found that cost doesn't necessarily indicate which wine will taste better," she said. "This was one of my grandfather's favorites." She looked toward the stove. "It smells great in here, by the way."

"Thank you. Everything is on a low simmer so we've got time before it's ready. Would you like a glass?" Hannah asked, pointing to a bottle of wine already opened. "I have a very bad habit of drinking wine while I cook."

Lindsey laughed. "Why do you say it's a bad habit?"

"I only say that because Margie thinks it is. She—"

Jack came hurrying back into the kitchen carrying two gloves and a ball. "Mom, Lindsey is gonna play catch with me."

"Good. I'll come watch." She looked back at Lindsey. "So? Wine?"

"Sure. Thanks."

The glove was a little tight on her hand, but she managed to catch the first ball Jack threw her way. She tossed it back at him and he caught it easily.

"You can throw it harder," he said. "I'm pretty good."

She glanced over at Hannah, who had taken a seat on one of the rockers. She was holding a glass of wine and the other she'd placed on the porch near the edge.

"Do you play with him?" she asked.

"Some. He says I throw like a girl."

Lindsey laughed. "Yeah, I never understood that."

"Well, in all fairness, I didn't have any brothers, and my father's idea of a sporting event is sitting by the pool with a cocktail."

Lindsey grinned. "My kinda guy."

"No...at least you'd be *in* the pool!"

After a few more tosses with Jack, she sat down on the porch and picked up her wineglass. "You wear me out," she told Jack. "I think tomorrow we should do the river and the rope swing. We'll practice catching a ball while you jump."

His eyes widened. "Oh...that'll be fun!"

She turned to Hannah. "That is, if it's okay with your mom."

Hannah smiled at her. "I keep telling you, you'll be sick of us before too long."

"And I keep telling you that won't happen."

* * *

Hannah opened the oven and checked the garlic bread. She turned the oven off but left the bread inside, thinking it could go another minute or two.

"Why don't you show Lindsey your room?" she suggested to Jack.

As soon as they walked off, she began taking plates out. It had been so long since she'd entertained anyone, she was looking forward to setting a nice table and serving a meal. She and Jack normally ate at the small breakfast table in the kitchen. Tonight, they would use Lilly's formal dining room. And if she dared, she'd use some of the china from the hutch...but no, she didn't dare. With her luck, Jack would break something and she'd never hear the end of it from Margie. She did wonder, however, what would happen to all of the china and the furniture. She thought that perhaps Dennis's sister would have already claimed it, but there'd been no mention of it to her. Not that it concerned her. She certainly didn't want any of it. She had her own wedding china boxed away in her parents' attic. And the hutch she'd used? It had been sold like most of their other furniture.

She paused in her task, thinking back to the house they'd lived in. It was the first house they'd bought after she and James married. As James's salary increased, he'd wanted to move to a bigger home, but she was settled there. She liked her neighbors. She was only a few blocks from Avery and Jennifer—her running buddies. And her parents' house was only a ten-minute drive away. She loved it there. It shouldn't have been as easy as it was to sell it and move.

But the house no longer held happy memories for her. It was simply a reminder of James's illness. And like Jack, she kept expecting to see James walk into the house, come into the kitchen while she was cooking...find him sitting in his recliner watching TV. No, with James's ghost there, it hadn't been hard to sell.

"Need some help?"

She turned, finding Lindsey watching her. She smiled apologetically. She was standing there still holding the plates in her hands.

"Sorry. I'm afraid I drifted off for a second."

Lindsey nodded in understanding. "Memories?"

Hannah took a deep breath. "Yes. I was thinking about Lilly's china and all of her furniture and somehow I ended up thinking about our house in San Antonio and…"

"And James?"

Hannah nodded as she finished setting the table. "I loved the house, really. James wanted to buy something bigger, something newer, but I always balked. I didn't want to move." She turned to Lindsey. "I was thinking about—even though I loved it—how easy it had been to sell it…to leave."

"Death will…stain things."

Hannah nodded. "Yes." She walked closer to Lindsey and touched her arm, letting her fingers rest there. "As we both know all too well."

Lindsey met her gaze, holding it. Hannah expected to see sadness in her eyes, but it was something else there instead, something she couldn't quite grasp. Then Lindsey blinked, breaking their stare.

"So…you need help with anything?"

It was a quiet question, and Hannah blinked too, trying to remember what she'd been doing. She realized her fingers were still wrapped around Lindsey's arm, and she slowly pulled them away.

"I was setting the table," she said, reminding herself of her earlier task. She pointed at the hutch. "I didn't dare use Lilly's china, but we'll be brave and use her cloth napkins." Then she smiled. "Well, you and I will. Jack will use paper. If he'd let me, I'd put a bib on him when he eats spaghetti."

Lindsey laughed. "You may want to put one on me too."

Deciding it was too much to bring all the food to the table, they made their plates in the kitchen, buffet style. The salad bowl and garlic bread were the only things placed between them on Lilly's table, which was big enough to seat ten.

Lindsey had opened the bottle of wine she'd brought, and she let Jack have a Coke, using a third wineglass for him instead of his usual one.

"Fancy," he said with a grin.

"Don't break it," she warned him.

"Oh, my God…this is so good," Lindsey said as she bit into a meatball. "Did you make these yourself?"

Hannah was pleased that she could tell. "Yes. I'm not a fan of frozen meatballs. Or sauce from a jar."

"No wonder this is Jack's favorite meal. It's delicious."

"Thank you."

"I can't decide if I like this one the best or the triple-cheese casserole," Jack said.

Lindsey met her gaze. "I definitely want to be invited for dinner when you make that."

Hannah laughed. "Yes, and it's obscenely fattening. We'll have to spend the entire next day working it off."

"So we'll hike to the river instead of taking the Mule," she said as she twirled pasta on her fork.

"Did Jack ask you about the Fourth?"

"He did."

"And?"

"And she's going!" Jack said around a mouthful of spaghetti.

Lindsey nodded. "I'd love to. Sounds like fun."

* * *

"As hot as it was today, it always cools down in the evening," Hannah said as she settled into one of the rockers on the porch.

"Yes, it's pleasant." Lindsey sat down on the porch itself, resting back against the railing as she watched Hannah put the rocker in motion.

"I know I don't have to say this, but Jack absolutely adores you."

"Yeah…and that's definitely mutual. He's a great kid, Hannah. You should be proud."

Hannah smiled. "I'm…thankful," she said. "I don't know about proud. I just lucked out with him, I think."

"He's wise beyond his years."

"Yes, he is. I'm not sure if it was James's illness that caused him to mature so quickly or the fact that he wasn't really ever around kids his own age. Of the group of friends we hung out with, we were the first to have a child," Hannah said. "Jack was nearly four before another one came along. By the time he was six, playing with two-year-olds didn't appeal to him and he tended to stick around the adults." She took a sip of her wine. "He hadn't even turned nine when James got sick."

"If you don't mind me asking, how long was he ill?"

Hannah sighed. "His headaches started long before he finally saw a doctor. Once he was diagnosed, he...well, I think he gave up. He lived fifteen months, but they weren't good months. He was in a lot of pain, especially toward the end." She leaned forward a little. "I never told Jack this, but I think James knew long before he first complained of the headaches. He took out a second life insurance policy about eight months before he went to the doctor."

"Intuition, you mean?"

"Yes. When I think back on it now, his personality was changing. He was always a happy, playful man. Nothing seemed to bother him. But then he changed. He started worrying about little things that before wouldn't even cross his mind. He stopped wanting to go out with our friends. He started working long hours." She paused. "I...I even thought that maybe he was having an affair, he'd changed so much. But then he couldn't hide the headaches from me any longer and when I finally made him go see a doctor...well...he already knew what the outcome was going to be." She sighed. "He suffered through the treatments because of me and Jack. I think if he'd been on his own, he would have just left...just drifted away on his own terms."

Lindsey finished the wine in her glass and set it down beside her. She couldn't decide which was worse—knowing a loved one was going to die and having to watch it or having it thrust upon you without a moment's warning. As devastated as she'd been when she got the news about her family, she tended to think that was better than having to watch them slip away from her for fifteen months. Of course she hadn't lost one person. Her grief was magnified ten-fold because it was all of them...at once.

"I'm sorry."

Lindsey looked up, meeting Hannah's eyes in the moonlight. The whispered words hung in the air between them. Had Hannah read her mind?

"Nothing for you to be sorry for," she said. "A loss is a loss, no matter the circumstances."

"Still...I only lost my husband. You lost...so many." Hannah sighed quietly. "I had my family to turn to. You had—"

"No one," Lindsey finished for her.

Hannah leaned forward again, bending closer to rest her hand on Lindsey's shoulder. "I wish I could have been there for you."

"You and Jack...you being here now...that's been so good for me. I can't tell you how much it means that you've let me into your life like this."

Hannah squeezed her shoulder. "And you've let us into yours."

When the back door opened, Hannah leaned back in the rocker, away from her. Jack stuck his head out.

"Is it time for ice cream yet?"

"How can you possibly have room for ice cream after all that you ate?"

"Just a little, Mom...please?"

"Okay. Just a little."

"Thanks!" He looked at her. "You want some?"

Lindsey shook her head. "No, I'm still full from dinner. Besides, I should get going."

He walked fully onto the porch. "Are we gonna play tomorrow at the river?"

"Yeah...we'll play at the rope swing." She looked to Hannah for confirmation and Hannah nodded. "I'll pick you up like usual. About eleven or so?"

"I'll bring lunch this time," Hannah offered. "Tuna salad okay?"

"Sure." She got up and rubbed Jack's hair affectionately. "See you then, buddy."

"Okay." He hugged her quickly. "I guess I should get Max. They're asleep."

"Both dogs are on your bed?" Hannah asked with raised eyebrows.

Jack bit his lip and backed away. "No," he said unconvincingly as he ran back inside.

Lindsey laughed. "He's too cute."

"Tell me about it."

Hannah stood and took the wineglass from her before heading back into the kitchen. "I'm glad you came over for dinner."

Lindsey followed her inside. "Thanks for asking. I enjoyed it. And if you couldn't tell by how much I ate, I loved the meal. Your sauce and the meatballs were superb."

"Thank you. It's nice to cook for someone who appreciates it." She put the wineglasses in the sink. "Not that Jack isn't complimentary, but he'd be happy with a rotation of three meals."

"Spaghetti and meatballs, the triple-cheese thing—which I can't wait to try—and what else?"

"Hamburgers."

"Ah. Well, we'll need to grill out again on the deck."

Jack came back with two sleepy puppies following behind him. Max came up to her and sat down, leaning heavily against her leg. She reached down to scratch his head.

"We should go. I'll see y'all tomorrow."

Jack was already in the freezer, taking out a tub of ice cream. He turned to her and smiled. "Good night, Lindsey."

"Good night, kiddo." She looked over at Hannah. "Thanks again."

Hannah surprised her by coming closer and drawing her into a quick, tight hug. "Good night, Lindsey. See you tomorrow."

As Hannah slipped away from her, Lindsey had an urge to pull her closer again. It wasn't anything inappropriate—this was Jack's mother, after all—but human contact, the comforting touch of someone, a gentle, unexpected hug...all things she missed. Instead of satisfying her need for contact, she gave the briefest of nods to Hannah, then headed to the door.

CHAPTER THIRTY-ONE

Hannah sat on the rock, watching Jack and Barney splash in the creek while they waited for Lindsey to pick them up. She had a small, soft-sided cooler packed with their tuna sandwiches and a Coke for Jack. She had put in a couple of water bottles, but knowing Lindsey as she did now, she didn't doubt that she'd have beer for both of them. That was a bit odd for her. While she and James enjoyed a beer now and then, especially at backyard get-togethers with friends, she wouldn't call herself a beer drinker. In fact, it was rare when there was even any at their house. Wine? Sure. She and James nearly always had wine with dinner. And once he'd gotten sick, she'd started the habit of having wine while *cooking* dinner. Cooking always relaxed her and the wine helped dull the pain.

She smiled as she leaned back on the rock. And what was her excuse now? There really wasn't one. The pain in her heart had subsided. But cooking still relaxed her, as did the wine, so she saw no reason to end the ritual.

And relax her—it must. Why else would she have dared to hug Lindsey like she had last night? It had felt nice to have that close contact with someone, she admitted. Even though her impromptu hug was simply an act of showing affection, she could still see the pain that Lindsey carried with her. She hoped the physical contact helped in some way. Lindsey had been alone in her grief, save for the uncle she'd mentioned. As rough as Hannah's own ordeal had been, she couldn't imagine going through it without the support of her family. For Lindsey to have suffered so much—alone—nearly broke her heart.

"I hear her," Jack called from downstream where he and Barney had ventured.

Hannah listened, hearing the faint rumble of Lindsey's Mule. An involuntary smile lit her face as she stood, taking the small cooler across the creek to the trail.

"Do you think we could do the float trip again sometime?" Jack asked as they climbed the hill.

"I would imagine so."

"That was fun playing in the rapids, wasn't it?"

"Yes, it was. You should ask Lindsey. We could probably take the Mule to that part of the river and just play there at the rapids," she suggested.

"Okay. But I really want to play ball on the rope swing."

Hannah laughed. "Too much to do, too little time, huh?"

He grinned at her. "Do I have to go back to school? This has been like the best summer ever."

As soon as he said the words, Hannah could see the emotion—and confusion—on his young face.

"I mean...not *ever*, but...you know..."

She put an arm around his shoulder. "I know, honey. It's okay. I think we needed this. We needed a fun summer." She leaned down and kissed the top of his head. "We had a crappy year. I think we deserve to have some fun, don't you?"

"Yeah." He met her eyes. "But it's not like I've forgotten Dad or anything."

"I know. We won't ever forget him."

* * *

Lindsey sat up as high as the fanny floater would allow, the ball held loosely in her hand. "Okay. One…two…three!"

Jack swung out over the river, his eyes on her. She threw the ball toward him as he let go of the rope. As before, he fumbled with the ball before it slipped out of his grasp and splashed into the water seconds before he did.

"Oh…that time was pretty close," Hannah said.

Jack swam over to his noodle and held on as he rested. "Maybe we need a bigger ball."

Lindsey laughed. "What? Like a big beach ball?"

Jack splashed her with water. "Maybe you need to throw better," he teased.

She splashed water back at him. "Don't blame me. That was a perfect throw."

He looked at her thoughtfully. "Can we go play in the rapids?"

"Had enough of the rope swing?"

"I think after ten tries I need a break!"

Lindsey looked over at Hannah. "Want to go play in the rapids?"

"Sounds like fun. Can we get to them without floating down?"

"Yeah. The Mule trail doesn't go right to the river there, but it's close enough to walk to. We won't take the tubes this time."

They took the fanny floaters and Jack's noodle and tied them on top of the Mule, then loaded the dogs. Before long they were bouncing along the rocky trail that she normally took if they were going upstream to fish…or for the longer float trip. For some reason, her grandfather had not made a side trail to where the rapids were. She could see the river through the trees, and she tried to get her bearings. Soon she spotted the flat limestone rocks where they'd had lunch that day.

"I guess this is as close as we can get," she said as she stopped the Mule.

Jack let the dogs off the back as she untied their floats. Hannah had her cooler slung over her shoulder—lunch—and Lindsey carried their two floats after handing Jack his noodle.

The dogs led the way between the trees and Jack followed behind them.

Lindsey looked over at Hannah, noting the smile on her face. She looked relaxed and comfortable as she walked beside her. Hannah was wearing the black and white bikini today, and her skin had turned a nice golden brown from their days in the sun.

"Thank you for indulging him," Hannah said.

"Is that what I'm doing?"

Hannah turned to her. "No?"

Lindsey smiled at her. "I like playing as much as he does, I guess."

Hannah laughed. "I've noticed that. It's a wonderful trait to have."

"It's a learned trait," she said. "My family...well, like I told you before, there was always laughter, always playtime. When we all got together out here, nothing was ever very serious. It was...it was a time of joy."

Hannah bumped her shoulder with her own. "Thank you for sharing all of this with me and Jack."

Lindsey stopped and watched as the dogs and Jack splashed into the cool, clear water. It didn't take much for her to envision her nephews out there instead of Jack. It didn't take much to picture her parents lounging in their floats as they watched the kids play. She could almost hear the laughter bouncing along the water. She smiled as the memories ran through her mind. Yes...it was a time of joy. Like now. Jack was laughing as Barney and Max chased him in the water. She looked over at Hannah, who was watching her.

"I don't miss them as much when you and Jack are around," she said honestly. "I'll always have my memories of them, but I like making new memories."

Hannah took a step closer and Lindsey wondered if she was about to hug her again. As their eyes met, she saw that was indeed Hannah's intention. However, two fanny floaters and a cooler were too much to maneuver around. So Hannah simply smiled at her, and Lindsey smiled back, her thoughts going to the hug she'd received last night. She was sorry she missed the opportunity for another one.

When they got to the limestone rocks, she thought they'd have lunch before they played—it was nearly one already—but Jack was out in the river, waiting on them.

"Let's do the train!"

Hannah turned to her. "Okay with me...but you get to be in the back this time."

"Being in the back is the most fun," she said.

"I still have a bruise on my ass from the last time," Hannah said.

"And you think I'm going to protect you from that?" she teased.

Hannah smiled at her. "I do."

Lindsey coaxed Max and Barney back to shore before going out and joining Jack and Hannah.

"Do you remember how to do it?" she asked them.

"Stick my legs straight out," Jack said. "Mom wraps around me."

"You wrap around me," Hannah said to her. Then she grinned. "And keep me from hitting the rocks."

Lindsey winked at her. "Sounds like I've got the best job."

"Oh, I don't know about that."

Lindsey maneuvered Hannah in front of her, holding her lightly at the waist. Jack was standing in front of Hannah, waiting. Hannah turned and met her gaze.

"Ready when you are."

She nodded, tightening her grip at Hannah's waist. She closed her eyes for a brief second. *Jack's mom. Jack's mom. Jack's mom*, she reminded herself. Then she opened them again and blew out a breath.

"Okay...on three," she said. "One...two...three!"

They plunged into the rapids so quickly she nearly lost her hold on Hannah. She pulled her up tight against her, barely managing to wrap her legs around her before they hit the chute. She bounced hard against one side of the rocks as Jack led them through, his joyful scream making her smile even as the river threatened to swallow her. They shot out into calmer water and she untangled from Hannah but still held on to her as she stood.

"That was fun! I didn't hit any rocks!" Jack said as he swam to shallower water.

"Me either." Hannah turned, eyebrows raised. "You?"

"Not too bad," she said, finally letting her hands slip away from Hannah. Hannah eyed her for a moment, then reached out and touched her upper arm.

"Here?"

Lindsey looked where she touched, seeing the red mark where she'd banged against the rocks. "Yeah. I was a little late getting wrapped up with you."

Hannah smiled at her. "Yes, I thought I'd lost you." She held her gaze. "Let's go again. I'll take the back this time, if you want."

"I'll ride in the back," Jack offered.

Hannah looked at her. "Can he?"

She nodded. "Sure. I used to take the lead and the kids would ride behind me. Eli loved to be the last one." She paused, picturing him screaming his head off as they blasted through the chute. "The longer the train, the more fun it is in the back, I guess."

"How many would you take at once?"

Lindsey swallowed, meeting her gaze. "Four. There were... five kids, but Abby was too young."

Hannah's eyes gentled, and she again reached out a hand to touch her. Hannah was one of those people who communicated with touch. Lindsey, too, had always been a toucher. Especially with the kids. And now with Jack. But with Hannah? No. She'd intentionally kept her distance. Hannah was attractive. Hannah was most often in a bikini. Hannah was Jack's mother. And she would be lying to herself if she said she wasn't in the least bit attracted to her.

Yeah. She'd be lying.

"If you think Jack can handle the back, you can take the lead," Hannah offered. "I won't let you get away from me."

Lindsey nodded but turned away from her gaze. Hannah had ridden behind her before, the first time they'd come to the rapids. It didn't take much for her to remember the feel of Hannah's arms around her. But they knew each other a little better now. They were more familiar with each other. They were…they were friends. Whatever hesitancy Hannah had displayed the first time would surely be absent now. That thought nearly made her shiver.

"Am I going to hit the rocks?" Jack asked.

She shook her head. "No. I only hit them because I wasn't holding on to your mom tight enough."

"Okay. Then I won't make that mistake."

"We'll start a little farther upstream so we'll have time to link up," she said. "And don't let go of her."

"I won't."

She went upstream of the rapids into deeper water, a little higher than her waist. Jack was bouncing on his toes to keep his head above water. Hannah held her arm out and Jack took it, using her to brace himself.

"Okay. Hannah, bend down a little, let Jack get on your back." She looked at Jack. "Hold her around her neck."

"Don't choke me!"

Jack laughed. "This is fun."

Lindsey moved in front of Hannah. "Okay…let's get a little closer. We're probably too deep here." She felt Hannah's hands at her waist as they walked through the water. She paused about ten feet from the chute. "Ready?"

She wasn't sure *she* was ready when she found herself being pulled up tight against Hannah. She could feel Hannah's breasts pressing into her back, and yeah…there was no hesitancy whatsoever in Hannah's touch. She took a deep breath—*Jack's mom, Jack's mom, Jack's mom*—then pulled Hannah's arms more firmly around her before counting.

"One…two…three!"

She lifted her legs up, sinking down onto the slick river bottom. Hannah's legs circled her thighs, and she gave up trying to ignore the nearly naked woman clinging to her. As they approached the chute, she held onto Hannah's legs with each hand, keeping them wrapped around her. As they were sucked into the chute, Jack was screaming as if he was on a roller coaster and she could feel Hannah tighten her arms as their bodies shot through the water.

It was over in a matter of seconds, and she found herself laughing along with the others as they untangled from each other.

"That was *so* much fun!" Jack said exuberantly. "Can we go again?"

"How much water did you swallow?"

He grinned. "Not much."

Hannah held onto her arm as they moved back toward shore. "I'm game for one more time." She smiled at her. "I like being behind you."

"Yeah...safest place is in the middle. But the least amount of fun."

"I wouldn't say that." Hannah winked at her. "I had a great time."

Lindsey pulled her gaze away. Yeah, it was a great time, all right. But this was Jack's *mother*, she reminded herself for the umpteenth time. It wasn't supposed to feel *that* great.

CHAPTER THIRTY-TWO

Jack couldn't seem to sit still, and Hannah finally walked behind him and held him in his chair.

"She'll be here soon."

"What if she's late? We're going to miss the parade."

"She promised you last night that she'd be here. It's not even seven yet. Finish your cereal."

"I don't want to spoil my appetite."

She laughed. "For all the candy you hope to get at the parade?"

"Funnel cake and cotton candy," he corrected.

She shook her head. "I should have never told you they'd have food booths at the square."

According to the website Lindsey had found, the Fourth of July Leaky Jubilee was an all-day affair, beginning with the parade at eight. The arts and crafts fair was on the courthouse square until late afternoon. The fireworks display was at the park on the river and a street dance—which they planned to skip—was scheduled back at the square until midnight.

"Did you pack my clothes?"

"I did. Quit worrying."

He grinned. "It's going to be fun, isn't it?"

"We're going to have a great day, yes."

She didn't know who was looking forward to it more—Lindsey or Jack. It was forecast to be a very hot day with temps reaching near one hundred. Lindsey suggested they wear their water shorts and sandals so they could cool off in the river that afternoon. The park—and river—would most likely be crowded, so they were going armed with blankets and camp chairs. And a picnic basket. She'd fried chicken last night for their dinner and had made enough to take along today. It was going to be a fun day, one she was looking forward to as well.

"I miss Barney."

"Yes, it is a little quiet here without him, but I'm sure he enjoyed spending the night with Max."

Since she had no fenced yard to keep him in, Lindsey had said she could secure her grandmother's garden enough to keep both dogs penned for the day. She had taken Barney with her last night when she left. Today, she would walk up through the creek like always and Hannah would take her car into town.

"Yay! Here she comes!" he said excitedly as he hurried to the back door, his cereal still uneaten. He opened the door, waiting. "I thought you were going to be late!"

"Of course not," Lindsey said. "We've got to get a front row seat for the parade." Lindsey glanced over at her. "Good morning."

"Good morning." She motioned to the coffeepot. "Want a cup?"

"No, I'm good. Thanks."

"Okay. Well, I think we have everything packed. This one was up before I was," she said, pointing at Jack.

"Excited?" Lindsey asked him.

"Yeah. Let's go already."

"Clean the table off first," Hannah told him. She looked at Lindsey. "How did Barney fare last night?"

"Oh, he was fine. They slept in the bedroom with me," she said. "I put their toys out in the garden. I think they'll be fine while we're gone."

* * *

For it being such a small town, Lindsey was surprised at the number of floats in the parade. Jack had been more interested in the candy that was being tossed from the floats than the parade itself. His pockets were bulging with the loot he'd scooped up.

"Jack...I think you have enough," Hannah said as he was about to scramble out for more. "Let someone else have it."

"Oh...*Mom*," he complained. "I hardly have any."

"That's because you've eaten it all!"

"You better save room for that funnel cake you've been talking about," Lindsey told him.

He grinned. "I guess you're right."

As the last float went past, they got caught up in the crowd as everyone made their way to the town square and the arts and crafts fair. Jack walked between them, holding each of their hands as people jostled around them. Hannah smiled over at Lindsey.

"I didn't expect this many people."

"Me either."

Once they got to the square, the crowd dispersed, everyone heading in different directions. Dozens of booths lined the grass around the courthouse and vendors in food trucks were parked along the street, which had been blocked off to traffic. A live band was playing country music from a stage under the oak trees and a large tent shaded tables and chairs—the beer garden.

"I certainly wasn't expecting a beer garden," she said. "Gotta love these small towns."

They strolled aimlessly among the booths, looking but not buying anything. Almost every booth offered some kind of home-canned item, from pickles and okra to squash and corn. There were various assortments of jams and jellies and homemade cookies and candies. One booth had several quilts for sale, and she paused over them, thinking one would look nice on her bed but in the end, she passed on it. Jack had found his funnel cake and was content to walk along with them while he ate. He must have enjoyed it...a ring of powdered sugar circled his mouth.

By one, they'd seen everything there was to see, and she was the one who suggested the park.

"I'm about ready to cool off in the river."

"Yeah...me too," Jack said.

Hannah nodded. "Then let's go."

CHAPTER THIRTY-THREE

"I miss the dogs," Jack said as they tossed a ball back and forth.

"I'm sure they miss us too."

Lindsey had expected the park to be crowded and was pleasantly surprised to find only a handful of families staking claim to picnic tables. Kids and adults alike were splashing in the river, though, and a group of teenagers were floating by in tubes not far from where they were playing.

"I kinda miss having our own private river," Hannah said with a laugh. "Well, *your* private river."

"Yeah, we're pretty spoiled, aren't we?"

"I think we need to do another float trip," Jack said. "That was fun."

"I think we need a lazy day in the pond," she countered. "In fact, I've been thinking about fixing it up around there."

"What do you mean?" Hannah asked.

"Well, there's nothing there really. That's how my grandfather wanted it. It was all we could do to talk him into putting in the little side deck by the pier." She tossed the ball back toward Jack. "I want to fix up the lean-to and make it into an outdoor kitchen. Bring a gas grill down." Jack tossed the ball back to her. "It would be nice to be able to grill burgers or something."

"Hot dogs!"

"Or hot dogs."

"What else do you want to do?" Hannah asked.

"There's a nice slope from the lean-to down to the pond. That would make a good deck there. It's very primitive now, which is how he wanted it, but I don't think it would take away from the area if I added a few more amenities. I could put my architectural skills to use." She raised an eyebrow. "What do you think?"

"I think an outdoor kitchen would be nice. A deck too. Lawn chairs or loungers. If you don't feel like being in the water, the deck is the next best thing. Especially with the waterfall. I can imagine how peaceful it would be to just sit there and watch and listen to the waterfall."

Lindsey nodded. "Yeah…peaceful." She looked over at Jack. "And…maybe we could camp out there some night. You know, in tents."

"Oh…*cool*! Can we, Mom?"

At Hannah's expression, Lindsey laughed. "You've never been camping before, have you?"

"No. And neither has Jack."

"Well, if we're going to sleep out in tents, we'll have to wait until the weather's cooler. Maybe November."

"Hey." They all turned as a young boy, maybe eleven or twelve, approached. "You want to play baseball?"

Jack stared at him. "Me?"

"Yeah. We need another player." He pointed to a group of kids, both girls and boys, tossing baseballs around.

Jack's eyes widened as he looked at Hannah. "Can I?"

"Of course. Have fun."

Jack jumped out of the water and followed the boy back to the group of would-be baseball players.

"Does he know how to play?"

Hannah shrugged. "He played one year of Little League. Last summer, James wasn't able to work with him much and we missed a lot of games." Hannah looked over at her. "He can catch and throw pretty good. Not sure about hitting."

"I can work with him, if you want," she offered.

"You're already giving him swimming lessons."

"That doesn't count," she said with a shake of her head. "Besides, I used to pitch batting practice with my nephews all the time."

Hannah stared at her for the longest time, almost making Lindsey uncomfortable. "Tell me about your family," she finally said. "And I don't mean about the accident."

Lindsey held her gaze, wondering at the request. Hannah must have sensed her hesitation.

"I just want to know more about them, more about you. About what makes you…you," she said quietly.

Lindsey looked over to where the kids were choosing sides for the baseball game. At least Jack didn't appear to be the youngest one there. She turned her attention back to Hannah, finding her watching.

"Is it too painful to talk about them?"

Lindsey shook her head. "Not so much anymore, I guess." She took a deep breath. "Lorrie was the oldest, but we were all very close in age. My brother Shane was only eighteen months older than me. Lorrie was two years older than he was."

"That must have been nice," Hannah said. "My sister and I are six years apart. Vast difference when you're kids."

Lindsey nodded. "Yeah, it was nice. And we all got along. I don't remember there being any major fights or anything. We were siblings, but we were also friends." She moved a little deeper, sitting on another rock, the water now past her waist. "I was closest to Shane, though. I was kind of a tomboy growing up, so I tended to play with him and his friends more than Lorrie."

"And coming out here to your grandparents' place? Was that something you always did?"

She nodded. "Since we were babies, yes. Even high school, college…we still gravitated back here. When Lorrie and Shane got married, had kids, the cycle continued."

"How many kids? You said five?" Hannah asked as she moved closer to her, sitting down on a nearby rock.

"Yes, there were…there were five kids. Lorrie, my sister, had two. Mark was the oldest…he was twelve. Allison was ten." She swallowed. "And Shane, my brother, had three. Jett was ten. Eli was seven, and Abby was only five."

She wasn't surprised when Hannah's hand reached her, circling her forearm under the water. Lindsey met her gaze, making no move to pull away from her touch.

"And who does Jack remind you of?"

Lindsey wanted to look away, but Hannah's eyes held her in place. "You would think Jett since they were about the same age, but Jack is more like Eli." She shook her head slowly. "I know what you're thinking. That I'm using Jack to…to fill this empty spot, but…" She let out her breath. "Maybe at first, yeah, I was. But Jack is Jack. I know he's not…well, I know he's not one of my nephews, but I love him like he is." She felt Hannah's hand tighten. "I hope that's okay."

"Jack loves you too," Hannah said quietly. "I can't imagine what we would have done this summer if you hadn't stumbled into our lives. We had an empty spot to fill too." Hannah's hand slipped from her arm, but she didn't move away. She came closer, their shoulders bumping as they shared the same rock. "You've righted our world somehow, Lindsey. I hope we've helped you in some way too."

Lindsey nodded. "You have. Things feel a little more normal now. Today, for instance. Two months ago, I think this holiday—which used to be so filled with family—would have sent me into a very dark place, a place where I would have wanted to curl up and hide from the world." She let her gaze travel past Hannah to where Jack was playing. "Being here with you two makes today…special." She looked back to Hannah. "I needed to get away. If we'd stayed at home, stayed and played in the river or the pond, it would have been…too much, I think."

"I know. That's one reason I wanted to do something. With you."

"Thank you. You could have easily left me behind and joined your in-laws."

Hannah shook her head. "I wouldn't have dreamed of leaving you behind." Then she smiled. "Margie is pissed off at me, by the way. She can't understand why Jack and I would rather be with you than with them."

"I know you said that she doesn't like me just because of my name, but do you think it's because I'm gay?"

Hannah frowned. "No. I doubt she even knows you're gay. If she did, God, I can only imagine what all she'd be saying."

"Well, her generation, living out here, I assume she's old school on that thought."

"Yes, I'm sure." Hannah raised an eyebrow. "Why? Are you worried she might influence me or something?"

Lindsey shrugged. "Well, she is family. I mean—"

"No," Hannah said with a shake of her head. "This sounds terrible, but I don't feel like she's family. If James were still alive, then sure. We had that link. But now? The only connection we have is in name only. Jack is her grandson. I don't feel an emotional connection with her. I know Jack doesn't." Hannah moved her hands back and forth under the water, causing ripples on the surface. "That sounds unkind, doesn't it? I mean, we moved here with the intention of getting closer to Margie and Dennis, not farther away."

"You regret moving out here?"

Hannah smiled. "I was just thinking about that the other night. If I had to do it over again, what would I do?" Her smile softened. "Well, we wouldn't have met you."

Lindsey laughed. "I doubt my existence in your life has a bearing on that decision."

"Don't be so sure. Jack...Jack needed this. You. This summer," she said. "If we'd stayed in San Antonio—even moving to a new house—it wouldn't have been a big enough change." Again, as if she couldn't help herself, Hannah's fingers found her arm. "And you needed this too. So I don't want to play the 'what if' game."

Her fingers slipped away. "But I will admit, it's crossed my mind more than once—staying in San Antonio." She tilted her head. "Do you wish you'd stayed in Dallas?"

Lindsey thought back to the first few days when she'd moved out here...dark, dreadful days when she thought her grief would swallow her whole. Lonely, empty days that seemed endless...lifeless. Would it have been any different in Dallas? Would it have been worse? She looked at Hannah. If she'd stayed in Dallas—wallowing in her grief alone—she would have never met Jack, never met Hannah. She wouldn't have Max. She would be hiding away in her apartment, wishing for her miserable life to be over with.

"No," she said honestly. "Moving out here was the best thing I could have done. Even if, at the beginning, it seemed like the worst thing."

CHAPTER THIRTY-FOUR

Hannah sat next to Lindsey on the blanket, the light starting to fade from the sky. Jack sat in front of them, crossed-legged, waiting on the fireworks to start. After Jack's baseball game, they'd eaten the chicken she'd brought, then they'd gotten back in the water and spent a lazy couple of hours playing with a Frisbee that Lindsey had produced from her pack. They'd then gone up to the public restrooms and changed into dry clothes. It had been an all-around great day, albeit a long one. She'd seen Jack trying to stifle a yawn on several occasions, and she'd be lying if she said she hadn't had thoughts of relaxing on Lindsey's deck with a glass of wine. As if reading her mind, Lindsey nudged her shoulder.

"We should have stashed some booze in the picnic basket," she whispered.

Hannah smiled at her. "I was just thinking a glass of wine sounded good." She returned the nudge. "On your deck."

"My deck?"

"It's bigger and nicer than my little porch."

"How about we do burgers tomorrow? I think I have everything except buns."

"Okay. But I'll do the grocery store run. I need some things anyway."

"Deal."

Jack turned around. "When's the show gonna start?"

"It's almost dark. I imagine very soon." She rubbed his hair. "Did you have a good day?"

"Yeah. It was fun." Then he turned his gaze to Lindsey. "Do you think you could teach me how to hit?"

"Baseball?"

"Uh-huh. I'm not very good."

"Sure. I can do that."

He grinned. "I figured you could. You can do pretty much everything."

Hannah smiled as—even in the waning light—she saw a blush light Lindsey's face.

"I don't know about that, buddy. I can't cook like your mom can."

"Well...no, I guess not," he conceded. The first firework shot up in the sky and Jack spun around. "Finally! It's starting!"

Conversation ceased as the show got underway. Soon, choruses of oohs and ahs were heard as bursts of colors exploded overhead. Hannah followed Lindsey's lead and leaned back on her elbows, watching the sky above them. She was suddenly aware of their nearness, aware of the arm that was so close to her own...close but not touching. She wasn't quite sure what was guiding her—wasn't sure what to make of her sudden need for contact—but she moved her arm ever so slightly. She nearly gasped when their skin touched. It was as if an electric current had passed between them. She didn't move her arm and neither did Lindsey. She swallowed, not daring to look over at her. She continued to stare overhead, barely registering the fireworks as they shot across the sky.

No...the only thing that registered was the quiet darkness, the woman sitting next to her, the arm pressed against her own. The crowd around her seemed to disappear, the voices fading into the background as Lindsey shifted, moving enough so that their legs now touched, however slight.

Hannah hadn't realized she'd stopped breathing until Jack turned around, a grin on his face.

"That one was awesome! It covered the whole sky!"

Hannah nodded, although she'd apparently missed the burst. She blinked several times, bringing herself back to the here and now, forcing her gaze up to the sky, trying to focus on the fireworks—and not on the woman sitting beside her.

Before long, the grand finale started and "wows" erupted as multitudes of bursts flashed across the sky simultaneously. Again, her breath held as Lindsey leaned closer, her voice whispering against her ear.

"Damn good fireworks for a town this small."

Hannah nodded, afraid to turn her head, afraid to look at Lindsey. She kept her eyes glued to the sky as the last few bursts of color exploded overhead. It wasn't until she felt Lindsey sit up that she dared to move. Jack had spun around, facing them now.

"That was great," he said. "But it didn't last very long."

"I think we'd all be shocked at how much it costs to put on a show like this," Lindsey said.

People were stirring around them, packing up chairs and blankets. She let Lindsey pull her to her feet and they began gathering their own belongings. Before long, they were following the crowd across the park. Jack was between them, holding on to Lindsey's shorts as she snaked her way through the throng and back to where they were parked. A small traffic jam ensued as everyone tried to leave at once. She finally inched the car out into the steady stream of vehicles, and before too long they were heading out of town.

It was unusually quiet on the ride back. Jack's normal chatter was absent, and she looked in the mirror, seeing him leaning against the window, his eyes closed. She smiled, then glanced over at Lindsey, not surprised to find Lindsey watching her. It was too dark to read her expression, and she gave up trying, instead, turning her attention back to the road.

She blocked out the thoughts that were trying to settle in her mind. She pushed them away, leaving her mind blank as she drove them home. Her mind was blank, yes, but that didn't mean she wasn't aware of the quiet woman sitting next to her in the car.

Her mind was blank. She wondered if Lindsey's was.

CHAPTER THIRTY-FIVE

Lindsey had no idea what time it was. The sun was over the cedars behind the garden. Her coffee was long cold. Max and Barney were wrestling beside the table, but still she sat, staring out at the woods, seeing nothing.

Seeing nothing, that is, except Hannah lying beside her on the blanket. It had been Hannah who had moved...moved so that they were touching. At first, she thought it had been an accident, that Hannah had simply shifted, inadvertently touching her. But no. Hannah didn't move away. She didn't change positions. She stayed there, letting the contact continue.

Lindsey had been nearly paralyzed. She had frozen in place, afraid to move...afraid *not* to move. She finally told herself to relax. It didn't mean anything. Hannah was Jack's mother, for god's sake. It didn't mean anything. They were friends. They were watching the fireworks. Jack was there. It didn't mean anything. She relaxed.

Oh, hell...she didn't relax. She moved closer. She relished the contact. A mistake, sure, but that didn't stop her. She'd been disappointed when the show had come to an end and she'd made some lame comment to Hannah about the quality of the fireworks, anything to let Hannah know that she was thinking nothing of their positions on the blanket...anything to let Hannah know that she wasn't affected by it in the least.

The show had come to an end, they'd packed up, they'd gone back to the car, they'd come home...all with only a handful of words exchanged.

She reached down, absently rubbing Max's head, her stare fixed on the trees across from the deck. It was the hug at the end that had been her undoing. She should have left. Jack had already said his sleepy goodbyes and had shuffled off to bed, so she should have left. But Hannah had offered a glass of wine and they'd sat out on the porch, neither talking. Then the whirling sound of a screech owl broke the silence and she'd found herself telling Hannah about the nighttime birds, the sounds that her grandmother had taught her. The awkwardness between them had disappeared, replaced with the easy conversation—the easy friendship—that they normally shared.

She sighed. Maybe it was her fault. She'd hesitated. They'd finished their wine, she was taking her leave...and she'd hesitated.

"I had a good time today. Thanks for including me."

"It was a great day, Lindsey. Jack had a wonderful time. So did I."

That should have been enough. But she hesitated. And their eyes met. And suddenly, everything was...unclear. She wasn't sure who initiated the hug. She'd like to think that it was Hannah, but hell, maybe she did. Regardless, she found herself being pulled close to Hannah, felt her arms go around Hannah...felt Hannah's arms around her. She completely forgot to breathe in the confusion. She forgot to breathe because Hannah was too close and the hug was too intimate. How many seconds it lasted, she didn't know. Too long? Yes, but not nearly long enough.

Hannah had seemed embarrassed as she slowly pulled away. Lindsey, too, had averted her eyes. She'd mumbled a quick good night and had spun on her heels, bounding off the porch and into the woods before her jumbled mind could make sense of it all.

And now here she sat—after a nearly sleepless night—still trying to make sense of it all.

Because it made no sense whatsoever.

Hannah was a straight woman. A recently widowed straight woman. A mother. Lindsey leaned back in her chair. She was obviously reading too much into it all. She had overreacted. Hannah was just being Hannah.

Lindsey sighed. "And I'm attracted to her," she mumbled.

Jack's mother. I'm attracted to Jack's mother.

"You're an idiot."

The ringing of her phone brought her out of her self-loathing, but the name that popped up on the screen didn't alleviate her anxiety. She cleared her throat before answering, trying to sound as normal as possible.

"Good morning."

"Hey. We're on our way to the grocery store. Wanted to see if you needed anything besides buns."

She got up, going back inside. "Yeah…let me check. I think a tomato." She opened the fridge and looked inside the drawer, finding the lone tomato that had seen better days. "Yeah…this one's a little on the ripe side. I have lettuce, though."

"Okay. I'll bring a jar of pickles too. Margie brought us three," Hannah said. "I also have some tomatoes from her garden."

"Okay, fresh tomatoes. Great." She paused. Hannah sounded perfectly normal. There was no awkwardness at all in her voice. So Lindsey tried to match it. "Ask Jack what he wants to do today…river or pond?"

Hannah laughed. "I decided it was my day. And I vote for the pond. I feel like a lazy day."

Lindsey smiled, feeling some of the tension leave her. "The pond it is."

CHAPTER THIRTY-SIX

Hannah was having a hard time keeping her eyes open as she floated near the waterfall. The afternoon was sizzling hot and the cold water of the pond was refreshing. She cracked her eyelids open enough to see Jack and Lindsey standing on the pier. Diving lessons again today. She smiled, then let her eyes close once more as Jack fell into the water, sending waves rippling across the surface, rocking her float.

A lazy day indeed, she thought. She'd done absolutely nothing other than perch on the float, alternating between the shade and the sun. She was way past mellow, and she wondered if it was the two beers she'd had that had her feeling so relaxed. Lindsey had joined her a couple of times, but for the most part, she'd been entertaining Jack and the dogs.

Clapping and an exuberant "yay" from Lindsey forced her eyes open again. Jack was in the water, grinning from ear to ear. Had he executed a dive finally and she'd missed it?

"Mom...did you see me?"

"No, honey. Can you do it again?"

"Oh, Mom...why weren't you watching?"

Lindsey laughed. "I think she was sleeping. Come on, let's try it again."

Hannah spun the float around, facing the pier. She tried to keep her focus on Jack as he got out of the water, but she found her gaze drifting over to Lindsey. She was such an attractive woman. She wondered what—before her family's accident—her social life had been like. Lindsey had told her that she'd been seeing someone. Was it serious? Was it someone Lindsey had been in love with and, in her grief, had pushed away?

She supposed she could imagine Lindsey doing that at the time...but not now. Now, she seemed stronger, more in control of her emotions. Time did that. Time would eventually heal any wound, however deep. Not just time, though. Time and people. She and Jack had helped Lindsey...just like Lindsey had helped them. Their days were filled with laughter now, not tears. In fact, it shocked her to realize that she didn't think of James nearly as much as she used to...nearly as much as she should.

She found Lindsey looking back at her and their eyes held. Yes, she was an attractive woman with dark, expressive eyes. Eyes that seemed a bit guarded today though. She offered a slight smile and Lindsey returned it, then Jack grabbed her attention and Hannah smiled at him as he went back to attempt another dive.

"Okay...watch, Mom."

"I'm watching."

Yes, she was watching Jack, but she couldn't stop her gaze from lingering over Lindsey too. Her skin was nicely tan and as she bent over, her bikini top shifted, revealing a sliver of white along her breast. For some reason, the sight of that caused Hannah's heart to race a bit too fast. She pulled her eyes away quickly.

What in the world is wrong with you?

"Okay...push off with your feet."

Jack bent his knees, his arms held out and over the water. She could see him silently counting to three, then he pushed off, landing away from the pier in a somewhat graceful dive. She clapped appropriately, as did Lindsey, when Jack's head popped back up.

"Did you see? Did you see?"

"Yes! Very good!"

Lindsey dove in too, but unlike Jack, she didn't surface. Hannah looked into the crystal clear water, seeing Lindsey swimming toward her from below. Soon, a hand touched her foot, and she smiled as Lindsey came up, taking deep breaths of air as she held on to Hannah's float.

"I need to work on my underwater swimming," she said. "I used to be in much better shape."

"Your shape looks pretty good to me," Hannah teased.

Lindsey arched an eyebrow. "Really? You're flirting with a lesbian?" She leaned closer, a smile on her lips. "That could be very dangerous."

Hannah matched her smile. "I think I can handle you."

Lindsey laughed. "Okay...probably so." She playfully splashed water at her, then swam back to the pier where Jack was waiting for her.

Hannah made herself turn away when Lindsey got out of the water. She blew out a breath. *Yes, Hannah...flirting with a lesbian?* It wasn't intentional, she told herself. It was just too easy and the words were out before she even realized it. At least Lindsey knew she was only teasing. That's all it was. Teasing. Playing.

She put the float in motion, going back toward the waterfall. But what about last night? What was that all about? The fireworks...that was nothing. They were sharing a blanket. Of course they were bound to touch. The fact that she'd moved to make it so didn't escape her, but she pushed that aside, her thoughts going instead to the hug they'd shared when Lindsey was leaving. It was...just a hug. They'd hugged before. Yet...yet it was different.

It was different, and she couldn't quite put her finger on *what* was different about it. It lasted a few seconds longer than it probably should have. Was that it? And they were very close. So close that there hadn't been any space between them. Was that it? Or was it the look in Lindsey's eyes that made it different? She'd seen that look in Lindsey's eyes before, and she wondered what it meant. Well...she kinda knew what it meant, didn't she? She wasn't *that* out of touch.

She turned slightly, absently watching Jack and Lindsey on the pier. The dogs were with them and it looked like they were trying to do a group jump, but Barney wasn't cooperating. She leaned back, wetting her hair as she looked up into the cloudless sky. Oh, what a gloriously lazy day it had been. And how very lucky were they to have their own private swimming pond, with a waterfall, no less?

She heard laughter and running, and she looked up in time to see the four of them jump off the pier together. Well, Barney was bringing up the rear, but at least he jumped. Jack and Lindsey tried to beat Max to the ball, but he was winning the race. His mouth closed around the ball seconds before Lindsey reached for it.

"Now we'll never get it back!" Jack laughed.

"It's about time to head to the house anyway," Lindsey said. "Burgers," she reminded him.

* * *

Hannah was glad she'd packed dry clothes for them. Even though the water shorts dried quickly, it was nice to get out of her bikini top and into dry clothes. She'd also remembered to pack Jack's iPad, and he was sitting on the sofa playing his game.

"My parents are coming to visit on Saturday," she said.

"Oh, yeah? Staying the night?"

"Yes." She poured them each a glass of wine. "Margie and Dennis will come for dinner too."

Lindsey was slicing the tomato, and she looked up from her task. "Do they get along?"

Hannah shrugged. "As well as can be expected for having absolutely nothing in common." She paused. "You want to join us?"

"Oh, no." Lindsey shook her head. "Nope. You're not dragging me into that," she said with a laugh.

Hannah laughed too, but she'd hoped she would say yes. Lindsey would be a buffer, for one thing. And, well, she and Jack were used to seeing Lindsey every day. And lately, they shared dinner quite often as well. Of course, would she really subject Lindsey to Margie?

"I don't blame you. God only knows what Margie would say to you."

"What are you serving?"

"Lasagna."

"If it's anything like your spaghetti and meatballs... tempting."

Hannah laughed. "You're too easy."

Lindsey wiggled her eyebrows. "Yeah...but not *that* easy!"

Before she was even conscious of it, her hand was on Lindsey's arm, her fingers tightening affectionately. "I'll save you leftovers."

"Deal."

As nonchalantly as she could, she released her hold on Lindsey, smiling as their eyes met. "Sorry. I...I touch when I talk."

Lindsey's expression turned serious. "I normally do too. But..."

"Do you? I haven't noticed. With Jack, yes, but not me."

"Well..."

"Oh. I see." She nodded, understanding Lindsey's hesitation. "Because you're gay, you think it'll make me uncomfortable."

Lindsey took a pickle from the jar and put it on the cutting board. "Yeah. I mean, straight women, sometimes—"

"Don't," she interrupted. "The fact that you're gay doesn't even register with me. You're just Lindsey, my friend." This time when she reached out to touch Lindsey, it was intentional. "I like you. You're not going to scare me off if you touch me."

"Thanks." She sliced into the pickle, then looked up at her. "I like you too."

CHAPTER THIRTY-SEVEN

Lindsey wiped the sweat from her brow as she leaned against the oak tree, enjoying the shade it provided. Perhaps tackling the garden on a hot July day wasn't the best plan she'd ever had, but at least it was a plan. She looked at the dent she'd made, thankful that the garden had appeared worse than it actually was. She would get the leaves and debris out, then see if she could get the old tiller started. A couple of runs with the tiller should break the soil up and deter weeds from growing. Then, come fall, she might actually make rows and plant something. Her grandmother would be proud.

Yeah...she would be. She had her bird feeders filled, the deer feeder was filled with corn and the water mister in the bird garden did a steady business. She looked over to the house, to the deck, almost expecting to see her grandmother sitting in the nook on the side, her binoculars in her lap as they often were. The chair was empty...a reminder.

It didn't have to be empty, though. She could take her morning cup of coffee out and sit there. That had been her grandmother's quiet time. Her grandfather knew to leave her alone until she was ready to come in and start breakfast.

She shook away her thoughts, not wanting to sink into a pit of depression. Not today. Not when the day loomed long and lonely. It was amazing how quickly she'd settled into a routine with Hannah and Jack. And how lost she felt when that routine was broken. But she supposed spending the day apart was good. She was getting far too attached to them as it was.

She smiled. *Attached*? Yeah...that was a safe word. Being attached to someone was completely different than being attracted to them.

"Who are you kidding?" she murmured. She was both and she knew it. Her fear was that Hannah would suspect. Despite her words that it didn't bother her in the least that Lindsey was gay, she might keep her distance, pull away from her. Hannah might decide that the three of them were spending too much time together. She might...

No. It was nearly the opposite. Hannah was getting closer, if anything. She couldn't remember the last time that they hadn't spent the day together. And dinner? Yes, sharing dinner had become a ritual for them too. And the goodbye hug? Yes, that was a ritual too.

Lindsey leaned on her rake, thinking back to last night. Dinner had been simple: hot dogs and a can of chili. Jack thought it was the best thing ever. Their after-dinner glass of wine turned into two as they chatted. Hannah had once again asked her to join them, saying she'd love her parents. Lindsey had almost given in. It wasn't her parents she wanted to meet... it was simply spending time with Hannah and Jack that she wanted. So she'd declined, using Margie as the excuse. But when she'd gotten ready to leave, Hannah's hug was a little tighter, a little longer. Lindsey could still feel Hannah's breath as it tickled her ear, her whispered words still fresh.

"We'll miss you tomorrow."

When they pulled apart, their eyes held. Lindsey thought for one crazy second that Hannah was about to kiss her. The moment passed and Hannah had squeezed her arm, telling her that her parents would leave before noon on Sunday.

Sunday. Tomorrow. It was her turn to cook. She thought she'd get the smoker going and see if she could duplicate her father's ribs. They'd have a play day on the river with the rope swing. And dinner out on the deck.

Tomorrow.

But today still seemed endless. And cleaning out the garden in the heat of the day seemed stupid. So, she tossed the rake down and went back to the house. Max was on the kitchen floor—in the cool air-conditioned house—watching her from the window. His tail wagged when she opened the door, but he made no move to get up.

"Want to go swimming?"

She'd pack a few beers and take the Mule down to the river and cool off. She could kill a couple of hours there. Then she'd grill some chicken for her dinner. Maybe watch a little TV. Head to bed early.

And then it would be tomorrow.

* * *

Hannah sat down in the rocking chair with a sigh, her gaze going up into the sky, glancing over the stars before landing on the woods, the trees, the trail that was obscured by darkness. Their trail.

She sipped from her wine, not really surprised by how much she'd missed Lindsey today. She was thrilled to see her parents, of course. But...something was missing. And it was Lindsey. Dinner had seemed a little bit empty, despite the conversation. Margie had even been tolerable...yet she missed Lindsey. She missed the easiness of their friendship, the companionship that Lindsey offered. Jack missed her too. He talked about her so much, Margie was starting to roll her eyes. She smiled as she recalled Jack telling everyone about them riding the rapids without tubes. She thought Margie was going to have a stroke.

The back door opened, and she turned, finding her mother standing there, a wineglass in her hand.

"It's a little warm to be sitting outside, but I thought I'd join you."

Hannah nodded. "I'm used to it, I suppose." She motioned to the other rocker where Lindsey sometimes sat. Then she looked down, picturing Lindsey sitting on the porch itself, leaning against the railing. That was her favorite spot. She looked over at her mother. "Dad go to bed?"

"He's in Jack's room, telling tales, no doubt."

"I'm so glad y'all came."

"It's been good to see you and Jack. We talk on the phone, but it's not the same."

"I know."

"And you're still coming for Labor Day, right? I've already told Trisha to save the weekend for us. It'll be cramped, but it will be so nice to have both my girls at home."

"Yes, we're still coming," she said, even though she'd forgotten all about the plans her mother had made. She wondered what Lindsey would do. The thought of Lindsey staying here—alone—for the holiday made her heart ache.

"You know, I was hoping we were going to meet this Lindsey person that Jack talks about nonstop. When you'd said that you'd made friends with her, I didn't realize you spent as much time together as Jack indicates."

Hannah nodded. "I invited her to dinner, but, well, she's... she's not big on crowds," she offered as way of an excuse. "But yes, we've become friends. I'm embarrassed how I acted when Jack first met her," she said with a laugh.

"I remember. You thought she was an imaginary friend of his." Her mother set her rocker in motion. "Is it true what Margie said? That her whole family was killed?"

"Yes. It's very tragic. And she still has some bad days but, for the most part, she's no longer grieving."

"And what about you?" her mother asked quietly.

"Me?"

"Do you have bad days? Do you still grieve?"

She opened her mouth to speak, but she wasn't sure what to say. No, there were no bad days. There were no more tears. Did she still grieve? She was almost ashamed to admit that, even at night, alone in her bed, she no longer felt the emptiness of James's absence.

"Honey, it's okay."

"Is it? He died in March. It's not even August and I'm—"

"Living your life. Death…grief. There are no rules."

"He was sick for so long and…and we knew what the outcome was going to be. I keep telling myself that that's why I'm not hurting like I should be. I was prepared. James was prepared."

"You had closure."

"Yes. I think that's the difference between me and Lindsey. A plane crash. The whole family." She turned to her mother. "I can't even imagine her grief."

"No, I don't think anyone could. But Jack seems quite fond of her. Maybe that's helped both of them. Jack is like a completely different little boy than the one who cried so at the funeral."

She nodded. "Yes. Lindsey has filled a void in his life too." She smiled. "I'm quite fond of her as well. She's been a savior for us this summer. We've become…close," she said carefully. What did that mean exactly? They were friends. Yet…they were more than friends. Weren't they?

"I worried about you leaving San Antonio, leaving your friends behind. I was afraid you wouldn't be able to find someone here that you could connect with." She laughed quietly. "I pictured you turning into a younger version of Margie."

"What? Bitter and unhappy?"

"Oh, she does have some issues, doesn't she? And my goodness, she nearly cringed every time Jack mentioned Lindsey's name."

"I know. She gets that from Lilly. Apparently some family feud from way back in the day."

"That's too bad. Just wasted energy."

"Yes, it is. But I doubt she has any interest in changing."

"Speaking of changing, has she gotten over you redoing the kitchen? It's looks very good, by the way."

"Thanks. And no. I guess you didn't hear her snide remark about Lilly not even recognizing her own kitchen. I don't know what the deal is with her, but she never lets me forget that this is still Lilly's house and not mine."

"Would you have interest in staying here permanently? I thought...well, I hoped you'd come back to San Antonio."

"I don't know. We said we'd give it a year. Once Jack starts school, we'll see how it goes. He'll make new friends here. If he likes it, do I move him again just because I might not like it here?"

"You're still so young, Hannah. In time, you'll want to date again, surely."

Hannah laughed. "That's what you're worried about? Whether I'll be able to meet some nice man here?" She shook her head. "That thought hasn't even crossed my mind. I'm focused on Jack right now."

"Eventually you'll need to focus on yourself, though."

"Mom...I'm doing okay. Emotionally, I'm in a good place now." She turned to her. "I didn't expect to feel so...so content here. And at first—as you know—I wasn't. But now...I'm happy. Jack's happy."

"Having your own private section of river helps, I'm sure."

She nodded. "Yes, having Lindsey in our lives is the biggest thing."

CHAPTER THIRTY-EIGHT

Jack did his best Tarzan yell as he swung off the rope, landing with a splash out in the river. It was yet another glorious summer day, and Hannah was sad to think that they were coming to an end. This was Jack's last week of freedom, as he called it. Even though he groaned and complained about school starting up again, she knew he was excited. He'd pretended not to enjoy the shopping trip for new clothes and school supplies, but she saw through his guise, catching him organizing his stuff in his new backpack.

She used her hands to paddle her float upstream a little, then relaxed, watching as Lindsey joined Jack at the swing. They'd hardly had any rain during the summer months, but the river was still flowing enough to float. The rapids, however, were now too shallow to be much fun, even though they'd gone there to play just the other day.

Play. Now that Jack would be in school, she imagined that their playtime would cease. At least during the week. She sighed, knowing she would miss it...would miss seeing Lindsey every day. She couldn't recall the last time that they hadn't spent the day with her. Even last week when she'd taken Jack shopping, they'd been back by noon and were in the water by one. She supposed the last time they'd been apart was the weekend her parents had visited, over a month ago now.

"Watch, Mom!"

She smiled and nodded as Lindsey and Jack shared the rope, swinging far out over the water before dropping. As was now the case nearly every time they played on the rope, both dogs jumped off the deck to join them. Jack laughed and grabbed Barney's tail, letting him pull him to shore. Oh, the dogs were going to miss this too.

"Why the frown?"

Lindsey swam over, holding on to Hannah's float.

"Oh, I was just thinking how much I'm going to miss this. School starts next week so…"

"So you think that means that playtime is over?"

"Doesn't it?"

"Just because Jack won't be here, that doesn't mean you and I can't come out. Unless you'd rather not."

Hannah touched the hand that was holding on to her float. "Do you want to? I thought maybe—"

"Of course I want to. In another month, the water—especially in the pond—will probably be too cold to enjoy." Lindsey smiled at her. "Besides, it's not only Jack I enjoy spending time with."

"Thank you." Hannah held her gaze. "The feeling is mutual."

Lindsey leaned closer. "Jack's going to be so pissed though," she said with a wink. "We might have to keep it a secret from him."

Hannah laughed. "I agree."

Jack jumped off the rope swing again, splashing them with water as he landed close by. Two dogs quickly followed him. Lindsey pushed Barney away before he could hit the float with his paws.

"They've gotten so big, haven't they? It's hard to remember them being little puppies."

"I know. Max hardly fits on his little dog bed anymore."

"What are we having for dinner?" Jack asked as he, too, came over and hung on the other side of her float.

"It's my turn to cook," Lindsey said. "You pretty much know what your options are with me."

"Hamburgers!"

"Jack, we just had burgers," Hannah said.

"We're having chicken on the grill," Lindsey said. "I've already got it marinating."

"I like your chicken," he said. "Are you going to put that gooey sauce on it again?"

"I am."

"And can I have extra cheese on my baked potato?"

"Don't you always?"

He grinned. "It's gonna be a good dinner!"

Hannah shook her head as he swam off. "You spoil him too much."

"Well, he's all I've got to spoil. Other than you, of course."

Their eyes met and Hannah smiled. "Do you spoil me?" she asked unnecessarily.

"'Oh, Lindsey...a steak sure does sound good for dinner, doesn't it?'" Lindsey mimicked.

Hannah laughed. "Very funny. I was simply making a suggestion the other night when you didn't know what to cook."

"Uh-huh. And what was your excuse the time before that?"

"So I like steak," she conceded. "And when you do that rosemary and garlic marinade...oh, that's so good. The best. Ever." She smiled sweetly at her. "In fact, Saturday would be a good night for steak. I'll bring the wine."

"Okay. I guess that sounds like a plan." She paused. "On one condition."

"What's that?"

"You make the triple-cheese casserole thing on Sunday."

Hannah laughed. "Now who's spoiled?"

* * *

Hannah stood beside her, watching as she flipped the chicken pieces over and brushed them with sauce.

"I have to agree with Jack. I like your chicken."

"Thank you."

"What do you put in the sauce?"

Lindsey shook her head. "Nope. It's a secret sauce. Sorry."

"My guess is, there is no recipe and you just made it up."

She laughed. "You'd be wrong. It's my grandmother's recipe."

"She shared it with you?"

"No. But I found the drawer where she kept her recipes. Mostly scribbled on notepads and whatever she could find. Nothing organized at all," she said as she closed the lid on the grill. "That's on my list to do. A winter project."

Hannah handed her the wineglass and Lindsey took a sip. As had become their custom when she grilled outside, they'd drink a glass or two of a lighter wine—usually a chardonnay, Hannah's favorite—before dinner and open a different bottle for the meal.

"When you talk about them now, you're not quite as...I don't know, sad. Emotional."

Lindsey nodded. "It's not quite as raw anymore, I guess." She shrugged. "Time does that, I suppose. The shock has subsided. The guilt has subsided. The—"

"Why guilt?"

"I'm still here."

"Why should you feel guilty for that?"

Lindsey met her eyes, seeing a gentleness there that made her feel...warm, safe. "I should be dead, like them," she said simply. "I was supposed to be on the plane too."

Hannah gasped. "Oh, my God. I had no idea."

"I had a deadline. A project." She swallowed. "Normally, they'd fly up to Dallas and pick me up and we'd go on to Colorado from there. This time, though, I...well, I couldn't leave as scheduled. I'd planned to get a flight the next day or two and join them."

"Oh, honey," Hannah whispered.

Lindsey didn't resist as Hannah pulled her into an embrace. She heard the murmured words "I'm so sorry," but they didn't really register. Hannah was too close—far too close—and Lindsey closed her eyes, relishing the contact as their bodies touched. Whenever Hannah hugged her—which was often—she felt such peace settle around her she never found the strength to pull away, to resist. She knew it wasn't healthy, this…this attraction she had to Hannah. She knew it. Nothing would—could—ever come of it. And if she wasn't careful, she was going to end up over her head. She was going to end up with a damn broken heart and a lost friendship.

But like always, she let Hannah end the hug. Only this time, it was different. When Hannah pulled away, her lips grazed her cheek so softly, Lindsey thought she'd surely imagined it.

"Why didn't you tell me this before?"

"I…I don't know. I guess I thought you knew."

"Did you tell Jack?"

Lindsey nodded. "Yes." That got her pulled into another tight hug.

"I can't even begin to imagine how you must have felt."

"Fate…it's a funny thing, isn't it?"

Hannah pulled away again but kept her hand on Lindsey's shoulder. "Fate is the reason we met. The only reason. That's kinda scary to think about, isn't it?"

"What? Because of death, we were destined to meet?"

Hannah smiled. "Yes, that's scary too. But I meant scary to think about not ever having met you."

"I have to agree," she said seriously. "This summer…well, you and Jack have become…well…"

"Family," Hannah said simply. "And it goes both ways, Lindsey."

CHAPTER THIRTY-NINE

"Mom...quit worrying."

"I should have taken Margie's advice and sent you to church camp this summer."

He rolled his eyes at her.

"It's the truth," she said as she stopped at the end of Dennis and Margie's long driveway. The school bus would pick Jack up there. "At least you would have met some of your classmates then. Now...you won't know a soul." She shook her head. "It's my fault. I should have—"

"Mom, I had the best summer ever."

"Did you?" She smiled at him and tousled his hair. "It was pretty awesome, wasn't it?"

"Lindsey says I swim like a fish."

"Yes, you do."

"She says I should take lessons. Real lessons," he clarified.
"Oh?"

"Like maybe someday be in competitions and stuff."

"She thinks you're that good, huh?"

"Uh-huh."

"That would mean moving back to San Antonio," she said. "I doubt, around here, we'd find anyplace that offered lessons like that."

"Oh." His face fell and the smile disappeared. "I don't think I want to move."

"No? You might hate school here."

"But Lindsey's here."

"Yes, she is. For now. She may decide to go back to Dallas."

"But…"

"Honey, don't worry about it. She's here now. We're here now. That's all that matters." She should have never planted that seed in his mind. Lindsey hadn't mentioned going back to Dallas any more than Hannah had mentioned going back to San Antonio. Right now, it was a non-factor.

"Okay." Then, "What are you going to do today without me?"

She smiled. "I'm going to miss you, of course."

He poked her arm playfully. "I heard you and Lindsey whispering. You're going to do something fun today, aren't you?"

She laughed. "We may take the tubes out and float the river."

"No fair!"

"Or we may go to the pond and have a lazy day there."

"Mom, no," he groaned. Then his eyes lit up. "Why don't you homeschool me? You're a teacher."

"Homeschool you? Homeschool is still school. It doesn't mean you can sneak off with Lindsey anytime you want. Besides, you need the interaction with kids your own age. You've had enough adult time this summer."

"I guess."

"I did think about it, though," she admitted.

"You did?"

"Yes. At first. But it's just you and me. I didn't want you to be that isolated."

"You and me and Lindsey," he corrected.

She smiled. He never failed to include Lindsey. She understood the depth of their bond now, but she sometimes thought it went deeper than even she imagined. If Lindsey went back to Dallas or they moved back to San Antonio, she wondered how Jack would handle that. Would it be another loss in his young life that he'd have to overcome?

"There's the bus!" he said excitedly.

"Okay. I guess it's time." She reached over to kiss him and he jerked away.

"Mom! Somebody might see."

She laughed. "I'm sorry. Whatever was I thinking?"

He stood outside and looked back in. "So…you'll pick me up right here?"

"Right here."

"Okay."

"Have a good day, honey."

He turned back and pointed his finger at her. "Don't have too much fun without me today."

She laughed. "Go on. I'll see you this afternoon."

Her smile faded as soon as the bus pulled away. She should have taken him to school herself. She should have gone in and met his teachers. Then she shook her head. He would have never allowed that. No, he would be fine. She'd pick him up this afternoon and he would talk her ear off and tell her everything that he did. Then he would demand to know what she and Lindsey had done without him.

"And then we get to have dinner with Margie and Dennis," she murmured, already dreading it. But Margie had insisted. It was Jack's first day and they wanted to hear all about it. Hannah couldn't say no. They'd hardly spent any time with Margie and Dennis as it was, something Margie never failed to mention.

She turned the car around, heading back down the narrow private road that would take her past Margie and Dennis's house and to the back of the property where Lilly's house was, at least a mile away. She saw Margie waving at her so she stopped, waiting as Margie opened the gate by their front fence and walked over.

"How was he?"

"He was fine," she said. "Even though he complained, I think he was excited to start school."

"I just wish he knew somebody. He had all summer to make friends. You should have—"

"Margie…it's too late. He's off to school."

"Yes," she said with pursed lips. "I'm sure it'll be an adjustment for you having him gone. What do you have planned today?"

"I'm going to knock down one of the walls and enlarge my bedroom." Margie gasped and brought a hand to her chest, causing Hannah to laugh. "Kidding, of course." She saw no need to tell Margie that she and Barney would be having a play day with Lindsey and Max. "I pick Jack up at three forty-five. I'll see you then."

"I was thinking, since the road is not that far, Jack could just walk here to the house every day and you could pick him up here. That way, you wouldn't have to be on such a strict schedule and it would give Jack a little time with us."

She groaned silently. Jack would kill her. But she nodded. "That's a good idea, Margie. We can tell him at dinner." Oh, yeah…Jack would kill her.

Margie's face lit up. "Good. Well, see you later."

"Can I bring something for dinner?" she offered.

"No, no. I've got it."

* * *

"So did you cry when you dropped him off?"

Hannah laughed. "I did not. Although he about had a fit when I tried to kiss him good-bye."

"Oh, no…you didn't?"

"I did. I won't make that mistake again." Hannah shifted in the seat. "So? What do you have planned for today?"

"I'm thinking the pond," she said. She grinned. "I'm thinking skinny-dipping at the pond."

Hannah's eyes widened. "Skinny-dipping?"

"Uh-huh."

"Skinny-dipping," she said again slowly.

"What?" Then she nodded. "Oh. It's because I'm a lesbian. You think I'll be ogling your body or something."

Hannah slapped her arm. "I thought no such thing. You've seen me practically naked anyway."

Lindsey laughed. "Naked and practically naked are two different things."

"If you think I'm afraid of you, you're way wrong. I hesitated because, well, I've never been skinny-dipping before. So it'll be fun. A new adventure."

"Good. And I promise I won't look."

"I don't care if you look. I'll be looking at you," Hannah teased with a laugh.

Lindsey wasn't sure what possessed her to suggest skinny-dipping. Well, the prospect of playing in the water naked—with Hannah—was appealing. It was also dangerous. She'd also expected Hannah to refuse. But no. They were going skinny-dipping. And Hannah didn't care if she looked. Hannah would be looking. Good God, what had she been thinking?

The dogs jumped off the back and were in the water as soon as she lowered the tailgate. Hannah walked over to the metal footlocker and opened it, taking out their two fanny floaters.

"Or do you want a regular float?" Hannah asked with a grin. "You know, so you'll be on top of the water."

Lindsey nearly blushed. "We don't have to go skinny-dipping. We can just—"

Hannah laughed. "Oh, so now you're trying to back out on me, huh?"

"I was only thinking of you. Since you've never done this before, I mean."

"No. I'm good. It'll be fun." Then she grinned. "But you go first."

Lindsey stared at her, then swallowed. "Okay. Turn around."

Hannah laughed. "You're not serious."

Lindsey pointed her finger at Hannah. "You're having too much fun with this."

"I just can't believe you're shy. I've seen you all summer in nothing but a bikini top."

"You're right. And I'm not normally shy."

Hannah met her gaze. "Then don't be shy with me." Then she smiled. "This was *your* idea."

"One I'm regretting by the minute," she mumbled as she pulled her T-shirt over her head and tossed it on the pier. With her back to Hannah, she removed her top and tossed it on the shirt. Then, with a deep breath, she slipped off her water shorts, leaving her standing there in nothing but her sandals. She took a quick step to the edge and dove into the pond. The cool water was like silk on her skin, reminding her of why she loved skinny-dipping in the first place.

When she came up, Hannah was blatantly staring at her, a grin on her face. "Very nice." She laughed. "The dive, I mean."

Lindsey swam to where she could touch bottom, noting that the clear water did little to hide her nakedness. "Your turn, smarty-pants."

"You know, I used to be shy. In fact, the very first time I went to the river with you and Jack, I was nervous about taking my top off."

"You were in a black bikini, top and bottom," she said with a smile. "Not that I was looking or anything."

"Uh-huh. Anyway, I was pasty white and you were young and tan and I was embarrassed."

"And now?"

"And now I'm comfortable around you and I have a very nice tan."

Her bikini top fell to the deck and Lindsey stood there, staring, forgetting to breathe. True to her word, Hannah wasn't shy as her shorts lowered. Lindsey finally averted her eyes, feeling like a gawking teenager. Hannah stood there—like a goddess—then dove into the water, surfacing a little ways away from Lindsey.

"Oh, God...that feels *great!*"

"Yeah, it does."

She went over to where Hannah had tossed their floats and shoved one toward Hannah. She got into her own, then paddled out into deeper water, out into the sun.

"You'd said one time that Jack and I were the only ones to come out here, other than your family. Was that true?"

Lindsey nodded. "Yep. Ever since we were kids, we were told that this place was a secret. We couldn't tell anybody about it. Even when we were in high school and college and we had friends out, we'd always go to the river. We never said a word about the pond."

"Why?"

"My grandfather wanted it to be a special place. A place just for the family. And it was. We didn't come here that often. We usually played in the river. So on those occasions that he said we were going to spend the afternoon at the pond, it became special."

"Thank you for bringing me and Jack here. It's…it's a beautiful place. So peaceful."

"Yeah. I'm glad you like it."

"We come here often, though. Will it lose the special atmosphere that your grandfather wanted to preserve?"

"I don't think so. I like sharing it with you and Jack," she said honestly.

Hannah moved her float a little closer to her, a smile on her lips. "By the way, you have perfect breasts."

Lindsey felt a blush on her face. "You did not just say that."

Hannah laughed. "I did. It's the truth."

Lindsey wanted to protest. Hannah was the one with the perfect breasts. She'd stared at Hannah standing naked on the pier long enough for the sight to be permanently imprinted on her brain. Hannah's breasts were fuller than they appeared in a bikini. Full and firm and…perfect.

She cleared her throat. "Let's stop talking about breasts."

Hannah laughed. "You're too cute sometimes, you know."

CHAPTER FORTY

Lindsey felt tears threaten as Hannah brought out the cake. She was nearly overcome with emotion when Hannah and Jack started singing "Happy Birthday" to her.

"And many more," Hannah added at the end. "Make a wish."

Lindsey held her eyes, shocked that Hannah had remembered her birthday. She'd only mentioned it to her the one time that she recalled. Yet here she was, after spending the day alone—feeling sorry for herself—celebrating with the two people who meant more to her than anyone in the world.

"Blow them out! Blow them out!"

She closed her eyes for a second, wishing for something she had no business wishing for, then took a deep breath, blowing out all thirty candles in one try.

Jack clapped. "Yay!" He scooted closer to her at the table, so close that their arms were touching. "This is my favorite cake. You're going to love it too. It's a double chocolate chip on the inside and the icing is made with cream cheese."

She nudged him. "I figured it had cheese in it somewhere." She looked up at Hannah. "Thank you. I'm touched."

Hannah smiled sweetly at her. "You thought I forgot."

"It's not like we talked about it."

She sliced off a big corner piece for Jack. "I'm sorry I couldn't spend the day with you, though."

"Did you get packed?"

"Yes."

"What time are we leaving?" Jack asked with a mouth full of cake.

"In the morning."

Leaving. Yes, for three days. Three whole days. The Labor Day weekend loomed long and lonely. At least she'd have Barney to keep her and Max company. And she'd already told herself she wasn't going to wallow in sorrow. She wasn't going to spend the weekend rekindling the grief she'd finally gotten past. She had gone that morning to the grocery store and stocked up. In years past, the Labor Day holiday—like all holidays—was built around food and fun. Just because she'd be alone didn't mean she couldn't keep some of the traditions alive. She'd bought a large pork roast and ribs. She'd get her grandfather's smoker going in the morning and slow cook the meat all day. Ribs and pulled pork sandwiches would be her weekend meals. And on Monday, she'd do burgers. Hannah and Jack would be back in time to join her when they stopped over to get Barney. It would be the first time Hannah had actually driven to her house.

"I wish Lindsey was going with us."

Lindsey and Hannah exchanged glances. "I do too," Hannah said.

Lindsey smiled. "And what would we do with Max and Barney?"

"Oh."

"I'll see you on Monday for burgers, remember?"

"Yeah...but what are you going to do while we're gone?" Jack asked.

"I'll find something to do. Maybe I'll get up early and go fishing."

"Are you still going to take me next weekend?"

"Of course." She took the small plate from Hannah. "Thank you." Lindsey took one bite of the cake and decided that double chocolate chip with cream cheese icing was her new favorite dessert. "This is *so* good."

"Told you," Jack mumbled as he shoved another bite into his mouth.

After they'd eaten, Lindsey helped Hannah clean up the kitchen. Dinner had been leftovers from the enchilada casserole they'd had the other night. Jack had announced that this was his second favorite casserole after he'd added more cheese to his plate.

"He's growing like a weed but thankfully up and not out," Hannah said.

"When's his birthday? You said November."

"The fifteenth. I can't believe he'll be ten already. Before you know it, he'll be a teenager." Hannah laughed. "And I'm trying not to think about it."

"He's a good kid. He won't give you any trouble."

"I hope you're right." Hannah folded the dish towel and placed it on the counter. "So? What do you have planned for the weekend?"

"I'm going to barbecue and drink beer and play in the river." She grinned. "Not necessarily in that order."

Hannah touched her arm, letting her hand rest there. "I'm sorry we won't be here."

"Nothing to be sorry about, Hannah. You enjoy your time with your family. That's what holidays are for." As soon as she said the words, her heart tightened in her chest. Yes, that's what holidays are for. But not for her. Not anymore. Suddenly, her brave words of earlier—that she was over her grief—haunted her.

"I'd rather stay here with you."

She looked at Hannah, trying to read her eyes. "I'll be okay. Me and the boys...we'll play."

Hannah moved closer, wrapping her arms around her shoulders as Lindsey's arms went around her waist. She sunk into the embrace, fighting back the sadness that she was feeling.

"I'm going to miss you," Hannah whispered into her ear.

Lindsey squeezed her eyes shut, savoring the moment. "I'm going to miss you too."

CHAPTER FORTY-ONE

Hannah stood at the window, looking out on her parents' backyard and pool. Jack was standing on the side, showing anyone who would watch his new diving technique he'd learned from Lindsey. Watching him made her heart ache. Watching him made her miss Lindsey even more and it was only Saturday.

"There you are," her mother said. "I was wondering where you got off to."

"I came in for...for a drink," she said, holding up the bottle of water she had yet to open.

Her mother came closer, studying her. "Are you okay? You've been awfully quiet."

"I'm fine." She forced a smile to her face. "Jack is having a wonderful time."

Her mother linked arms with her. "You can't fool me, honey. What's wrong? Is it the holiday? Are you missing James?"

Hannah stared at her, blinking several times. My God, she hadn't even given James a thought in days. She should lie. She should say yes. Her mother would understand. But she didn't want her mother's sympathy. There was no need for it. She couldn't possibly tell her mother the truth though. That, she would *never* understand.

"I'm fine, Mom," she said evasively. "Is there something I can do to help with dinner?"

"No, no. There are three large pizzas out in the extra fridge. Your father's newest passion is grilling pizza. They're quite good. I hope everyone will like them."

"I'm sure we will." She headed to the door with her mother, then paused. "I'll be right out." Her mother looked at her questioningly. "I want to call Lindsey real quick. Make sure everything's okay there. She's babysitting Barney, you know."

She went back to her old room, the room she was sharing with Jack. Her phone was on the dresser and she picked it up, wondering if Lindsey might still be out at the river. No. She was probably back, already sitting on her deck. Drinking a glass of wine? Maybe a cocktail? Was she cooking? She could picture Lindsey sitting in her chair, the dogs lying beside her, her gaze on the deer feeder, waiting for the first one to come out to eat. Then she smiled. No, the dogs were probably in the kitchen, in the air-conditioned house.

She sighed. She was enjoying seeing her family. She really was. But she'd be lying if she said she wouldn't rather be at home...with Lindsey. She didn't want to think too much about it. She didn't want to analyze it. It was just...there. She didn't want to put it into words. She didn't want to go there...not yet.

She did, however, want to call Lindsey, to hear her voice, to know that she was okay. After three rings, her disappointment grew. Was she still out? Was she in the shower? Was she okay? Had she had an accident?

"Hey there."

Hannah let out a relieved sigh. "Hey." She squeezed her phone tighter. "Is everything okay?"

"Are you checking up on me?"

Hannah could hear the smile in her voice. "Busted."

"I'm fine. I've got thirty more minutes on the ribs and the dogs are already drooling."

"I'm sure they are." She paused. "Did you get out to the river today?"

"I went to the pond instead."

Hannah smiled, her voice low. "And did you skinny-dip?"

"I did. It wasn't nearly as much fun alone."

Hannah laughed. They'd gone three times to the pond to skinny-dip and she felt nearly shameless at how uninhibited she'd become. "I'm sorry I missed that."

"The dogs don't think I'm nearly as much fun as Jack, though. I think they're bored with me." Lindsey paused for a second. "So...are you having a good time?"

"Yes," she said automatically. "No," she said truthfully.

"What's wrong?"

Hannah sat down on her bed, chewing her lower lip. "Lindsey...I...I miss you."

She heard Lindsey take a deep breath. "I miss you too, Hannah." The words were soft, quiet, and they caused Hannah's heart to race.

She cleared her throat and stood up quickly. "So we're having grilled pizza for dinner," she said, changing their conversation to a safer subject. A *much* safer subject.

"Grilled pizza, huh? Sounds interesting."

"I'd rather have ribs."

Lindsey laughed. "No, you'd rather have a steak."

"True." She cleared her throat again. "Well, I guess I should get back out there. I just wanted to check on you."

"Thank you for calling. And for worrying about me."

"Enjoy your ribs. I'll be thinking about you as I'm eating my pizza."

After a quiet "goodbye" from both of them, she ended the call. She sat down heavily on the bed again and lay back, staring up at the ceiling. "Oh, Hannah...what are you going to do? What in the world are you going to do?"

* * *

Lindsey…I…I miss you.

The words echoed over and over in her mind. Things between them were changing. It wasn't a sudden change, so it shouldn't scare her as much as it did. No, things had been changing ever so slowly all summer. They either needed to put a stop to it…or…or what? Did Hannah even know what was happening? Surely, she did. Their time at the pond, their trips there to go skinny-dipping…there wasn't anything "normal" about it any longer. Subtle flirting—from both of them—should have been a clue, as should the hugs that had ceased being between friends a long time ago.

What would they do now? Would they continue to ignore it and pretend it wasn't there? Or would they talk about it? Get it out in the open?

"I vote to ignore it," she murmured.

At least for a while. At least until she could wrap her mind around it.

Lindsey…I…I miss you.

CHAPTER FORTY-TWO

So this is what the road to Lindsey's driveway looked like. Now she knew why they always met at the creek. If either of them were to actually drive to the other's house, it would take at least thirty minutes. They were on completely opposite sides.

"Can you believe all the people that were in the river?" Jack asked. "I'm glad we don't have to share our part with anyone."

"*Our* part? Don't you mean Lindsey's part?"

He grinned. "Yeah, but she kinda acts like it's ours too."

"She does. But it's not." And yes, the river was crowded with people. And why not? It wasn't even noon yet. It was a holiday. It was over ninety degrees already.

Yet she'd rushed away from her parents' house and pool, barely taking the time for breakfast. Jack had seemed anxious to get back too. She, herself, was beyond anxious. The weekend seemed to drag by and she'd only barely resisted the urge to call Lindsey last night. To check on her, she told herself. It had to be emotionally hard for her to be there all alone on a holiday. From what Lindsey had told her, holidays were special in their family. She imagined the weekend had been hard for her.

"Mom?"

"Huh?"

"I kinda miss Lindsey."

She smiled. "Just kinda?"

"Do you miss her?"

She nodded. "I do. And we'll see her in a minute."

"Do you think she'll want to go to the river this afternoon?"

"You spent the entire weekend in the pool. Aren't you sick of the water?"

"No. We could play on the rope swing a little."

"Okay. Ask her. We're just going to pick Barney up and head home. She was planning on picking us up at the creek. We're having burgers, remember?"

"I remember."

Hannah turned off the main county road they were on at the landmark Lindsey had told her. The dirt road was bumpy, and she slowed as she crossed the cattle guard, signaling the entrance to Lindsey's property. The house was more than a mile down the road and as they got closer, she recognized the side trail that they took to get to the river.

"Now I know where we are," she said.

"That way to the river," Jack said, pointing.

As they approached the house, she saw Lindsey's Jeep out and she wondered if she'd gone somewhere. She most often kept it in the garage. Next to the Jeep was the Mule and Hannah parked beside it. Lindsey was out on the deck and she felt her anticipation grow. Jack jumped out as soon as she stopped and he ran up the steps and nearly flung himself at Lindsey. Hannah's heart swelled as she watched them hug. Then Jack was rubbing on Barney and Max and Lindsey's eyes were on her.

She walked up the steps, never breaking eye contact. She didn't hesitate as she walked into her arms. Their hug was tight, long...and totally inappropriate between friends. She was aware of every spot their bodies touched, and she was in no hurry to break the embrace. But the dogs brushed against them, demanding attention too. When they pulled apart, she realized how much things had changed between them. As she looked into Lindsey's eyes, she knew that Lindsey recognized the change too. Oddly, that didn't frighten her.

* * *

"Pizza on the grill. It was good too," Jack said. "We should try that sometime."

"I don't know if we can buy fresh pizza around here," she said.

"I bet Mom could make one."

Lindsey looked over at Hannah, who had floated to the other side of the river. She had a smile on her face as she watched them.

"What is Mom going to make?"

"A pizza," Jack said. "So we can grill it."

"How about we just stick to regular stuff on the grill and leave Mom out of it?"

"You know what I want," Lindsey said to Jack. "Spaghetti and meatballs."

"Oh, yeah. Maybe she could do that this week."

Hannah floated back over to them. "Are you two starving or what? That's all you've been talking about is food."

"I like to eat," Jack said.

"No kidding."

Lindsey's laughed. "He's a growing boy."

"And what's your excuse?"

"You're an exceptional cook. I've become very spoiled."

Hannah gave her a flirty smile. "Yes, you have. At least you recognize it."

"I think I reciprocate."

Hannah held her gaze. "Yes, you do."

"What does reciprocate mean?" Jack asked.

"It means she cooks me a steak when I want one."

He frowned. "Well, I don't want to reciprocate. I'd rather have a burger, I think."

Lindsey's laughter bubbled out before she could stop it and Hannah splashed water at her.

"Come on, buddy. Let's go off the rope swing. It's time you learned how to do a flip."

"Oh...*cool*!"

CHAPTER FORTY-THREE

Hannah leaned her head back into the water with a contented sigh. When Lindsey had suggested a lazy float trip down the river—probably their last one for summer—Hannah had been oddly disappointed she hadn't offered the pond. The pond and skinny-dipping. But after yesterday's encounter, perhaps skinny-dipping wasn't the best option. Besides, floating on the river like they were, it would be a perfect time to talk. Neither of them could get away, could walk away. Whether that was a good idea or not, she wasn't sure. But she felt they needed to talk. Ignoring what was happening wasn't solving anything. The problem was, she had no idea how to begin. She took a deep breath. Might as well jump in with both feet and see what happened.

She looked over at Lindsey, who was a few feet away from her. The dogs were on the bank, sniffing next to a cypress tree. The river was getting lower, the flow slowing down even more. She paddled over to Lindsey, holding on to her float, keeping them together. Lindsey looked at her expectantly.

"Something's happening to me," she said. Probably not the greatest of lines, but it was a start.

Lindsey raised her eyebrows but said nothing.

"I feel like I have all these changes happening inside of me." She met her eyes. "I don't know what to do about it."

Lindsey held her hand up. "Hannah, we don't need to talk about this."

"No?" She reached out, taking Lindsey's hand. "Are you attracted to me, Lindsey?"

Lindsey had a panicked look on her face. "No! Of course not. I mean…you're Jack's mother. He…I would…I mean—"

Hannah squeezed her hand, stopping her disjointed sentence. "It's okay to tell me the truth."

Lindsey shook her head. "Look…yes, we've grown closer. I know that. But I'm…I'm…you're—"

"Lindsey, it's a simple question that requires a yes or no answer. I don't need an explanation one way or the other. Please, just tell me."

She saw Lindsey swallow, could feel her nervousness. "Yes. Yes, I am."

Hannah nodded. Yes. She was surprised at how thankful she was that the answer was yes and not no. She released Lindsey's hand, leaning her head back to look into the blue sky, a sky that had a smattering of clouds floating around.

"My roommate in college, she wanted me to go out with her. Like…on a date," she said. "We lived together for two semesters. But I had already met James, we were dating." She looked over at Lindsey. "I hadn't thought about her in a really long time. But now…well, I think back on her and us living together and I wonder—if I hadn't met James—would I have gone out with her?" She shrugged. "I don't know. I don't know." She cleared her throat. "I'm attracted to you too. I'm not sure what to do about it. I don't know where to put it. I don't know if it's just everything that's happened to me, to you. I don't know if that's what pulled us together."

She shrugged again. "I don't know. We've gotten so close this summer, but is that all it is?" She held Lindsey's gaze. "I see you like this…in your bikini top. I see you when we're skinny-dipping…and…" She smiled. "Well, I have…inappropriate thoughts," she admitted with a laugh. "And please don't ask me to tell you what they are."

Lindsey gave a quiet laugh too. "Are we...are we really talking about this?"

"Yes. I think so. I think we need to talk about it. We can keep pretending that there's nothing here," she said, motioning between them. "But we'd be lying. I'm not blind, Lindsey. I've seen the way you look at me." When a blush lit Lindsey's face, Hannah grabbed her arm. "No, I didn't mean to embarrass you. It's just...I see that. And if you can't see the same when I look at you..."

"I have. I just didn't know if it was real or not."

"I don't know if it's real," she said honestly. "I don't know anything. I just know...being with you makes me happier than not being with you. This weekend—in San Antonio—was endless." She let her hand rub against Lindsey's arm. "And in case you haven't noticed, I like to touch you. That scares me."

Lindsey smiled. "I have noticed. It scares me too."

Hannah returned her smile, letting their fingers entwine. "I'm glad we talked about it. I don't know if it did any good or what purpose it served, but at least it's out there in the open." She tightened her fingers. "I don't want things to change between us, Lindsey. I don't want you to be guarded. I don't want you to think that everything you do, say, that I'll take the wrong way. Or me...I don't want us to change. I need your friendship most of all. I need what we have right now. I just don't know if I need more. If *you* need more."

"Hannah—"

"It scares the hell out of me. Jack...what would Jack think? What would he do?"

"Let's don't go there," Lindsey said. "Maybe we were just drawn together because of our grief. We healed together. Maybe we're reading too much into it."

"You think so?"

"I don't know. Maybe?"

Hannah nodded. "Maybe so. Maybe that's all it is." Then she smiled. "The fact that you look fabulous in a bikini—and better out of it—has nothing to do with it."

Lindsey laughed. "Well, perfect breasts and all," she teased.

Hannah squeezed her fingers again. "I love that we can talk about this. Can tease about it. But I don't know—"

"Neither of us knows, Hannah. If it happens, it happens."

"And that's okay with you?"

"Honestly, I don't know. I need you in my life. But if I need more…and you can't give me more…then I don't know. I guess we'll cross that bridge when we get there."

Hannah said nothing, thinking, yes, that was the logical thing to do. If—when—the situation arose, they would deal with it then. She had a fear that it would be upon them sooner, rather than later.

CHAPTER FORTY-FOUR

Lindsey held her hands up. "What's the problem?"

"I can't do it. It'll be a belly buster like Jack."

"When you're over the water, push off the rope with your feet. Do a flip."

"I'm old," Hannah complained. "You're going to laugh."

"I'm not going to laugh. If you hurt yourself, I'll come rescue you."

"Well, I would hope so."

At that, Lindsey did laugh. "I've done it three times. It's easy."

"You're an athlete."

"I'm not an athlete. I had a desk job."

"Yes, but I've seen you naked and your body begs to differ."

Lindsey put her hands on her hips. "Why, Hannah Larson, have you been peeking at me when we skinny-dip?"

"You know I have." Hannah let the rope slip from her hands and she walked closer. "Do you have any idea how adorable you are?"

"Like…irresistible?"

The levity between them suddenly vanished as Hannah met her gaze. "I've…I've never kissed a woman before," she whispered. Lindsey stared at her, not backing away. When she thought it would be sooner rather than later, she had no idea it would take only two days.

"Hannah…" Lindsey warned.

"What? Too soon?"

Lindsey nodded, then grabbed her arms and ran with her to the edge of the deck, throwing them both into the water. Hannah came up sputtering.

"Oh, God! You did *not* just do that!"

"You were about to kiss me."

"And?"

"And when we kiss, it's not going to be out here at the river."

Hannah swam into shallower water and stood. "I've lost my mind. I've completely lost my mind."

"How so?"

"It's all I think about."

"What?"

"You. Kissing you." She paused. "Other stuff."

"I think about it too."

"Then why haven't you done it already?"

Lindsey came up to her, her hands resting on Hannah's hips. She pulled her closer. "Is this where you want to do it? The first time? In the river?"

"Yes. I don't care."

Lindsey smiled. "That bad, huh?"

"You're teasing me. I'm being serious."

"I'm trying to hold on to sanity."

"You think I'm not ready?"

"Two days ago you weren't. What's changed?"

Hannah slammed the water with both fists. "I hate that you're being so mature about this."

"Hannah…"

"I know. I know. You're right." She took a step away from Lindsey. "Quit being so damn adorable then."

Lindsey leaned closer, her smiling eyes twinkling. "Never."

Oh...God, she is adorable. And I want to kiss her.

But Lindsey took her hand and led her to shore. "Come on. Try the flip again."

CHAPTER FORTY-FIVE

"I can't believe it's raining," Jack complained. "Do you think it'll rain tomorrow?"

"What? It's not supposed to rain on a Saturday?"

"No. We have a play day."

"You should be worried about me and Max. We have to cross the creek in this mess and drive the Mule back."

"I can drive you around," Hannah offered.

"Oh, it's not that bad. Not much more than a light drizzle."

"What are we gonna do if it rains tomorrow?"

"If it's raining, we'll call Aaron's mother and cancel. We can do it another time," she said.

"But...we don't have much time left. It'll be fall soon."

"Honey, I'm sorry." And she was. Jack had made a friend at school and he wanted to bring him over for a play day in the river. It's all he'd talked about all week.

Lindsey and Jack were on the sofa and she put an arm around his shoulders. "If it doesn't rain, we'll go out like we planned. We'll play at the rope and we'll do a short float trip. And we'll go to my place and do burgers. If it's raining just a little, we can still play at the rope swing. We'll be right there at my parents' cabin in case it gets worse."

Jack's expression turned serious. "Do you ever go in there?" he asked quietly.

Hannah was surprised the question didn't seem to affect Lindsey. She gave Jack a small smile. "Not much. I'm going to get it cleaned out this winter, I guess. For as much as we go to the rope swing, we could use that place instead of going all the way back to the house."

"We can help you," he offered.

"Yeah?"

Lindsey looked over at her and she nodded. "Yes."

Lindsey leaned back with a sigh. "I have a lot to do. My grandparents' house…there's so much stuff in there that needs to go. I've pretty much been living in the kitchen, bedroom and bath only," she said. "Even the bedroom…it's still got some of their stuff in there."

"Did you bring anything with you?" she asked.

"Clothes. A few books. My laptop." Lindsey looked at her. "I got rid of everything that I had in Dallas. Most of my personal things, things that meant the most to me, I kept at my parents' cabin. I had my own room there."

Hannah wondered why, when Lindsey moved out here, she went to her grandparents' house instead of the room she used to use. Maybe most of her memories were there. From what she'd learned, their family gatherings were held on the deck at the big house. Maybe Lindsey felt closest to them there. But yes, when she was ready to clean out their rooms, she and Jack would be there with her. That was no chore to do alone, as she could attest.

"I should get going," Lindsey said as she stood up. "Thank you for dinner."

Hannah got up too. "Salmon patties on a Friday night. Nothing special."

"Are you kidding? That homemade mac and cheese was sinful."

Hannah smiled. Lindsey and Jack both had three helpings of the stuff. She figured Lindsey would like it as much as Jack did.

Lindsey tousled Jack's hair. "See you tomorrow, buddy."

"Good night, Lindsey." He stood up and gave her a quick hug, then went back to the corner of the sofa. He looked up at her. "Can I watch TV for a little bit?"

"Sure. I'm going to walk Lindsey out. I'll be right back."

He nodded, but he was already flipping through channels.

"I don't let him watch TV much on school nights," she explained as they went into the kitchen.

"I'm not much of a TV watcher myself," Lindsey said. She opened the back door and the dogs ran out. "Well...I guess I'll see you tomorrow. Call me when Aaron gets here and I'll come pick you up."

Hannah nodded. "I hope it doesn't rain. Jack will be so disappointed."

"Yeah. We'll find something to do."

Their eyes met and they both hesitated. The good-bye hug was getting harder and harder to take. At least for her. There was no pretense from either of them that it was only a friendly hug. They were well beyond that. Still, it was all they'd allowed themselves—the hug.

Lindsey walked out onto the porch and Hannah followed. She closed the door behind them. The drizzle had turned into a misty rain and the damp air was cool around them.

"Good night, Hannah," Lindsey said quietly from the edge of the porch.

The light from the kitchen window was too faint for her to make out Lindsey's expression, but her voice sounded different. It sounded as if Lindsey was tormented...aching. Hannah went to her, sliding her hands up her arms and around her shoulders. Lindsey pulled her close. She knew immediately that this hug would not be like their usual good-bye hugs. She pressed her body as close as she could get to Lindsey. Their breasts were touching, their hips were touching...their thighs. It was as if— even though they weren't kissing—their bodies were. Hannah couldn't stop herself. She shifted, moving her hips ever so slightly. She heard Lindsey gasp, heard her own breath catch.

"*God...*" Hannah breathed.

Their mouths were only a fraction apart. Hannah knew that was the defining moment. If they were alone...if Jack wasn't in the house, there would be no more holding back. She literally ached to kiss Lindsey, ached to touch her. If they were alone, this would be the very moment that their relationship changed for good.

But they weren't alone and Jack *was* in the house. It took all of her willpower to turn away from those lips that were so near. She pulled back, separating them. They didn't speak. What would they say? There was no sound but their uneven breathing. And all of that from a hug.

Lindsey turned and walked down the steps, whistling for Max. Hannah walked down the steps, grabbing Barney by the collar when he would have followed. She stood there in the light rain, watching Lindsey disappear into the woods, then she went back on the porch. She paused once, turning back around, looking out into the night, then went back inside the kitchen.

She stood there, her eyes wide. It was a hug. It was the most intimate hug she'd ever had. And she knew that there would be no going back from it. But the weekend was here, and they'd have no time alone. How were they going to face each other after that? What would they say? And come Monday, when they would be alone...then what?

"Oh, God," she murmured.

* * *

Lindsey stood at the edge of the deck, watching the lightning streak across the sky. Rain was something they'd seen little of this summer, and she hoped the thunderstorms building would drift this way, enough for a shower or two. And of course be gone by morning so Jack could have his play day.

She sipped from her wine, enjoying the cool night air. The earlier rain had stopped completely by the time she'd gotten home, but the radar on her phone showed strong storms to their south. She went to her chair and sat down, ignoring the dampness of it. She leaned back and closed her eyes, still able to feel Hannah pressed against her. So close. They'd been so close, it was like she could feel every inch of Hannah's body. And so close to kissing. So close, it was painful.

Now what? Had they crossed the line with that hug? Would Hannah pull away from her? Or would she go forward? Would they take this…this thing between them to the next level? Or would it be different between them? Strained? Uncomfortable?

She had no answers. She knew what she wanted the answer to be, of course. She knew what she wanted that hug to mean.

But in the light of day, would it be the same?

CHAPTER FORTY-SIX

Hannah had been afraid that things would be a little…well, a little tense between them today, but she needn't have worried. Lindsey was her normally cheerful self when she picked them up and she was entertaining the boys on the rope swing like nothing out of the ordinary had happened last night. She wasn't certain what to make of that. Maybe the hug hadn't affected Lindsey like it had her. Maybe Lindsey hadn't spent a sleepless night, tossing and turning, her body making demands that she felt she could no longer deny.

God.

She spun her float around, her back to them. She couldn't get the damn hug out of her mind. No. It wasn't the hug. It was the feeling of being so close to Lindsey that she couldn't shake. It was that moment of certainty, that moment when she realized that the desire was real. It was a physical, emotional yearning that was weighing heavy on her today. How could she possibly deny it?

But how could she possibly give in to it? Because if she gave in to it, then everything would change. Her life would be flipped upside down. And then Jack's would. Could she even seriously contemplate having a sexual affair with Lindsey?

She turned her head, watching Lindsey on the deck trying to show Aaron how to flip off the rope. She looked like she always did…bikini top and water shorts. After their skinny-dipping sessions, it didn't take much imagination to picture Lindsey naked, without her top. So yes, she could envision a sexual affair with Lindsey. She already *had* envisioned it. But something told her it wouldn't be an affair. She and Lindsey were both too emotionally invested for that. Maybe that's what made her hesitate. She was already in too deep. If they went forward with this…and it didn't work out, then she was the one who stood to be hurt, not just Lindsey.

"Hey, Mom! Watch!"

Aaron and Jack were both on the rope at the same time and Lindsey pulled them back, then gave them a push out over the water. Jack, like usual, did a Tarzan yell before hitting the water. Aaron seemed like a nice boy and she could tell he was enjoying himself. It was good for Jack, she knew, to spend some time with someone his own age.

"Can I join you?"

She smiled at Lindsey. "Of course."

The boys went back to the deck for another jump, and she and Lindsey floated away from them to avoid their splashing.

"Do we need to talk?"

Hannah was surprised by the quiet question. Lindsey had given no indication that she was unsettled by last night. Or was the question for her benefit? Did she think that Hannah was the one who needed to clear the air? She decided that there was no reason to talk it to death. They both knew the score. So she moved closer, allowing herself a quick touch of Lindsey's hand.

"That was the best hug ever," she whispered.

Lindsey seemed relieved by her statement. "Oh, yeah?"

"We need…" Hannah met her gaze, holding it. "We need to be alone."

She thought Lindsey would protest, but she nodded. "Like maybe a trip to the pond on Monday?"

"Like maybe...we could just go to your place for the day." Lindsey seemed shocked by how brazen she was being and she smiled. "I didn't sleep at all last night," she murmured.

"So you don't want to take baby steps with this?"

Hannah again held her eyes. "I don't know if I'm ready to make love with you. I don't know if I'm ready for that. But...I need...I want more than what we have." She looked over to where Jack and Aaron were in the water, making sure they couldn't hear. "Last night told me that I want more than what we have. It told me you do too."

"Yes."

Hannah relaxed. "Good. And I'm not opposed to also going to the pond." She wiggled her eyebrows teasingly.

CHAPTER FORTY-SEVEN

"I had a good weekend, Mom."

"Did you? Good."

"It was fun having Aaron out," he said. "I wish I could have taken him to the pond though."

"You know the rule about the pond."

"I know. It's a secret."

"Lindsey's grandfather wanted it that way and Lindsey wants it that way. We have to respect that."

"Yeah, but we don't go out there much anymore."

She smiled. "Well, probably because that's where Lindsey and I go during the week while you're at school. Besides, you like swinging off the rope down at the river, don't you?"

"Yeah. But I like the pond too. It's like a big swimming pool." He turned to her. "Are y'all going there today?"

She nearly blushed at his innocent question. "I don't know." And it was the truth. Their plan was to go back to Lindsey's house. Whether they made it out to the pond or not was to be determined. Because that depended on what they actually *did* at Lindsey's house.

Oh, it was suddenly very hot in the car, and she looked down the road, hoping the school bus wouldn't be late today.

"Isn't it about time for the triple-cheese casserole?"

She laughed. "Is that all you think about? Food?"

"Lindsey likes it too."

"I know. But it's not on the menu tonight. Baked chicken."

He turned up his nose. "There's no cheese involved with baked chicken."

"I'm making the creamy rice with it."

"Oh. Okay. I like that." He opened the door when the school bus came into view. "See you later, Mom."

"Have a good day."

She waited until the bus pulled away before she turned the car around. He was such a damn cute kid. And a damn good kid. How did she get so lucky?

As she drove past Margie's house, she realized she wasn't lucky after all. Margie was waving her down. She groaned, then lowered the passenger side window.

"Good morning," she said with forced cheerfulness.

Margie stuck her head in the window. "I couldn't help but notice you had company out on Saturday. Wasn't that the Burketts?"

"Yes. Aaron Burkett is in Jack's class. He came out for the day."

"How nice for Jack. That's good. What did you do all day? It was very late when they came back to pick him up."

"We were out at the river most of the day, then had burgers."

"The river? Over on the McDermott's land?"

"Yes, Margie. With Lindsey."

She shook her head disapprovingly. "I don't understand your relationship with that woman."

She shrugged. "We're friends, Margie. Why is that hard to understand?"

"I heard from Tom Merkel that she's from Dallas."

"She is."

"And she moved out here by herself. Wonder why?"

"She felt close to her family here. This is where she wanted to be."

Margie shook her head. "It just seems strange, her living out here by herself."

"I'm sure people think that about me and Jack, living back here in the woods like we do. Lindsey's been a godsend for us."

"It's not like you live alone, Hannah. Dennis and I are right here. Of course, it's not like you come by to visit, though."

"Margie, Jack walks to your house after school. I see you every day." God, it was times like this that she wished she'd never moved out here in the first place. But then, she would never have met Lindsey. The thought of Lindsey not being in her life...well, she couldn't imagine it. "I need to go," she said. "Busy day planned."

She didn't offer an explanation to that statement as she pulled away. Oh, Margie was never going to change. She didn't know why she was still bothered by their encounters. Maybe because there was some truth to what she said. They didn't visit like they should. Jack hadn't gotten to know them like he should. They'd been out here all summer and they were still like strangers. It just wasn't something she could force though. Margie was not warm and fuzzy. She wasn't someone you wanted to be around. It had always been that way. She didn't know why she thought it would change if they moved out here.

Oh, well. She pushed thoughts of Margie from her mind. She had a date with Lindsey to get to.

* * *

Lindsey could tell as soon as she saw Hannah that she was nervous. Her smile was a little hesitant and she wouldn't meet her gaze. Lindsey was actually thankful that Hannah was feeling a little anxious. It helped relax her somewhat as she had nearly had a panic attack that morning herself.

"So...it's like summertime hot today, isn't it?"

Hannah nodded. "Yeah. Yeah, it is."

"So...I was thinking maybe we should just go to the pond. Enjoy the cool water and...and relax."

"Yeah. Good idea," Hannah said quickly. Then she laughed. "I'm nervous. I guess you can tell."

Lindsey smiled. "I can tell, yes."

"I'm sorry."

"No. Let's don't force things, Hannah. If we go to the house, we'll force things. Let's just…go to the pond and have a day. A play day, as Jack would say."

Hannah visibly relaxed. "Okay. A play day." She reached over and touched Lindsey's thigh lightly. "Thank you."

Lindsey was aware of the hand on her leg…the hand that didn't move, the hand that felt warm and soft against her skin. She kept her eyes focused on the trail ahead of them instead of picturing that hand sliding between her thighs. She nearly shivered at the thought.

CHAPTER FORTY-EIGHT

Hannah had expected their play day to include skinny-dipping, but Lindsey gave no indication that's what she had in mind. Instead, she dove into the pond, as was her ritual, then swam under the waterfall before coming back to shore.

"It's cold," Lindsey said. "Colder than the river."

"Are you saying summer is nearly over?"

"Yeah, well, September is nearly over. I guess it's time."

Hannah walked to the edge of the pier, mentally bracing herself for the cold plunge. As she'd learned long ago, it was best to jump in quickly and get it over with. Still, the cold water was a shock to her on such a hot day. She followed Lindsey's lead, going to the waterfall and holding on to the rocks as the cold stream of water hit her head. The volume had decreased steadily over the summer, but Lindsey had said she'd never seen it stop completely, not even during the worst of droughts.

She swam over to where Lindsey stood with their floats. The hot sun felt good on her skin and she relaxed. She'd worked herself into a bundle of nerves by the time it got to eleven, the time that Lindsey picked her up at the creek. It had been her suggestion that they go to Lindsey's house, her suggestion that they needed to be alone. At the time, it had sounded like a good idea. In fact, at the time, she'd been ready to go right then. Her body was certainly ready. Her mind, however, was lagging behind.

What if it's all wrong? What if it's awkward? What if she freaked out and...and ran away from Lindsey or something?

Or what if it's perfect and wonderful? What if it's the best thing she's ever felt? Then what? What does that say about her life? About her marriage? She knew that was the real problem. She was more afraid that it would be fabulous than not. If it felt wrong, if it was awkward, she could handle that. But what if it wasn't?

Their time at the pond, however, wasn't awkward in the least. Lindsey made sure of that. They chatted like always. Lindsey told her stories from her childhood. They floated and swam, they jumped off the pier with the dogs, and they dove underwater for rocks. They played. And they flirted. And they touched. And when Lindsey stood on the pier, about to dive in again, Hannah stopped her.

"Take your top off."

If Lindsey seemed startled by the request, she didn't show it. An arch of one eyebrow and a quick smile were her only reactions.

"As you wish."

The offending top was tossed carelessly to the pier and Lindsey stood there, meeting her eyes for a moment before turning her attention to the water. Yes, she really did have perfect breasts, Hannah thought. Small but not too small. Round, firm. Nipples that were...*God*. She found herself blatantly staring, but she couldn't pull her eyes away. Then Lindsey dove into the water, taking those perfect breasts with her.

"Oh, *God*," she murmured, shaking herself.

Lindsey surfaced not far from her, a smile on her face. "Now I can't be the only one topless. That's against the rules."

Oh, God.

Well, she was the one who started this. She walked out onto the pier like Lindsey had done. She didn't have to look at her to know that Lindsey was watching. She removed her top slowly, letting it fall. She took a step to the edge, then paused, chancing a glance at Lindsey. Their eyes locked together and Hannah nearly stumbled. Lindsey's eyes were transparent and filled with desire. Hannah took a deep breath, then dove into the water. She scarcely noticed the cold. Her body was on fire.

When she came up, she found Lindsey standing in water barely to her waist. There was never a doubt that she would go to her. They stood there, several feet apart, watching each other. Lindsey finally took a step closer, her gaze lowering to Hannah's breasts, her rigid nipples. She had a slight smile on her face.

"The water...it's very cold."

Hannah smiled too. "I assure you, cold has nothing to do with it. I feel like the water is boiling around me."

Lindsey took another step closer, finally pulling her eyes back to Hannah's face. Hannah was certain she'd never felt more sensuous than she did at that moment, standing in the water, topless, face-to-face with a beautiful young woman who was also topless...a beautiful young woman with desire in her eyes.

"I think about you," Hannah said quietly. Lindsey tilted her head questioningly. "I...I'm not going to lie. I think about... about making love with you."

Lindsey didn't say anything; she just continued to stare at her.

"Do you...do you think about...making love with...with me?"

Lindsey's smile nearly melted her heart. "Every damn day."

There wasn't really anything else to say, was there? Hannah took a step closer, moving until they were nearly touching. Her heart was hammering in her chest, and she wondered if Lindsey could see it, hear it. She was surprised that she was the one who reached out first, pulling Lindsey to her.

When their mouths met, she thought she'd be prepared. She'd thought about kissing Lindsey often enough. But she was woefully unprepared for her heart to leap into her throat, unprepared for the rush of blood to her face, her ears, drowning out all sound. She wasn't ready for the soft lips that claimed hers with barely controlled passion. She wasn't expecting desire to course through her veins like it did. She wasn't expecting her knees to wobble when she felt Lindsey's tongue brush her lip. And she certainly wasn't expecting to be aroused—not *this* aroused—from a kiss.

When Lindsey pulled her closer, when their breasts touched…their nipples brushing, she felt faint, light-headed. And when she opened her mouth, letting Lindsey inside, the loud moan that she heard surely wasn't from her. Was it?

But yes, there—in waist-deep water—they stood, their bodies pressed together, their mouths still fused, mingling moans drifting around them as they kissed…and kissed…and kissed. She thought crazily that if Lindsey let her go, she might very well drown. She held on tightly, not caring that they were so close their breasts were smashed together. When Lindsey's hands moved to her hips, when she cupped her and pulled her body impossibly closer, she felt the world spin around her.

Then Lindsey slowed, her lips moving lightly now, easing away even as Hannah tried to prolong it.

They stood there, their foreheads touching, their breath coming quick in short gasps, hands resting at each other's waist. It was several seconds before a cognizant thought materialized, several seconds more before she could form words…a sentence.

"If I'd have known kissing you would be like that, I'd have insisted we do it months ago."

Lindsey smiled. "Months ago you would have slapped my face."

Hannah lifted her head, looking into Lindsey's eyes, eyes still shimmering in desire. "Let's go to your place," she whispered. When Lindsey would have spoken, Hannah held a finger against her lips. "No. Don't say anything. Let's go to your place. Now."

* * *

Hannah stood by the bed, watching her. Lindsey hadn't expected Hannah to be so sure of herself, so in control. But she was. Lindsey had been the one fumbling, getting tangled in her shorts as she took them off.

"Are you nervous or in a hurry?"

"Both."

Hannah smiled at her. "Do you know how incredibly sexy I find you?"

"Sexy, huh?"

"Yes. And I'm aroused and I don't have a clue as to what to do."

Lindsey stood still. "Do what you want to do. Touch where you want to touch." She took a step closer, her eyes never leaving Hannah's. Her hand lightly touched Hannah's waist, then slid higher. "Like this," she murmured. She brought her other hand up, cupping Hannah's breasts, feeling the weight of them. When her thumbs brushed both nipples, Hannah gasped but didn't move away. "Like this." Then her hands slid around behind Hannah, moving over her skin, down her back, past her hips. "Like this."

She could see Hannah's pulse in her neck, could hear the change in her breathing. She watched as Hannah's eyes darkened. Yes, Hannah was aroused. She wasn't frightened. She was aroused.

So Lindsey leaned closer, finding her mouth, her light kiss deepening when Hannah's mouth opened. She felt Hannah's arms slip around her shoulders so she pulled her closer, their bodies touching, head to toe, no barriers between them.

She shifted, moving them to the bed. They lay on their sides, facing each other. Lindsey smiled reassuringly at Hannah when Hannah's hand touched her waist, rubbing slowly back and forth, before finally moving to her breast.

"God...so soft," Hannah whispered. Her fingers grazed her nipple. "So hard."

Lindsey's breath caught as those fingers moved to her other breast.

"Incredible." Hannah's eyes moved to Lindsey's. "So soft," she said again.

Lindsey touched Hannah's hip, her thigh, moving slowly. Hannah's hand, too, moved along the curve of Lindsey's hip. They touched and caressed, getting familiar with each other, getting comfortable touching each other like this. Hannah was the one to move closer, her lips finding Lindsey's. A quiet moan, a brush of her tongue, a hand on her breast. Lindsey rolled them over, resting her weight on top of Hannah as they kissed. She nudged Hannah's thighs apart, and as she settled there, she could feel Hannah's wetness against her skin.

She left Hannah's mouth, moving lower, finding her nipple with her tongue, swirling across the peak as Hannah's fingers threaded through her hair. Her mouth closed over the nipple, and Hannah arched into her, holding her close.

"*God...*Lindsey," Hannah breathed. "Feels so good."

Lindsey felt Hannah's hips moving against her, felt her own arousal flood her. When she left Hannah's breast and returned to her mouth, their kiss changed. There was an urgency now, their lips moving faster, harder, their tongues meeting almost frantically. Hannah's hands were on her back, rubbing up and down, pulling her closer with each stroke. Her thighs parted even more, her hips arching into Lindsey.

Lindsey pulled away, her breath coming in quick gasps between her lips. She moved to Hannah's ear, kissing her there, letting her tongue wet it.

"The first time," she whispered. "The first time, I want to make love to you with my mouth."

Hannah groaned. "Oh...*God*."

"Can I? Please?" She felt Hannah tremble beneath her.

"Yes...*yes. Anything*," Hannah moaned.

Lindsey kissed her again, then pulled back, meeting her eyes. She saw no fear there, no hesitation. No uncertainty. Hannah's eyes were dark, cloudy with desire.

"Yes," Hannah said again.

It was Lindsey who trembled now as she moved lower, her lips taking their time, teasing Hannah's nipples. Hannah's fingers were again running through her hair, holding her tight against her breast. She sucked a nipple into her mouth and Hannah moaned, her hips once again rocking against her.

She moved lower, her tongue, her lips nibbling against her skin, across her smooth belly, to the valley of her hip. She heard Hannah whimper, could feel her trembling as she got close. She kissed her inner thigh, the scent of her arousal making her want to devour her, but she moved slowly, surely, her lips kissing skin lightly, her hands gently spreading Hannah's legs. Hannah's hips arched, as if trying to find Lindsey's mouth.

"Please...*yes*," Hannah breathed.

Lindsey cupped her hips and pulled her close, her mouth immediately covering Hannah's clit. She sucked it into her mouth, holding on to Hannah as she jerked violently against her.

"Sweet...*Jesus*."

Sweet Jesus indeed, Lindsey thought as the taste of Hannah nearly made her delirious. Her tongue swiped up and down, teasing her clit at each pass, then plunged deep inside her. Hannah's thighs squeezed tight against her face, her hips rolling as she tried to take her tongue deeper. Lindsey pulled out of her, going to her clit again.

Hannah was moaning, her breath hissing between her teeth, her hands clutched in Lindsey's hair. Lindsey's tongue flicked against her, then she covered her again, sucking her clit hard, her tongue moving against it at the same time. Hannah was writhing against her and Lindsey held firmly to her as her mouth—her tongue—continued to stroke her.

Hannah's hips lifted off the bed and a guttural scream left her body as she climaxed. Her legs were squeezed so tightly against her that Lindsey could hardly breathe. Hannah's hips jerked again, almost violently as Lindsey sucked her clit, bringing out the last of her orgasm.

When Hannah relaxed, when she released Lindsey, she lay still on the bed. Lindsey lifted her head, shocked to see tears running down Hannah's face. She got to her knees, moving closer, but Hannah turned, curling into a ball, her arms wrapped around herself. The sobs that Lindsey heard made her heart stop. *Oh, God. No.*

"Hannah...I'm so sorry. I don't know—"

Hannah lifted a hand and shook her head. "Don't."

Lindsey reached out to touch her but stopped. Hannah's shoulders were shaking as she cried, and Lindsey didn't know what to do.

"I'm sorry," Lindsey murmured again. "God...I'm sorry."

She got out of bed, going to her dresser. She opened a drawer and pulled out a T-shirt, slipping it over her head as she walked out of the room. She paused at the door, looking back at Hannah, who had her back to her. She closed the door quietly, shutting out the sight of Hannah's tears.

"What have I done?"

CHAPTER FORTY-NINE

Hannah couldn't explain her tears…not even to herself. She also couldn't stop them as they continued to fall. Her heart felt like it was being squeezed out of her chest, and she wrapped her arms tightly around herself, rocking on the bed, trying to get her emotions under control.

Oh, my God.

"Oh…Lindsey."

She wiped at her eyes. It was…it was just too much. Too good. Too incredible. She felt like someone had plugged her into an electrical socket and left her there. How could she possibly have just had her first earth-shattering orgasm? What did that say about her marriage? About James?

She turned her face into the pillow and cried. Was that it? Was she feeling guilty? Was it too soon? No. No, that wasn't it. The guilt she was feeling was because…because Lindsey drove her to heights she'd never even imagined. And she did it with her mouth.

She rolled onto her back and forced her eyes open. Lindsey made love to her. Lindsey. A woman. At one point, when

Lindsey's mouth first touched her, Hannah thought she was going to pass out. Lindsey made love to her with her mouth.

"Oh…God…and it was so incredible." So much so that she'd thought she might possibly die from pleasure right then and there. When her orgasm hit, it was so intense, so powerful, she felt like her body was being ripped apart by the explosion.

The explosion came all right. In the form of tears.

What must Lindsey think? She sat up and rubbed her face. Oh, she knew what Lindsey was thinking. She got up quickly. She needed to find her, to explain.

"God…I never cry," she murmured as she opened drawers, stopping when she found a shirt.

She went out into the kitchen, seeing Lindsey through the window, sitting on the porch, the dogs beside her. She stared at her for a moment, feeling overcome with emotion at the sight of her.

How am I going to explain this?

She finally opened the door. Lindsey didn't turn, but Hannah knew she'd heard as there was a slight tilt of her head. Hannah walked up behind her, slipping her arms around her neck.

"I'm sorry. The reason you think I cried was not the reason at all. It was…it was too much. I wasn't expecting it. I wasn't expecting it to feel like that. It was different. It was a good different." She smiled. "It was a *great* different. And…and I was overwhelmed by it. And…and I couldn't stop." She bent down, her mouth to Lindsey's ear. "Come back to bed. We're not finished." Lindsey turned then and Hannah saw the streaks of tears on her cheeks. "Oh, honey…no. I'm so sorry." Their eyes met and Hannah moved closer, kissing her gently. "It was so… so intimate. I loved it," she whispered. "Now come back to bed."

* * *

Hannah was still at her breast and Lindsey looked down, her heartbeats nearly choking her. She jerked slightly when Hannah's fingers pulled out of her. Hannah lifted her head and their eyes met.

"So…so was it…"

Lindsey smiled. "What? That scream didn't give me away?"

Hannah nestled beside her. "That was incredible. To be inside you like that…to feel how wet you were." She moved her head, kissing her lips. "You're so soft. Your skin…"

Lindsey ran her fingers across Hannah's cheek. "Are you okay? With…with us? With everything?"

"I'm okay. Right now, I'm okay. Honestly, I'm not sure that it's even registered with me yet that we're…that we're lovers. When I see Jack…tonight, when I'm alone…I don't know. Right now, it feels almost like I'm in a dream." She smiled. "A very, very nice dream."

"If it's too much, Hannah…if you need to go back, we can try. We can—"

"We can what? We can ignore this attraction between us? We can pretend that we didn't just make love to each other? I love being with you, Lindsey, like this. What we did today, I don't want to undo it." She sat up and leaned on her elbow, her hand lightly grazing Lindsey's stomach. "I want to be honest, though." She looked up and met her eyes. "I don't know what I can give you. I don't know how far I can take this. I may wake up tomorrow and say 'what the hell were you thinking?' or…or I may be overcome with guilt and cry in my cereal." Hannah's hand moved to her breast. "I don't want to hurt you, Lindsey. Most of all, I don't want to hurt you."

Lindsey knew there was a very good chance she was about to get her heart broken. But as Hannah had said, could they ignore this? The attraction between them had been building for months. Talking about it now, though, after they'd just made love wasn't the time. She didn't want anything to take away from what she was feeling. And that was a quiet contentment that she hadn't felt in so long, she hardly recognized it.

So she took Hannah's hand—the fingers that had been inside her only moments ago—and brought it to her mouth, kissing it gently before entwining their fingers.

"I think we should get you back. The school bus will be around soon."

"What time is it?"

Lindsey looked past Hannah to the clock on the nightstand. "Almost three."

Hannah sighed. "Yes. I should go." She leaned forward and kissed Lindsey. "You asked if I was okay. What about you?"

"I'm scared," she answered honestly.

Hannah nodded. "Me too." She sat up, then cupped Lindsey's cheek. "It was a beautiful day, Lindsey. Thank you for that."

CHAPTER FIFTY

Hannah stared out into the darkness. She wasn't certain what she was feeling. Earlier, she'd had a touch of nervousness when she picked Jack up at Margie's. She had feared that Jack would take one look at her and know exactly how she'd spent her afternoon. But his normal chatter never ceased as they drove home and he told her about his day at school. And he didn't even notice that their dinner had been leftovers and not the chicken and rice she'd promised. He did, however, notice that she was being quiet. He'd asked her in a rather adult voice if she was feeling okay.

He was now in bed and she was in the rocker, trying to make sense of her day. As she'd told Lindsey, she didn't want to undo it. It had been too special for that. In fact, just thinking about it, about making love with Lindsey, made her heart flip.

It was the guilt that had her confused. Or rather, the fact that she had no guilt. She tried to picture James's face...his smile, his blue eyes. In her mind, she saw Jack instead. Jack was nearly a carbon copy of his dad. She'd had a good marriage, she told herself. She was happy. She and James were good together.

Toward the end, James had told her to move on from him, he'd told her to find someone else to make a family with Jack. He'd been so firm in his request, she'd agreed, even though—at the time—she couldn't imagine there being someone else in her life.

Certainly not a woman—not a beautiful, sensitive, passionate woman. Lindsey was falling in love with her, Hannah could tell that. Lindsey was probably already in love with her, whether she would admit it or not.

Hannah leaned back in the rocker, putting it in motion. And what about her? Was she falling in love? She thought back over the summer, back to the first time Jack had mentioned his new friend, back to the first time she'd met Lindsey, back to when she'd first gone swimming with them at the river. They'd gotten so close, so fast, she had a hard time recalling a time when Lindsey hadn't been there for them. Picnic lunches, play days, dinners. Good-bye hugs. When had that started? She didn't remember a time that they didn't hug. And when did the hugs change? The Fourth of July? She felt the attraction way back then, she knew.

Was she falling in love? Had she been slowly falling in love all summer and not even known it?

She took a deep breath and folded her arms around herself. What was she going to do? Go forward with it? Sneak around and hide it from Jack? Hide it from her family? God…hide it from Margie? Or…she could play it safe. She could tell Lindsey that they should stop.

She felt her heart ache at the thought. Lindsey would stop coming around as much. Lindsey would withdraw from her… from Jack. Eventually, there would be no more Lindsey over for dinner or play days. Eventually she would simply disappear from their lives. She wiped at a tear that escaped. Could she handle that? If Lindsey walked away, would she let her?

The truth was she didn't want Lindsey to walk away. She didn't want to tell Lindsey that they should stop this before they got in too deep.

Because the truth was, she was already in too deep. Today told her that. Yes, she was falling in love with Lindsey…a woman. And she didn't want to stop it. It felt too good.

She didn't know what she would do…about Jack, especially. How in the world would she be able to tell him, to explain to him that she and Lindsey were in a romantic relationship? He couldn't possibly understand it.

No one would understand it.

She took a deep breath, then stood, going to the edge of the porch. She leaned against the railing, looking up into the night sky. What was Lindsey doing? Was she out on her deck? Most likely. Most likely she was worrying about tomorrow… wondering what Hannah was going to tell her.

Well, she didn't want Lindsey to worry. She pulled her phone out of her pocket. They'd agreed not to call. They'd agreed to take the night to think about it, to sort it out. They'd said they'd talk about it tomorrow.

She smiled. There'd been no mention of texting.

* * *

Lindsey heard the bell on her phone. She picked it up, wondering who was texting her this late. Actually, wondering who was texting her at all. Her friends in Dallas had long ago stopped trying to contact her.

"Today was the best day ever. Can we do it again tomorrow? I'm dying to know how you taste."

"Good Lord," she murmured. She let out her breath as she read the words a second time.

Then she smiled, sending back a one-word reply.

CHAPTER FIFTY-ONE

Hannah looped her arms around Lindsey's neck and sighed. "I hate the weekends."

"Really? But Jack loves them."

"Oh, I know. But we don't have a second alone on the weekends." She leaned closer, kissing her. "We can't make love on the weekends."

Lindsey laughed. "You're insatiable."

"Yes, I know. It's all your fault."

And it was. The last two weeks had been pure bliss. Oh, they'd attempted to keep things normal…like going to the pond. The problem was, they couldn't keep their hands off each other. Thankfully, the weather had cooled enough that the water was too cold now in the pond. That was the excuse they used, anyway. A light north breeze had chased away the summer temps, and there was a hint of fall in the air. Today, though, Lindsey had a picnic planned for their Friday. A blanket. A bottle of wine. And no dogs. They'd left them inside the garden fence.

Lindsey spread the blanket out on the pier and they sat down cross-legged, their knees touching. Lindsey was wearing a white T-shirt. Lindsey *wasn't* wearing a bra. Hannah pulled her gaze away, wondering when she'd become so wanton... wondering when she'd become so, well, so sexual. She and James had a good sex life, but it was never like this. It was more physical, less emotional. Making love with Lindsey...everything about it seemed more passionate, more intense, as if Lindsey was reaching into her very soul when they touched.

"What are you thinking about?"

Hannah looked at her, looked into her eyes. "I was thinking about how I feel when we make love. How...passionate it is. How...different."

Lindsey's eyes gentled. "Compared to James?"

Hannah nodded. "But I'm not making comparisons really," she said quickly. "Being with you, being with him...two completely different things." She touched Lindsey's arm lightly, rubbing her fingers across her skin. "Different physically, certainly. But different emotionally, too. I feel...closer to you, more connected. Being with you—making love—I feel a bond with you that...that I think was missing with James." She looked away for a second. "That scares me. I feel like I'm a different person. Inside...I feel different inside." She leaned forward and kissed her lightly, her lips moving slowly across Lindsey's. She pulled away, again meeting her eyes. "I need to tell you something."

Lindsey held her gaze and Hannah saw a trace of fear there. Fear for all the wrong reasons, Hannah knew.

"I'm...I'm falling in love with you. Every day, I feel I fall more and more. Then I think, what would Jack do if he knew? What would my parents say? What would they think?" She bit her lip. "I know that shouldn't have a bearing, but it does. I'm not used to this. I'm not used to keeping things from Jack, from my mother." She again squeezed Lindsey's arm. "I don't want to hurt you."

Lindsey swallowed and Hannah could see the uncertainty in her eyes. "I don't want to get hurt either. I don't think my heart can take it."

"I know, honey." She took both of Lindsey's hands and held them. "Tell me what you're thinking. Tell me how you feel."

"Do you really want to know?"

"Yes. Tell me."

"I'm already in love with you," Lindsey said simply.

Hannah touched Lindsey's face, rubbing her thumb across her lips. "I know. We can't hide that when we make love, can we?"

"No."

"I'm scared, though, Lindsey. I'm scared about Jack, about my family. I'm scared for you. If this is wrong, if it's a mistake, what's going to happen to you? I don't want to hurt you," she said softly. "What if we screw up everything and we lose each other?"

"We don't have to tell Jack. We don't have to tell anyone."

Hannah stared at her. "No? This is enough for you?"

"Yes."

Was it really enough? These stolen afternoons they had when Jack was in school...was that enough? She didn't have time to contemplate it though. Lindsey leaned closer and kissed her, chasing away any doubts she might have had.

CHAPTER FIFTY-TWO

"Tell me about your life."

Lindsey leaned up on an elbow, watching Hannah. Her voice was thick, still emotional from their lovemaking. Lindsey smiled contentedly as her hand brushed across Hannah's nipple.

"You mean before? In Dallas?"

Hannah nodded.

"Oh...you know, just normal stuff. I had a nice apartment. I worked for one of the largest firms there." She smiled. "I had no business getting a job there when I did. I didn't have enough experience at the time, but I knew somebody who knew somebody," she said. "Anyway, I had a group of friends. And a group of work friends." She shrugged. "And I dated, here and there, on and off. And I spent a lot of time out here, at the river. Holidays, for sure. Birthdays. Any other occasion that my grandfather decided the clan needed to get together. And sometimes just by myself. Drive down on a Friday night, spend Saturday in the water, part of Sunday. Enjoyed my grandmother's cooking," she said with a smile. She ran her hand along Hannah's waist. "What about you? What was your former life like?"

Hannah sighed. "It's hard for me to even recall the early days. It seemed like James was sick for so long, when I think back on it, that's mostly what I remember and that's so sad. We had a group of friends that we hung out with…backyard barbecues and get-togethers on Sundays for football games. Some were James's friends and some were mine and we all intermingled eventually. Once Jack came along, well, I told you we were the first to have a kid, so that changed things a little." She rolled over to her back. "We spent a lot of time with my parents. They have a big house and a pool, so that was the gathering place in the summer." Hannah turned her head to look at her. "Normal stuff."

Lindsey smiled. "I guess you never imagined this."

"God, no." She met her gaze. "Sometimes, though, when I'm with you, I can't imagine this not being my life." Hannah rolled again to her side, facing her. "I feel so comfortable with you…like this. It feels natural to me." She paused. "I loved my husband. We had a good marriage. There were no fights, no major disagreements. We were compatible. And when he got sick, I told you, he changed. I can't blame him, of course, but he became someone I didn't even know anymore. The last six months or so, he was…he was so different from the man I married. It was really hard to go through that, to watch him change like that right before my eyes. And I know he couldn't help it." She paused. "The last couple of months, the last month, for sure, he was in such pain, we were just waiting for the end, really. And Jack…poor Jack, I don't think he really knew—or understood—everything. It was a…it was…and I'm ashamed to even say this, but it was—"

"A relief?"

"Yes. It was. I think I told you that before…I was relieved when it was over. I feel terrible for saying that. But he was in such pain. You always hear people say, well, at least their pain has stopped. Yeah. Everything has stopped. But I felt selfish when it was all over with because I felt relieved. Then…well, then I felt…"

"What? Guilty?"

Hannah nodded. "Then I felt guilty, which is why we ended up out here. But I tried to put all of that behind me. The change was good. It was needed." Hannah took her hand. "Meeting you…that was the best thing that could have happened to me and Jack."

"And this?" she asked quietly as she touched Hannah's nipple with her finger.

Hannah leaned closer, brushing her lips. "I can't imagine us not having this, can you?"

"No."

"Lindsey…I'm in love with you. I didn't think I'd ever fall in love with anyone again…certainly not a woman. But when I'm with you, whether we're playing or having dinner…or making love, everything feels so *right* in my world."

Lindsey was still as Hannah moved closer, welding their bodies together. Yes, Hannah was in love with her. She was in love with Hannah.

Now what?

Hannah kissed her softly. "I know what you're thinking," she whispered.

"Do you?"

"It's going to be okay, Lindsey."

Lindsey pulled her tight against her. "I hope so. Because I'm madly in love with you."

CHAPTER FIFTY-THREE

"I like it when you make burgers," Jack said as he sat in a chair, watching her put the patties on the grill.

"I guess so. You ask for them enough." Lindsey glanced over at him. "You excited about tomorrow?"

His eyes lit up. "Yeah! I've never been on a camping trip before. Aaron says they go a lot."

"We should have practiced," she said. "But you'll have fun."

"Have you been to Lost Maples before?"

"Yep. We used to go over there when the leaves changed. Do a hike. It was fun."

"Yeah…we're going to go hiking too."

"So how many are going?"

"Six of us boys, then Aaron's dad and Joey's dad."

"Good. You'll have a great time."

His young face turned serious. "Will you and Mom be okay without me? Especially Mom. She's not used to being by herself at night."

Lindsey hid her smile. "You know what? Maybe I should invite her to stay with me tomorrow night. She and Barney."

He nodded. "Yes. That's a good idea. Do you think she will?"

"I don't know. Let's ask her."

"Ask me what?" Hannah said as she brought out the platter with the hamburger toppings.

Jack looked at Lindsey and she nodded at him.

"We were thinking…since I'm going to be gone tomorrow night, maybe you should just spend the night over here with Lindsey. You and Barney."

Hannah raised an eyebrow, then turned to Lindsey, a smile playing on her lips. "Is that what you were thinking?"

"Yeah. Jack was worried about you being there by yourself." She could no longer hide her smile. "You know, I've got lots of room here. I think I could stand you for one night."

Hannah laughed. "Well, then I guess I'll plan a sleepover tomorrow." She pinched Jack's cheek. "Don't want you worrying about me while you're gone."

Lindsey rubbed his hair affectionately. "I've got something for you. Be right back."

She went inside and down the hall to Shane's room. She paused only a second before opening the door. She'd been in there twice. Once to get swimming trunks for Jack way back when they first sneaked off to go to the river. Then again when they went fishing, she got the rod and reel she'd given to Eli for Christmas. She went to the closet and opened it. In the back, against the wall, were the two hiking sticks she'd given to the boys several years ago. She took the bigger of the two—it was Jett's—and wrapped her fingers around the top of the shaft, holding it tightly for a moment. It was from one of the many juniper trees on the property. She cut it, sanded it smooth, then stained and varnished it. A leather strap was wound through a bore hole at the top and she'd carved a *J* onto the handle. *J* for Jett.

She held it close to her chest for a moment, remembering Jett's smiling face when she'd given it to him…remembering the times he'd used it when they hiked up the Mule trail to Antler Peak.

She took a deep breath, rubbing her finger along the handle for a second. Now... *J* was for Jack. Jett wouldn't mind that she was giving his stick away and she knew Jack would cherish it.

She held it behind her when she went back out to the deck. Hannah was sitting in the chair she normally used, holding a glass of wine. Jack was waiting, looking at her expectantly. She smiled at him, then brought the hiking stick out from behind her back.

"I want you to have this," she said. "You might need it tomorrow."

As expected, his eyes were filled with wonder as he took it. He saw the *J* and looked up and met her eyes. She nodded.

"Yes, it was Jett's. I made it for him a couple of years ago. I want you to have it."

"Wow," he whispered as his hands felt the smooth wood. Then he looked up. "Are you sure?"

"I'm sure."

He hugged her tightly and she had to hold back her tears. "Thank you, Lindsey."

"You're welcome."

She went to the grill, flipping the burgers over even though they could have gone a minute more. Anything to get her emotions under control. Then she felt Hannah beside her. She leaned closer, until their shoulders were touching. Hannah seemed to know she needed that contact and she pressed against her.

"Can I go try it out?"

Hannah was the one who answered. "Sure, honey."

Jack and the dogs bounded off the deck and he headed down the path toward the garden. Lindsey found herself engulfed in a tight hug as soon as he was gone.

"I love you," Hannah whispered into her ear. "You are the sweetest person I've ever met."

Lindsey held on to her, burying her face against Hannah's neck. She hadn't cried in so long, the tears snuck up on her now. Hannah rubbed her back soothingly, letting her cry.

She finally took a deep breath. "Sorry."

Hannah pulled back a little, wiping the tears gently from her cheeks. "Jack knows how much you loved your nephews. For you to give him that...well, he knows what it means."

She nodded. "Thank you. I needed a hug."

"I know." Hannah took a step away from her. "So...a sleepover tomorrow night, huh?"

Lindsey smiled, pushing the sadness away. "Yes. How about that? Wasn't that nice of Jack to suggest it?"

"Yes, it was." She wiggled her eyebrows. "I was going to suggest it myself."

Lindsey held her eyes. "So we'll have the whole day?"

"And night. And most of Sunday," Hannah said. "How shall we spend it?"

Lindsey shrugged. "You want to go out? Maybe drive to Uvalde...have dinner?"

"Like a date?"

"Yeah...like a date."

Hannah stared at her. "I think I'd like that." Then she lowered her voice. "Although if we end up at a Mexican restaurant, we must never tell Jack."

* * *

"That was nice of Lindsey to give me this, wasn't it?"

Hannah smiled as the hiking stick was stuck between his legs as he finished off his bowl of ice cream.

"Yes, it was."

He looked at her. "Was she sad?"

"What do you mean?"

"I saw you hugging," he said. "Was she crying?"

Hannah swallowed down the panic she felt. So he'd seen them hugging, huh? But to his eyes, it wasn't out of the ordinary. He'd seen them hug before. He apparently had sensed that Lindsey needed comfort. She nodded.

"Yes, she was crying. But she wasn't sad that she gave you the hiking stick, honey. She was just remembering her nephew, that's all."

"Will it always make her cry?"

"I don't think so."

He was quiet for a moment, then he looked over at her. "When I remember Dad, I don't cry anymore."

She walked behind his chair and put her hands on his shoulders. "I think maybe she was crying because of you," she said gently.

"Why?"

"Because she loves you. This was a gift she'd made for him…and now she was giving it to you…because she loves you, like she loved him." When he looked at her he had tears in his eyes. She bent down and kissed his cheek. "And it's okay to cry, honey."

CHAPTER FIFTY-FOUR

Hannah's breath caught when Lindsey entered her, her hips jerking hard, pushing Lindsey deeper inside. Then a hot mouth settled over her nipple and she closed her eyes, savoring the feeling of Lindsey at her breast, Lindsey's tongue flicking back and forth. She moaned when Lindsey sucked her nipple into her mouth, and she held her tightly, her chest heaving upward, urging Lindsey to take more.

The fingers inside of her were curled, stroking her, faster now as Lindsey devoured her breast. Hannah's hips rocked against her hand, almost frantically as her orgasm built. Lindsey shifted, straddling Hannah's thigh, and she moaned with pleasure as she felt Lindsey's wetness coat her skin. She moved her hand, slipping it between her leg and Lindsey, finding her clit with her fingers. Lindsey rubbed against her in hard, short bursts, her own fingers moving even faster inside of her.

Hannah was trembling as Lindsey's mouth continued its assault on her breast, her nipple rock-hard as Lindsey sucked it. Her vision swam as her orgasm threatened. She tried to hold on…a little longer, just a little more…but it was too much. The feel of Lindsey's wet clit against her fingers, the feel of Lindsey's mouth at her breast, the feel of Lindsey's fingers as they plunged inside of her…it was too much.

Her body felt like it split into pieces when she climaxed. She could no more have held in the scream than she could have stopped breathing. It tore through her, echoing in the room, mingling with Lindsey's moans as she continued to rub her clit against her fingers, continued to suck on her nipple, continued to stroke her. Hannah was gasping for breath, shocked to feel her body respond again, shocked to feel a second orgasm threaten.

"God…*yes*," she hissed as her senses came alive again. Lindsey at her breast, Lindsey's wet clit, Lindsey inside of her… *hold on, hold on, hold on.*

Lindsey's mouth left her breast, and she let out a loud moan as she climaxed, pushing down hard against Hannah's fingers. Hannah let go, her hips arching one last time as her second orgasm rifled through her.

They were panting, their bodies glistening with perspiration. Lindsey slowly slid her fingers out, causing Hannah to jerk as she brushed her clit. Then Lindsey's weight was on top of her and Hannah held her close, her hands rubbing lightly across her back.

"That was…fantastic," she murmured. "I'm so glad I don't have to leave your bed and go home. I don't think I have the strength."

Lindsey leaned up, away from her. She kissed her mouth lightly. "I love you, Hannah."

Hannah brushed the hair away from Lindsey's eyes, meeting them. "I love you too."

* * *

Lindsey stood at the door, listening to Hannah's even breathing, then closed it quietly and made her way into the kitchen, startling the dogs in the process.

"Just me," she whispered.

She took a bottle of water from the fridge and went outside to the deck. Both dogs joined her and immediately ran out into the darkness. She hadn't looked at the time. One? Two? Certainly after midnight. She was tired, yes, but she couldn't sleep.

No, that wasn't true. She *could* sleep...that was the problem. Going to bed with Hannah, turning out the light, making love... sleeping in each other's arms; it was something she wanted every night, not just tonight. The reality was, though, that she couldn't have that with Hannah. Not with Jack in the house.

She took a deep breath. Was this enough? Could she go on like this, she and Hannah sneaking off during the day while Jack was at school? Having the occasional night together when Jack was at a friend's house? Was that enough?

It had to be. There was no other alternative.

She heard the dogs rustling next to the deck and she quietly called them back up. They settled around her and Max, of course, had a stick in his mouth. She leaned back, watching the twinkling of stars overhead. Off in the distance, she heard the call of a nighttime bird...the common poorwill. That sound, of course, brought up images of her grandmother and she smiled in the darkness, remembering walking with her down the trails as her grandmother's binoculars swung from her neck.

"Whip-poor-will?"

She felt Hannah's arms slide around her from behind and Lindsey touched one of her hands.

"It's a common poorwill, but yeah, same family. The whip-poor-will doesn't come this far west," she said, remembering her grandmother's explanation.

"You learn that from your grandmother?"

Lindsey smiled. "She tried her best to turn me into a birdwatcher."

Hannah squatted down beside her chair and rested her hands on Lindsey's thighs. "What's wrong? It's three in the morning."

Lindsey took one of her hands and squeezed it. "I'm sorry. I didn't mean to wake you."

Hannah stared at her. "What's wrong?" she asked again.

"I don't know." She shrugged. "I don't want to get used to sleeping with you, I guess."

"Oh, honey...I know." Hannah knelt down and brought Lindsey into a hug. "I know. We have stolen moments, don't we? That's all." Hannah pulled back, meeting her eyes in the shadows. "We need to tell Jack."

Lindsey's eyes widened. "What? No," she said. "No. I...I don't know if I'm ready for that."

"Maybe it's time."

Lindsey blew out a nervous breath. *Tell Jack?* God...

Hannah squeezed her hand. "We'll talk about it." She stood and tugged at Lindsey's arm. "Come back to bed. For now, this is all we have. I don't want to waste a minute of it."

CHAPTER FIFTY-FIVE

Hannah had just poured a cup of coffee when her phone rang. It was her mother and she smiled before answering.

"Hey...I was just thinking of you," she said truthfully.

"Am I catching you at a bad time?"

"No, no. I just got back from dropping Jack off for the school bus." She paused. "I've been meaning to call you."

"Well, that's why I called. It seems like I haven't talked to you in weeks. Is everything okay?"

She swallowed down her nervousness. She'd always been able to tell her mother everything. For days now she'd wanted to talk to her about Lindsey, but she wasn't sure how to even begin. She had no idea what her mother's reaction would be.

"Hannah...what's wrong?"

She took a deep breath. "There's something that I wanted to talk to you about...something that I need to tell you."

She heard her mother's sharp gasp. "Oh, my God...you're not sick, are you? Jack?"

"No, Mom, nothing like that." She hesitated only a second. "It's about Lindsey."

"Lindsey? Your friend? Your neighbor?"

"Yes." *Oh, God…how do you tell your mother you've fallen in love with a woman?* "Lindsey and I…well, I don't know how to say this other than to just say it." She could feel her heart beating nervously and she tried to ignore it. "Our relationship…well…"

"What is it, Hannah?"

"I'm in love with her." There was complete silence on the phone for several seconds. Seconds that seemed to drag on for minutes. "Mom?"

"In love?" her mother asked quietly. "Like…in *love?*"

"Yes."

"Oh, my God," her mother gasped.

"I just need to talk to you about it. Okay? I need to talk to someone."

"Oh, my God," she said again. "Hannah…in love? With a *woman?*"

"Yes."

"Are you sure, honey? I mean, maybe it's just because of James…because you're lonely. Hannah…a *woman?*"

"I know. And at first, I thought that too. It's not like I just jumped into this, Mom. It's been happening all summer and I kept ignoring it. I was attracted to her and I pushed it aside. We both did. We kinda danced around it…but it was there. We both knew it."

"Hannah, have you…I mean, are you…intimate with her?"

Hannah smiled. "Intimate? Are we having sex?"

"Are you?" her mother whispered.

"Yes."

"Oh, God. And?"

"And? Do you want details?"

"Oh, my God! I most certainly do not! But—"

"Mom, when we're together, it seems perfectly natural to me. I'm more satisfied with her than I've ever been." She paused. "Ever."

"I see."

Hannah shook her head. No, she clearly did not. "That's not what I wanted to talk to you about. It's about Jack. I've got to tell him."

"Oh, Hannah…he's too young, isn't he? How is he going to understand? I can't even understand this."

"I don't want to hide this. I don't want to have to watch every single thing I say. When the three of us are together, I don't want Lindsey and I to have to pretend that we're not in love. Mom…I want it to be real. I want her to be able to stay here at night. I want me and Jack to stay the night with her. But it's just so…so complicated."

"Is Lindsey…is she gay?"

"Yes."

"I see. And did she—"

"If you're going to ask if she forced me or coerced me or anything like that, the answer is no. In fact, I was the one who pushed things along."

"Hannah…but you're not *gay*," her mother said.

"Mom, I'm not looking for labels or trying to explain it. I just wanted to talk about Jack."

"Okay. Okay." She paused and Hannah could hear her taking a deep breath. "To say that I'm floored by the news is an understatement. But honey, if you're sure about this, then it shouldn't be complicated. If you think it's right and you want more than an affair with her, then yes, you need to tell Jack."

"It's more than an affair, Mom. I could handle an affair because I could walk away from an affair. I can't walk away from this…from her. At the beginning, I thought maybe I should try to push these feelings away, ignore them. These feelings were new for me, different…foreign. But just because it might be a shock to you, to Jack…to everyone…I'm not going to push it away." She touched her heart. "It feels right to me, Mom. Inside. In my heart, it feels right."

"What about James?"

"James is gone, Mom. I loved James. But James is gone."

"And Lindsey…you love her like that?"

"Yes. Mom…she makes my heart smile. After James died, I didn't think it would ever smile again."

"Oh, honey…"

"So back to Jack…how in the world should I tell him?"

CHAPTER FIFTY-SIX

"I've missed the pond."

Hannah was standing on the lone board they'd put up for the new deck they were building, gazing out toward the waterfall.

"We've been here every day this week."

Hannah turned and smiled at her. "We've been here *working* every day this week. Not the same thing."

"But it's coming along. Jack's gonna be so surprised when he sees it."

"He'll be happy to help this weekend." She balanced on the board as she walked back over to her. "Have I told you how handy you are with tools?"

Lindsey laughed. "What kind of tools are you talking about?"

"Oh, don't go there!" Hannah laughed too. "But God, that was fun."

Lindsey helped her off the board, then pulled her close and kissed her. "You're pretty handy with tools yourself."

Hannah looped her arms around her neck and laughed. "Should being in love be this much fun?"

Lindsey's smile faltered a little. "I don't know. I've never been in love before."

Hannah held her gaze. "I don't remember it being quite like this." Her hand moved into Lindsey's hair, bringing her closer for a kiss.

Lindsey closed her eyes, letting Hannah have her way as they kissed. Hannah's hands found their way under her shirt and soon she was touching her breasts.

"I love it when you don't wear a bra."

Lindsey smiled against her lips. "I think I was ordered not to wear one."

"Maybe you should ignore my orders. We'll never get the deck finished otherwise." Hannah finally pulled away from her. "When do you want to talk about it?"

Lindsey sighed. Talk about Jack, she meant. Talk about telling him. Lindsey had been hesitant to even have the discussion. Because if they talked about it…if they agreed to tell him…and he freaked out or something…

"What are you afraid of?" Hannah asked quietly. "Tell me."

"I'm afraid that…that'll be it. For us." She looked away, staring at the waterfall for a second, then brought her eyes back to Hannah. "I'm afraid he won't accept it and then you'll… you'll end things and…"

"Oh, honey, no. That's not going to happen." Hannah took a step closer, touching her cheek. "You're inside my heart. You're inside my soul now."

"I'm afraid though. Jack is your son. I know you want to tell him. But whatever happens after that is out of our hands." She took a step away from Hannah, trying to gather her thoughts. "I love you very much. Whatever happens, I love you. That won't change. But—"

"Lindsey—"

"I told you…before—I was in a dark place. I'm not sure what would have happened to me if you and Jack hadn't come into my life. This summer…I don't think I would have made it. I don't think I'd still be here."

"Oh, honey." Hannah came closer, holding her tight again. "Please don't say that. I can't even think about that."

"I'm afraid I'm going to lose this, Hannah," she said honestly. "And then I'm afraid of what's going to happen."

"Sweetheart, if anything happens to us, it won't be because of Jack."

Lindsey felt tears in her eyes. "You're my only family. You've come into my life and made everything right. My world was upside down...and I feel normal again. I know my family is gone and I miss them every day. And I know they're not coming back. All I've got are memories...that's all I'll have, no matter what. But they're good memories. Good, good memories. If I get past the sadness, those memories make me happy." She wiped at a tear that ran down her cheek. "I'm ready to focus on the future...my future, without my family." She swallowed down her tears. "You and Jack, you're my family now...and I'm afraid I'm going to lose that," she finished with a sob. "So I'm scared to tell him."

Hannah held her close as she cried and she felt Hannah's own tears against her neck.

"Okay, honey, it's okay. We won't tell him. Please don't cry."

CHAPTER FIFTY-SEVEN

"Have I told you lately what a good cook you are?" Lindsey asked as she tried to steal another piece of chicken from the platter. Hannah slapped her hand before she could snatch it.

"There won't be enough for the enchiladas if you don't stop." Hannah handed her the block of cheddar. "Here, shred the cheese. I'd ask Jack to do it, but he'd eat half of it."

Lindsey looked over to where Jack was sitting at the table, playing on his iPad. The rain that had chased them in from the pond—and their work on the new deck—had changed from a downpour to a light drizzle. They'd gotten more work done than she'd expected, and she assumed it was because Jack was there helping. The rain had started about four and after packing up their tools and hurrying back to the house, they were all soaked. By the time they'd showered and changed clothes, the chicken in the slow cooker was done, and soon the enchilada assembly would begin.

"I think the rain has stopped," Jack said. "Can I go on a hike with the dogs?"

Hannah looked at him, then glanced out the window. "I don't know. It's kinda messy outside. Those are the only clothes I brought for you."

"Just a short one. I won't get dirty."

"Okay, but don't be gone too long. It'll be dark soon. And dinner will be ready."

"I won't." He came over to the counter and stole a wad of the shredded cheese. "Put extra cheese on my half."

"Half?" Lindsey shook her head. "No, no. I get half. You and your mom get the other half."

Jack laughed. "No! You and Mom share. It was my turn to pick dinner so I should get the most."

"Who are you kidding? You pick dinner every night."

He stole another wad of cheese. "That's because I pick the best meals!"

She swatted at him playfully and he ducked out of the way with a laugh. "Go on, take your hike."

"Come on, boys," he said as he held the back door open for the dogs. He took his hiking stick that was leaning in the corner and waved at them before closing the door again.

"The two of you are a mess," Hannah said.

"A mess? Well, we're going to be a fat mess if you don't stop cooking all these delicious meals."

Hannah looked her over with a smile. "Fat? I can't see it." She wiggled her eyebrows. "I think we get enough exercise, don't you?"

"I certainly can't complain about the amount of exercise we get, no."

Hannah laughed. "I would hope not." She held her gaze steady. "I never thought I'd be the type of person who would want to have sex...like every day."

"Oh, yeah?" She took a step closer. "Every day, huh?"

Hannah wiped her hands before looping them around her neck. "I get aroused just being near you. Like now."

Lindsey heard a loud clap of thunder, but she ignored it. She heard the patter of rain on the roof, but she dismissed it. She pulled Hannah closer, fitting their bodies together. The kiss they shared nearly melted her bones. Hannah pressed against her, her tongue snaking into her mouth.

Maybe because they were here in her kitchen, maybe because this was so familiar to them, maybe because this was their place where they could be themselves…but she lost sight of the fact that Jack was there.

They heard the door open, they heard a sharp gasp, but they couldn't pull apart quickly enough.

"No! What are you doing?"

Jack's voice was loud, shrill. He looked first at Hannah, then turned accusing eyes to her. Lindsey wished she could crawl into a hole and hide from his eyes. He tossed down the hiking stick and it rattled on the floor. Then he turned and ran back outside, into the rain, the dogs chasing after him.

"Jack!" Hannah yelled, going after him but Lindsey stopped her.

"No. I'll go. It's me he's mad at."

"Honey, I'm so sorry. This is my fault. I started it. I forgot…"

"I know. I did too."

"We should go together. You shouldn't have to face him alone. I know how you feel about him knowing."

"If I'm ever going to get past my fear of this, then I've got to do it."

"Where do you think he went?"

"He went to the pond," she said with certainty.

"It's getting dark. It's raining. What if he didn't go there? What if he's running home?"

Lindsey looked out into the approaching darkness, the drizzle that was getting harder. She stared outside for a moment, then turned back to Hannah. "He went to the pond."

"Take the Mule. You'll catch him before he gets there."

She hesitated. "I think maybe he needs to get there first. I think maybe he needs some time alone."

"Lindsey…he's nine years old. It's getting dark."

Lindsey pulled her into a tight hug. "He'll be ten in a few weeks. Don't let him catch you saying he's only nine."

Hannah smiled at that. "Okay, I'll quit worrying. And you're probably right. He could use a few minutes alone." She stepped away. "I'll get you a couple of towels."

Lindsey slipped on a sweatshirt that was hanging on the coatrack by the door and grabbed a baseball cap too. "Thanks," she said as she took the towels from Hannah. "Can you hold dinner? Jack and I will both be pissed if we miss out on the enchiladas."

Hannah nodded, then leaned closer and kissed her. "I love you. Please bring him back safely."

"I will." She paused. "I just hope he doesn't…you know…"

"Honey, Jack isn't going to dictate my personal life."

Lindsey let out a nervous breath. "Okay. Be right back."

She ran out into the rain. The Mule was parked on the side where she normally kept it. While it had a roof and a windshield—that they normally kept folded down—there were no doors. The seat was wet from the rain and she used one of the towels to sit on.

She drove slowly, the lights of the Mule cutting through the rain as it came down harder. She was trying to think of what she was going to say to Jack when she found him, but she couldn't gather her thoughts. All she could imagine was him lashing out at her, him wanting nothing to do with her anymore…him telling her to stay away. That would break her heart. But then what? Would she and Hannah continue their affair during the week, only to be absent in each other's lives on the weekends? How long would that last?

She turned on the road that would take her to the pond. She slowed even more, wondering if he'd had enough time to get there. If he'd run, then yes. But it was getting dark. Was he scared? Was he sure of the route? *Quit worrying*, she told herself. He'd been out to the pond dozens of times. He knew his way around the trails as well as she did.

The headlights of the Mule reflected off the water, and she turned toward the new deck and the lean-to. She let out a relieved breath when she saw him. He was sitting against the back of the lean-to, his knees drawn up to his chest, his arms wrapped around them. The dogs were with him, and they ran out when they saw her. She left the lights on and got out, absently rubbing both of the dogs' heads, keeping her eyes on Jack.

She walked slowly toward him, then stopped when he held up a hand.

"Go away," he said. "Leave me alone."

She stood there in the rain, trying to decide what to do. "We should probably talk, Jack."

"I don't want to talk to you."

She squatted down, wanting to get to his level. The dogs had gone back under the lean-to with Jack, and Max was looking at her questioningly, as if wondering why she was out in the rain.

"It's my fault, Jack," she said. "I'm the one who wanted to keep it a secret from you."

He raised his head a little to look at her. "Why?"

"I…I didn't want you to be mad at me. I thought you would hate me." He put his head back down but didn't say anything. She stood back up. "I love your mom, Jack. And she loves me. She loves me like she loved your daddy…but different."

He looked up again. "No."

"Yes." She spread her hands out. "Come on, Jack. You've been around us, you've seen us. I know you're young, but I think even you can tell when two people are falling in love."

"No!"

"Yes," she countered.

A rumble of thunder overhead seemed to open up the clouds and a downpour ensued. She stood there, getting drenched, waiting on him. He stared at her for the longest time before speaking.

"At least get out of the rain," he said, his voice quiet…small.

She nodded. "Thank you."

She went under the lean-to and moved Barney out of the way so she could sit down beside Jack. She leaned closer to him. He didn't pull away from her.

"I love you, Jack. If it wasn't for you…I don't think I'd have made it this summer."

He turned his head. "What do you mean?"

She stared at him but shook her head. "Nothing. Never mind," she said quietly. "But you...you're very, very important to me. And your mom has become very important to me. The two of you...that's what keeps me going. I don't have anyone, Jack. You're my family now." She took a deep breath, trying not to cry in front of him. "Everyone just wants to be happy. Aren't you happy with me being in your life?"

"Yeah," he mumbled.

"The three of us, we're happy together, aren't we?"

He nodded. "Yes. We're a family."

She put her arm around him and pulled him close. "We're a family." She heard him crying, and she turned, gathering him into her arms.

"I'm sorry," he said through his tears.

"No, I'm sorry. But it upsets your mom when you run away like that."

He nodded against her. "I know. But I was...I was scared when I saw you."

She pulled away enough to see his face, his eyes still swimming in tears. She brushed his cheek. "What were you scared of? You knew what it meant, right?"

He nodded, but when he tried to look away from her she finally understood.

"Were you scared that your mom was taking me away from you?"

He nodded again and she saw his lower lip tremble.

"Oh, Jack...nothing's going to change. You and me, we're buddies."

He wiped his nose with the back of his hand. "And you and Mom?"

She smiled at that. "Well, we're different kind of buddies," she said. "I love her. She loves me. Do you understand what that means?"

He nodded. "Are you going to sleep with her at night?"

"Would that bother you if I did?"

"No. Because you'd be there when I went to bed at night and you'd be there when I woke up."

"That's right. You and your mom wouldn't have to be alone anymore."

"Okay. Barney would probably like having Max over too," he conceded.

She smiled. "Yes, he would. Do you think your mom would let Max sleep with you and Barney?"

"We'll probably have to tell her he sleeps on the floor even though he'll get in bed with me."

"Okay. It'll be our secret." A loud clap of thunder made them both jump. "We should probably get back home. Your mom will be worried."

"She'll be mad," he said.

"I just hope she hasn't started eating our enchiladas yet."

* * *

Hannah was pacing in the kitchen, and she let out a relieved sigh when she saw the lights of the Mule. The rain was pouring down so she stayed inside, waiting. Jack was the first to come to the door, and when he opened it, she met his eyes, trying to read them.

"You said if I ever ran away again, you'd beat the crap out of me."

Hannah grabbed him and held him tight against her, not even noticing his wet clothes. "I love you, Jack."

He clutched her shirt as he cried, and she had to blink her own tears away. She saw Lindsey at the door and she looked up. Lindsey simply nodded and went back outside, standing under the porch while it rained.

She leaned down, wiping the tears from his face. "Are you okay, honey?"

"Why didn't you tell me?"

"We didn't think you'd understand. Lindsey was afraid—"

"That I'd hate her."

Hannah nodded. "She loves you, Jack."

"I know. I love her too."

At that, Hannah couldn't hold back her tears any longer, and she hugged him tightly again. She saw movement outside the window, and she looked up, seeing Lindsey watching them. She smiled through her tears and motioned her inside.

CHAPTER FIFTY-EIGHT

"I can't believe I let you and Jack talk me into this," Hannah said as she helped Lindsey set up Jack's tent near the river.

"Your fault," she said. "You asked him what he wanted to do for his birthday, remember."

"Yes, but I didn't know that would involve chaperoning six boys for two days."

"At least we won't be sleeping out with them," Lindsey said.

No, they would be staying at her parents' cabin. They'd spent the last few weeks getting it cleaned out and rearranged. She and Hannah were using the master bedroom and they'd fixed up her old room for Jack. There had been a few tears but not many. Hannah had been patient with her as she'd taken her time sorting through everything. They had it like they wanted it now. Come next summer, she imagined they would spend more time here.

But for this weekend—Jack's birthday—they'd spent four days getting ready. They'd hauled large rocks from the riverbank to make a fire ring, and she'd cut up a dead oak tree to use for their campfire. Jack had wanted to have hot dogs over the fire and roasted marshmallows for s'mores. Tomorrow, five of his buddies were coming over. He was as excited as she'd ever seen him to show off his river playground to his friends. He'd already asked if he could have "the guys" out in the summer for a play day. Lindsey had been all for it, but Hannah had balked. "What if somebody drowns?" So they'd compromised. Jack could invite three friends, and they'd also invite their parents for a day on the river and burgers afterward.

"You spoil him, you know," Hannah said, interrupting her thoughts.

"Is that right?"

"And don't expect me to get up at the crack of dawn to go fishing."

"No. You'll get up to cook breakfast for everybody."

"Six is too many. We should have said three."

"Quit worrying. No one will sleepwalk at night and fall into the river. No one will get attacked by a mountain lion. No one will accidentally start the woods on fire. No one will get lost on a hike." She laughed. "Did I miss any of your other concerns?"

"I know. I worry too much."

"You do. They're kids, and I'll watch them like a hawk."

Hannah walked over to her and hugged her. "I know you will." She kissed her. "I'm only happy I'm not being subjected to hot dogs for dinner."

"Got your eye on that steak, huh?"

"That was an excellent idea you had."

"Well, they're not going to have any fun if we're hovering about. The house is close enough to watch them. Besides, Jack knows how to behave."

"I can't believe y'all practiced having a fire and cooking hot dogs."

She laughed. "It was fun."

Hannah's smile faltered a little. "I need to talk to Margie, you know. It's time."

Lindsey's smile faded completely. "She's not going to take it well."

"No. But I need to tell her. It's time."

"We can both tell her," she offered.

"Honey, you don't want to do that, trust me. I was thinking that maybe Jack and I should tell her. Together. She may be more accepting of it then if she knows that Jack is okay with it all. Actually, I'm surprised that Jack hasn't already let it slip. He talks about you all the time. She knows that we stay at your house some nights too." She shook her head. "I swear, the kid can't keep a secret."

"It doesn't matter who tells her, she's not going to accept it."

"I know. And when I tell her we're planning to move in with you, she's going to go berserk." Hannah smiled. "Unless, after I tell her about you and me, she throws me out. Then I won't have to tell her we were going to move anyway." She came closer again, moving into her arms. "Are you sure it's not too soon?"

"We're together all the time anyway, either at your place or mine. Jack is all for it. Max and Barney are all for it."

Hannah smiled and kissed her. "Well, if the dogs think it's okay, then I guess I shouldn't worry."

"What are you worried about?"

"I don't know. I'm so blissfully happy, I'm afraid it's not real. I mean, everything is perfect. You and me...Jack. What if—"

"We can't live with 'what ifs,'" she said. "We live for today. Tomorrow is never guaranteed." She held her tightly. "I love you. Being with you is the best thing that's ever happened to me. I want us to be together. Always." She pulled back, meeting her eyes. "I'm ready to move forward with our little family."

Hannah touched her cheek, then pulled her closer for a kiss. "I love you too. So much pain we had to go through to find each other. There is no more pain in my heart, Lindsey. Just love. For you."

Lindsey hid her face against Hannah's neck, trying to keep her emotions under control. She knew Hannah loved her, yes. But sometimes, when she told her, when she could see it, hear it...yes, it made her realize that there was no more pain in her heart either. Just love.

"We should probably go," she said finally. "The school bus will be around soon."

"Yes. And tomorrow is our little man's birthday, and we'll be chasing after six boys for two days."

They held hands as they walked back up to the cabin. She turned, looking back toward the river. The dogs were splashing by the shore, and Jack's red tent stood out against the fading green of November. She smiled, her gaze going to the fire ring and the stack of wood and the old picnic table they'd hauled out for the boys to eat on. It looked like a real campsite. It looked like...well, it looked like it used to when the kids would camp out. She was pleased that that thought made her happy and not sad.

"You okay?"

Lindsey turned back around and nodded. "Yeah. I'm good. Everything is perfect."

Hannah leaned closer and kissed her cheek. "You make everything perfect. You always have."

Lindsey smiled and continued on their walk. "Well, what can I say? It all starts with having perfect breasts."

Hannah laughed, the sound bouncing through the air around them. "That, my love, you most certainly do."

Lindsey arched an eyebrow teasingly. "You want to see them?"

Hannah was smiling as she kissed her. "How much time do we have?"

"As much as you want. We'll just leave Jack at Margie's longer than usual."

Hannah laughed again. "Oh, God...he'll kill us." But she pulled Lindsey inside the cabin. "He'll get over it."